DURING THE REIGN OF KUBILAI KHAN HE CAME TO CHINA A SLAVE AND STAYED TO BECOME A CONQUEROR. . . .

Edmund de Beauchamps, an English knight captured during an ill-fated crusade to the Holy Land. Tortured, degraded, and finally sold as little more than a pack animal, he journeyed farther than almost any Christian had gone before—to the legend-shrouded empire of Cathay.

Edmund de Beauchamps—the lusty adventurer whom the Chinese called *Chin man-tze,* the Golden Barbarian. With lance and broadsword he fought his way up from servitude to become a general in the army of Kubilai Khan, only to discover that, in China, the Imperial Court could be as dangerous as the battlefield.

Books by Franklin M. Proud

RALLY-HO
TIGER IN THE MOUNTAINS
  (*with Alfred F. Eberhardt*)
BRAVO ONE
THE GOLDEN TRIANGLE
THE TARTAR
THE WALKING WIND
WHERE THE WIND IS WILD

WARLORD OF CATHAY

Franklin M. Proud

A DELL BOOK

Published by
Dell Publishing Co., Inc.
1 Dag Hammarskjold Plaza
New York, New York 10017

Dell ® TM 681510, Dell Publishing Co., Inc.

ISBN: 0-440-19423-7

Printed in the United States of America

First printing—December 1984

WARLORD
OF CATHAY

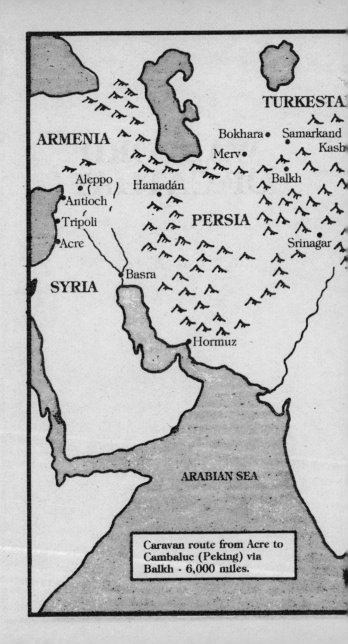

ARMENIA

TURKESTA[N]

Bokhara • Samarkand
Merv • Kash[?]

Aleppo
Antioch
Tripoli
Acre

Hamadán

Balkh

PERSIA

Srinagar

SYRIA

Basra

Hormuz

ARABIAN SEA

Caravan route from Acre to
Cambaluc (Peking) via
Balkh - 6,000 miles.

Chapter One

In the spring months of the Year of Our Lord 1269, news of two events reached me. Except that I was taken completely by surprise by both, the events were unrelated.

At the time, I was attending Oxford, an undergraduate at Merton College undergoing instruction in classical Greek. I had every reason to believe that my seclusion in the world of academe would continue without interruption at least until my eighteenth birthday in the coming autumn. That was not to be. The two events were to have an unexpected and profound effect on my immediate future.

In the first week of April a terse communication from my father advised me that he had remarried in February. Other than her name, Ethelwyn of Hebb, he said nothing about the lady who had become both my stepmother and the Countess of Hartleigh through this union. I had not known my father had contemplated such a step and was all the more astonished since, in the nine years following his serious accident in a tournament and my mother's death shortly thereafter, he had displayed scant interest in the opposite sex. There was no reason that he should have consulted me in the matter, but I was nonetheless miffed that I'd not been privy to his plans. After all, as his only son and heir to the earldom, I felt that the least he could have done was take me into his confidence.

Naturally I was curious about the woman my father had taken as his second wife. Ethelwyn of Hebb? It sounded to me like a Welsh name. We had long been at war with the Welsh—or, at best, in a state of uneasy peace with our quarrelsome Celtic neighbors. The de Beauchamps' family seat, Ravenscrest Castle, was perched on the Welsh border. It well could be that the marriage was founded on political expediency rather than on considerations of love or passion. After all, since his crippling accident and his bereavement, my father's passions seemed to have been confined almost solely to the hunt.

Curiosity concerning my newly acquired stepmother would not have sufficed to send me scurrying to Ravenscourt. It was the second piece of momentous news which reached Oxford early in May that caused me to take leave of my fellow undergraduates, the master with whom I was reading Greek, and the Principal and maniciple of my hall, and set spur to horse.

Of course, since many of the undergraduates at Oxford hailed from France, we all knew that France's King Louis IX had taken the cross—for the second time in his reign—and was preparing to launch yet another crusade. What came as a surprise to us all was that England's Henry III had agreed to make common cause with the French in this Holy War against the infidel foe. England's Plantagenet royal house long had been at loggerheads with the French kings, contesting the suzerainty of disputed Normandy, and Henry III, when not at odds with his rebellious barons at home, had taken to the field in Gascony in opposition to the army of Louis IX. We were all amazed, therefore, when word reached us that the English were to join with the French in the campaigns of this, the Eighth Crusade. Henry III, now into his sixties, would not lead the English knights. That signal honor would go to Prince Edward, known familiarly as Edward Longshanks. All Oxford was abuzz with this unexpected and welcome news. As was the case with most of my fellow students, I burned to be a participant in this great adventure.

There was, however, one serious obstacle in my path. I'd yet to be knighted. Until invested with knighthood, I could not wear the knee-length chain mail—the coveted hauberk signifying knighthood—nor could I joust in tourneys. And, until knighted, I was barred from taking the cross.

It had been my father's wish that I be knighted at the age of sixteen. It had been his desire that I should bring added honor to the de Beauchamps name and heraldic insignia in the lists now denied him due to his crippling affliction. Already, at that age, I had attained considerable skill at arms and would have brought credit to our name and colors. Why, then, was I attending Oxford instead of taking my rightful place in the lists?

There is a simple answer to that question. Brother Bartholomew, the Dominican monk who had been my tutor, mentor, and confessor since my childhood, had opposed the investiture. The good monk had argued that, since I had displayed an interest in the writings of Thomas Aquinas and had an aptitude for languages, I should be allowed to expand my knowledge through the study of classical Greek at either Oxford or Cambridge before assuming the obligations of knighthood. He reinforced his argument by stating flatly that advanced schooling would have been my mother's wish. It was the latter argument that swayed my father. I, of course, was not consulted. I am not of bookish bent. Had I had any say in the matter, despite my admiration of and affection for Brother Bartholomew, I'd have sided with my father in favor of knighthood.

The upshot of the difference of opinion between the monk and my father was a compromise. I was to attend Oxford until I reached the age of eighteen—and *then* be knighted.

As I rode toward Ravenscrest, I fully appreciated that the conditions had not been met. I was still five months short of my eighteenth birthday. Nonetheless, under the existing circumstances, I felt that Brother Bartholomew would voice no objection to my investiture. My father, I was confident, would be delighted that I sought knighthood in order to take the cross. De Beauchamps knights had ridden at the side of Richard Coeur de Leon in the Third Crusade, and had won much honor in its various campaigns. That, however, had been more than two generations in the past and not since then had the coat of arms and colors of our immediate branch of the family, the direct descendants of the illustrious Godfrey de Beauchamps, been in evidence in those eastern Mediterranean realms known as the Outremer. I knew that my father, had his sad affliction not precluded it, would have jumped at the chance to serve both the church and the crown in freeing Jerusalem from infidel thralldom. He would welcome the fact that I, Edmund Viscount de Beauchamps, would represent the family in his stead.

The May air was heady with the breath of spring. The fields and trees were liveried in green. Spring flowers brightened the scene with vivid splashes of mauve, yellow, and palest blue. The hawthorns were dusted with white and pink blooms. It was good to be alive.

As I rode along the turnpike toward the Cotswold Hills, my mind was awhirl with grand visions. Once I'd attained knighthood I would distinguish myself in both tourneys and on the fields of battle. I would heap added honors on our illustrious name. I, Edmund de Beauchamps, would become a legendary figure. Our heraldic device of three sable ravens on a field of gold, emblazoned on my shield and embroidered on my tabard and surcoat, would command the respect of my peers and strike fear in the craven hearts of my enemies. My lance would rip unerringly into the guts of my foes and my sword would drip crimson with Saracen blood. I was filled to overflowing with high purpose. Adventure beckoned me.

I thought, as well, with warmth and affection of my family. My mother, Eleanor of Staines, had been of Saxon blood. It was from her side of the family that I'd inherited my blue eyes, fair complexion, and blond hair. It had been her doing that had given me my gift for languages, for, while French was spoken by the gentry in the great hall of the castle keep, in the privacy of her chambers my mother patiently had instructed me in English. I would have learned that tongue in any event since most of our retainers and tenants were of Saxon stock, but theirs was a rougher English than that imparted to me through my mother's teaching.

In every way imaginable my father was the opposite of my mother. Where she was slim and of but average height, he was a bull of a man who soared well over six feet. Where mother was blue-eyed and fair of hair, my father was swarthy, brown-eyed, and with hair and beard as black as charcoal. In contrast to my mother's gentle, retiring nature my father was a boisterous man much given to roistering and all manner of sporting activities. It was my father who bequeathed me my height, breadth of shoulders, and well-muscled physique.

I am, of course, describing my father as he was before his accident—the way I like to remember him.

I was a lad of but eight, my sister Catherine just turned two, when my father was cruelly crippled, and some months later my mother sickened and died. That was in the Year of our Lord 1260, a year of infinite sadness burned deeply in my memory.

It was in September of that year that my father jousted in a tournament held at Gloucester. He was not unseated in the lists. As the accident was described by his squire who witnessed the incident at close range, the trampled ground was muddied by a sudden downpour, and when executing a turn at the end of a charge, my father's steed stumbled, then fell heavily. My father, encumbered by his weighty armor, was pinned beneath the struggling stallion. My father's right leg was fractured and his hip was crushed. Attended by a physician, and in great pain, my father was borne to Ravenscrest on a litter.

The knitting of his broken bones was a painfully slow process. He never did recover the use of his right leg. It remained stiff and twisted. His right foot dragged and he walked with great difficulty with the aid of a stout stick.

During the months of my father's protracted convalescence there was little mirth at Ravenscourt. My mother's face wore an almost constant worried frown. The servants wore long faces. No laughter echoed in the castle keep. No hunts were conducted in our forests; no feasts were served in the great hall. The servants and men-at-arms spoke in hushed tones. As often as not I ate my meals in the servants' quarters while mother attended to my father's wants. I saw but little of her during those months. She scarcely left my father's side.

I remember that long autumn as being cruelly cold. Even though roaring fires were kept blazing in the grates, the castle was drafty and damp. My mother, wan and tired, developed a persistent cough that worsened as autumn gave way to an early winter. In December she was stricken with a fever and took to her bed. She died in her sleep on Christmas Eve.

My father, claiming she had weakened herself in nursing him back to health, blamed himself for my mother's untimely demise. He was moody, withdrawn, and short of temper. During those years of my early youth I learned to keep well clear of him.

To add to my father's torment was the fact that he no longer could participate in his beloved tourneys. However, though walking tried him sorely, he still could sit a horse. Hunting became practically his sole diversion. Where, in former times, he'd been a gregarious man much given to lavish entertainment, following my mother's death he tended to shun all but his most intimate companions of the hunt.

In the light of that background it's little wonder that I suspected his remarriage had been inspired by political motives rather than romantic considerations. I could not but speculate concerning my stepmother. Did she resemble my mother in appearance and temperament? E'en though it must be a loveless marriage, would she bring my father a measure of well-deserved happiness? More to the point, how would she and I get along together? The last thing I wanted was to add to my father's burden by introducing friction into our household.

I topped a rise and reined in my palfrey. The familiar valley spread out before me. I looked down on the rooftops and spires of the market town of Hartleigh and beyond to where the village and abbey of Coombs nestled on the rising slopes of the forest-mantled hills. Off to the left, perched atop a treeless promontory, the battlements of Ravenscrest Castle loomed forbiddingly. It was strange. Always, in the past, I'd found the sight of Ravenscrest reassuring. Now, for some reason, even in the glow of afternoon sunshine, the gray stone turrets and battlements looked alien and menacing.

As I touched spurs to horse and started my descent toward the valley floor I couldn't suppress a shiver—but whether it was due to anticipation or apprehension I could not say.

Chapter Two

I was greeted with unexpected and unwelcome news. A few days earlier, accompanied by his chamberlain, constable, and an armed escort, my father had left the castle to journey to Windsor in order to petition the king with respect to some disputed property in one of our Yorkshire estates. Since his participation was an essential feature in my investiture as a knight, his absence was a development anything but to my liking.

Nor was his absence the only surprise in store for me. For some reason he'd not seen fit to take my stepmother with him on his journey. Accordingly, within an hour of my arrival, I met Ethelwyn of Hebb.

A footman conducted me to her chamber and announced my presence. She was seated by a casement window at the far side of the cavernous chamber. She was engaged in embroidery. While the frame and linen on which she was working were in sunlight, she was in shadow and I could not see her distinctly until she rose and stepped into a slanting beam of sunlight that streamed through a west-facing casement.

I took a pace forward, then stopped dead in my tracks. Mouth agape in shocked surprise, I must have looked the veriest of oafs. A smile played about her lips as she glided toward me.

The mental image I had formed of Ethelwyn of Hebb was so far removed from actuality that it verged on the ludicrous. She was the most startlingly beautiful woman I'd ever seen, and to my added astonishment she appeared to be not much older than I. She was, in fact—as I was to learn later that evening—barely into her twentieth year.

Her hair, loosely coiffed, was a rich shade of dark red. Beneath delicately arched eyebrows her wide-spaced eyes were a hue of blue-green one sometimes sees in calm, deep pools of seawater. In an oval face her nose and chin were finely formed. Her mouth was full lipped and, parted as her lips now were in a smile of welcome, revealed even teeth of dazzling whiteness.

As she advanced toward me, I hastily revised my earlier assumption. Whatever other considerations had prompted the marriage, my father surely must have been captivated by this exquisite creature.

Over her cream-colored gown, girt at the waist by a silken sash of emerald green, she wore a dark-green cloak trimmed with vair. The cloak was caught at the throat by a gold brooch. It billowed around her as she walked, revealing the low-cut bodice of her gown where her firm breasts pushed defiantly against the constraining linen.

She extended her right hand in greeting. "Edmund," she said simply, "what a delightful surprise." Her voice was low and melodious, with the lilting quality that is a distinguishing feature of the Welsh.

Dazedly I took her proffered hand in mine and brushed her fingers with my lips. I murmured something—I know not what—in polite response and released her hand quickly.

I'd found even that fleeting contact of the flesh oddly disquieting and was sure I was blushing.

From the amusement mirrored in her eyes I was sure that Ethelwyn was aware of my discomfiture. She chose to ignore it, and as though oblivious of the unsettling effect she had on me, she turned imperiously to the footman who still stood just outside the arched doorway. She ordered that a fire was to be laid and lighted in my chamber, that clean linen and aired furs were to be fetched to prepare my couch, and that fresh rush matting be supplied to cover the flagstones. And, observing that I must be travel-stained and weary after my long ride, she ordered that a tub and buckets of hot water were to be taken to my chamber without delay. I couldn't but admire the way she handled herself. It was obvious that she was no stranger to authority and had experienced no difficulties in adjusting to her role as chatelaine of Ravenscourt.

When we dined that night in the great hall, my father's chair was, of course, unoccupied. I don't recall all those that were present—uncles, aunts, cousins, and invited guests—but it was a goodly number. I do recall that a visiting nobleman, Simon de Broulay, earl of Croftshire, and his nephew, Arthur de Broulay, were present. Arthur, almost a year younger than I, already had been knighted—a status of which I was envious. Also at the table were a number of unfamiliar faces belonging, I assumed rightly, to kinfolk of Ethelwyn of Hebb.

On two counts my earlier speculation concerning my stepmother proved to have been correct. She was indeed a daughter of Wales, and regardless of any romantic attachment that might have been involved, the marriage had cemented an alliance with a border clan that had long been bitterly opposed to the English crown.

I recall only the seating arrangement of those guests closest to my position. Ethelwyn sat to the immediate left of my father's vacant chair, with me to her immediate left. On my left, between me and Arthur de Broulay, was my twelve-year-old sister, Catherine. Simon de Broulay, the guest of honor, sat to the right of father's empty chair. On de Broulay's right was the abbot of Coombs Abbey.

Ethelwyn, somewhat to my surprise, spoke at least four languages with practiced ease. To me, the de Broulays, and many of the gentry present, she spoke French. With the servants and some of the other guests she discoursed in English. With the majority of her kin she conversed in Celtic—a tongue I hadn't mastered. But what surprised me the most was that when speaking to the abbot, or to Brother Bartholomew, she switched to Latin, in which she displayed scholastic fluency. It was rare indeed to find a woman, other than a nun, who had been vouchsafed tutoring in Latin.

During the repast Ethelwyn conversed but sparingly with me. She directed most of her attention to Simon de Broulay, leaving me to talk of Oxford and the like with Arthur de Broulay and try as best I could to include Catherine in our conversation. Nonetheless I was acutely conscious of my stepmother's presence at my side and it was with difficulty that I kept my gaze from wandering in her direction. Of a truth I've only the vaguest recollection of what dishes were placed before me, but remember that my goblet was seldom empty and that I drank more wine than was my wont. What does stand out in my memory is the brief incident that took place at the conclusion of the meal.

A troupe of musicians and Gypsy dancers was ushered in to entertain us. At the conclusion of their spirited performance a troubador was brought in. Seated on a low stool before the roaring fire he strummed a lyre as accompaniment to his haunting refrains of undying love. I recall thinking that it had been some years since the great hall had witnessed entertainment of this nature and was inordinately pleased that Ethelwyn was breathing new life into the castle after its years of somber mood.

I reached toward my goblet and, as I did so, felt pressure against my right thigh. Believing the contact to be accidental, I moved my leg slightly. Ethelwyn's knee followed, maintaining the contact. I turned toward her. From beneath demurely lowered lashes she was watching me—the barest suggestion of a smile hovering on her slightly parted lips. She placed her fingers lightly on my sleeve. "Patience," she said softly in English, then turned abruptly to respond laughingly in French to some sally of Simon de Broulay's, and left me to puzzle out the meaning of her cryptic remark. I confess I knew not what to make of it. The only interpretation I could put to it—wrongly, as it transpired—was that, sensing my keen disappointment with respect to my father's absence, the pressure of her knee had been to attract my attention and her remark was an expression of sympathy concerning the delay in my investiture. But I should have known better. I must have been befuddled by wine. The subject of my knighthood had not been discussed between us.

When I retired to my chamber off the great hall, I was the worse for the wine I had consumed. I remember that I staggered when I flung fresh logs on the grate and that, when I disrobed, I left my garments in careless disarray on the rush matting at the foot of my couch. I crawled between the linen sheets and awkwardly adjusted the fur covering. No sooner had my head hit the bolster than the fatigue of the day's journey and a skinful of wine took their toll and I dropped into a dreamless sleep.

* * *

I awoke with a start to find a hooded figure standing beside my couch. The cry of alarm that leaped to my throat was stilled by fingers pressing lightly against my lips and a soft admonishment in a woman's voice, "Shhh . . . we mustn't alert the guards or servants to my presence in your chamber." I recognized the voice as that of Ethelwyn and my panic subsided to be replaced by bafflement. Why *was* she here?

In her hand was a lighted candle. She placed the candle holder on the low bench at the head of my couch. Before waking me, she must have placed fresh firewood on the embers, because the fire in the grate danced and crackled casting a ruddy glow over the far end of my bedchamber.

Ethelwyn pushed back the hood of her cloak, unclasped the brooch, and let the cloak whisper downward to the matting. Unabashedly naked, she stood there smiling down at me. In my breast my heart leaped like a startled stag. She left not the slightest doubt concerning the purpose of her nocturnal visit.

She was unbelievably beautiful in both face and figure. Perfection! Limned by soft candlelight and wavering firelight, she was like a glowing statue carved out of rose-colored marble. Her hair, now loose, cascaded down to her waist. Her proud breasts were capped with aureolae that looked like low hillocks of burnished copper from which her pink nipples thrust outward. From her narrow waist her hips curved outward to taper down to her long, slender legs and trim ankles. Where her inner thighs met the firm curve of her abdomen a soft tangle of russet hair coyly masked her pubis. My eyes were drawn to that beckoning triangle. Fire flooded my loins.

Noting the direction of my gaze Ethelwyn laughed softly

and canted her hips forward provocatively. Then, pulling aside the sheet and furs, she slid onto the couch beside me.

She pressed herself tightly against me. Her flint-hard nipples dug into my chest. Her lips found mine. She kissed me hungrily as her hand moved down my waist.

I didn't need her caress to stiffen me. Even as she'd slid alongside me, my rod had been as rigidly erect as a pavilion centerpole. When her fingers slid up my straining shaft and grasped the throbbing glans, she gasped aloud and pushed her tongue deep into my mouth.

Breaking off the kiss, she worked downward to kiss my chest and lick my tautened nipples. Then, facedown, she swung around. Her crotch was scant inches from my mouth. She fondled my testes as her flicking tongue moved up and down my shaft. I slid my hands slowly across the ripe smoothness of her buttocks, then parted the moist lips of her vulva with trembling fingers. I probed with my tongue until I located the sensitive buttonlike protrusion I was seeking.

When my tongue made contact with her clitoris she quivered like a plucked bowstring and moaned, "Yes . . . yes . . . dear God—*yes!*" then her mouth enveloped my glans and she sucked like a starving calf at a cow's teat.

She must have sensed that I was nearing my climax. She lifted onto her hands and knees, then pivoted to straddle me. She held my phallus upright. Her silken hair brushed my chest as she inserted the swollen head of my shaft into her dripping vulva, then inched slowly downward until I was fully sheathed.

She matched my desperate upward thrusting with a rocking motion. Deep in her throat she made a noise that was somewhere between a moan and a rasping growl. Gradually the tempo of my thrusting quickened until, finally, I gave a strangled gasp as I pumped my juices deep within her.

I was no stranger to the art of coupling. I had first been introduced to its pleasures at the age of thirteen. The event took place in a secluded corner of the keep undercroft—my willing partner and instructress the fifteen-year-old lissome daughter of the chamberlain. Thereafter I abandoned masturbation in favor of copulation and expanded my activities to include two of the chambermaids and the head gamekeeper's niece. At Merton College wenching forays into Oxford town were routine. The bawds and doxies of the town were ardent and adept proponents of the gentle art. I was no novice, but I was unprepared for what happened next with Ethelwyn. I'd never experienced anything even remotely like it and would not have believed it possible.

As my engorgement ebbed I shifted my position, intending to disengage. Ethelwyn, still astride me, tightened her vaginal muscles to constrict the opening and hold my phallus firmly in place. How she came by this unusual skill I know not, but it was exceedingly effective. By alternately constricting and relaxing the muscles she coaxed me into a second erection in a surprisingly short space of time. Soon I was thrusting madly upward with renewed vigor. Astride me Ethelwyn rocked, gyrated, and trembled as with an ague.

Suddenly she stiffened, arched backward like a strung bow, then lifted clear of me. She grabbed the bolster, flung herself on her back, slid the bolster beneath her buttocks, and spread her legs wide. "Hurry!" she gasped. "Hurry!"

I needed no second urging. I rolled atop her and rammed my juice-slicked penis home, scarcely missing a stroke.

She moaned and gasped, rising to meet my quickening, hammering thrusts.

She locked her legs behind my back. Digging her nails into my buttocks, she cried out, "Now—*now!*" It was as though her cry were a command. A strangled shout sprang involuntarily to my lips and, with a final lunge, I shot my seed within her with explosive force.

My heart thundered like the hoofbeats of a war-horse in full charge. The blood pounded in my ears. Completely spent, I sagged onto her as I fought to suck more air into my laboring lungs. Slowly I came down from the Elysian heights of ecstasy to which I'd been transported. Withdrawing, I rolled off and collapsed at her side.

Gradually my ragged breathing grew easier and I became aware again of time and place. The sweat was cooling on my body and I realized that the bedchamber was chill and damp. Even as the conflagration that had raged in my loins had burned itself out, so had the fire in the grate subsided to glowing embers and small curling flames. The candle on the low table had burned down almost to the holder rim.

Shivering, I got up and padded over to the fireplace. I stirred the glowing coals and added fresh logs. Then I went over to the stand where the basin and pitcher of water stood, took a woolen towel from the rack, and rubbed myself dry.

While I was engaged in these activities, Ethelwyn relieved herself in my chamberpot, straightened the rumpled sheets, rearranged the covering furs, and slid back between the sheets. Taking a fresh towel from the rack, I walked over to the couch and handed it to her.

When she'd patted the film of perspiration from her belly and between her breasts, Ethelwyn handed the towel back to me and raised the sheet invitingly. Dropping the damp towel on the mat, I sank gratefully onto the couch at her side. She pulled the furs up to cover us and snuggled up to me. Sighing contentedly, she murmured, "It has never been like that before, Edmund. Never! It was wonderful."

She had voiced my very sentiments with respect to our lovemaking—but thoughts that until now I'd pushed from my mind intruded. "Do you love him?"

"Who? Oh, Geoffrey . . . your father. No. I respect him, of course, but it wasn't a question of love. Our marriage was to seal a bargain between your father and mine—a truce between our feuding clans, an alliance to bring peace to this portion of the border region."

"But did he . . . ? Did you—?"

Ethelwyn laughed softly. "Was the marriage consummated? Is that what you are trying to ask me?"

"Yes. I guess so."

"It was . . . after a fashion. I will not deny your father his conjugal rights. But he lacks the vigor to satisfy my needs. Thankfully that frailty does not extend to you."

We lapsed into silence for some moments, then Ethelwyn drew my attention to the faint gray light rimming the closed shutters of the casement window. "It is time I left you," she said, a note of regret in her voice. "I do not want to—but dawn must not find me still in your chamber."

She was right. To stay any longer was to court disaster. Already she might have stayed too long. I'd not noticed the approach of dawn. Of course, any of the servants who might have been stirring, or any men-at-arms in the vicinity of my chamber, must know full well by now what activity had engaged their young lord. Our lovemaking had not been conducted in silence. But unless she was found in my chamber, or recognized on leaving it, Ethelwyn could not be identified as the wench with whom I'd coupled.

She stepped from the couch, donned her cloak, and pulled up the hood to hide her features. She kissed her fingers and placed them lightly on my lips. "You should sleep now," she said softly. "There is nothing that the morn requires of you. Sleep late. This afternoon we'll ride together in the forest. I know a secret glade."

She turned, glided to the door on her bare feet; then, wraithlike, she was gone.

Chapter Three

Sleep eluded me. No sooner had Ethelwyn left my bed-chamber than disquieting thoughts crowded in on me.

I got up, dressed, and shrugged into a linsey-woolsey cloak. Leaving the keep, I made my way to the battlements. Sunk in dark musing I restlessly paced the battlements in the gathering light of dawn. The enormity of what I'd done became increasingly evident to me and remorse weighed heavily upon me.

Forsooth, it was Ethelwyn who'd taken the initiative by coming unbidden to my chamber. She, not I, had been the aggressor. But that didn't absolve me. She wouldn't have come, confident that her advances would not be rejected, had I not encouraged her in some way by look, word, or action. True, I had drunk more wine than was my wont at dinner but I couldn't use that as an excuse. The effects of overindulgence had largely worn off by the time she'd appeared wraithlike at my bedside. I had been startled, yet in command of my senses. I could have discouraged her advances. I had not done so. I'd been a willing partner.

I had sinned grievously. Not only had I committed adultery with my father's wife, but I'd done so wittingly. In cuckolding him, I had dishonored my father.

Hugging my cloak to me to ward off the predawn chill, I walked along the parapet of the west-facing battlement with dragging footsteps. What was done could not be undone. The best I could hope for was that my father never learned of the transgression. A saying came to mind: "Where there are servants, there can be few secrets." It might still remain our secret, but if the affair continued, it soon would be known and become the subject of gossip within the castle's walls. Eventually word of it was almost certain to reach my father's ears. Therefore the rash act of last night must not be repeated. Easier said than done, I thought glumly. Ethelwyn had made her intentions abundantly clear. As far as she was concerned our illicit relationship had just started.

Never had I encountered such an insatiable sexual appetite. She'd been like a bitch in heat. I'd responded like a rutting bull in a cow byre. There had been a feral quality to our lovemaking that had made it, at least for me, a fantastic experience. The mere thought of it sent blood surging to my groin. Would I be able to resist the temptation to possess her yet again?

I asked myself that question as I reached the southwest corner of the battlements. After a moment's hesitation I stepped out onto the projecting bartizan. From this coign of vantage the view was spectacular. The western battlement was a soaring extension of a sheer cliff. Looking westward through the crenels of the bartizan, one had the impression of being suspended in thin air above the narrow valley that brooded at the base of the promontory. It was a sensation that rarely failed to thrill me, but that morning, burdened as I was with guilt, it did nothing to lift my spirits. I gazed moodily down at the mist-shrouded valley far below. All the panorama did was to serve as a reminder that what I was gazing at was Welsh territory—and that my stepmother was a daughter of Wales.

I sighed dejectedly and turned to rest my back against the stonework of a merlon. I knew the answer to the question I had posed myself. If I stayed at Ravenscrest I would be unable to put temptation behind me. Heedless of the consequences, I would couple again with Ethelwyn— and again—and yet again.

If I didn't want to compound my sins beyond all hope of redemption I mustn't stay even as much as another day under the roof that sheltered Ethelwyn of Hebb. If I valued my immortal soul, I had no choice other than immediate departure.

What, then, of my resolve to be knighted and take the cross? If I stayed with friends in Hartleigh while awaiting my father's return to Ravenscrest, that, as well, would generate unwelcome gossip. In addition Hartleigh was much too close to Ravenscrest and my alluring stepmother. The logical alternative would be for me to journey to Windsor, seek out my father, and have him arrange for my investiture there rather than at Ravenscrest. That, however, was an alternative I was most reluctant to pursue.

The thought of facing my father, either in Windsor or on his return to Ravenscrest, made my stomach churn. In my distraught state I was convinced that once I found myself in my father's presence my guilt, in some way, would betray me. In time, I supposed, that danger would lessen; but for now I wanted to maintain a goodly distance between us.

The cinnabar disc of morning sun was struggling to free itself from the eastern hills. As with me, I thought morosely, the night is loth to loose its grip. If only, I mused, my

investiture could be conducted without my father's participation. If only—

At that moment the realization came to me that I was
staring fixedly at Coombs Abbey in the middle distance.
Limned by the red-bronze light of sunrise, the abbey stood
out like a beacon. Of course! Why hadn't I thought of it
sooner!? The answer to my dilemma was staring me in the
face. There *was* an avenue to knighthood that would make
no demands on my father. Moreover, it was a path to the
taking of the cross which should provide me with a means
to expiate my sins against God's holy commandments.

I clattered across the drawbridge spanning the berm and
moat protecting the castle's eastern approaches and turned
my horse's head toward Coombs Abbey.

It was no great distance. The sun had climbed but a
quarter of its way toward its noontime zenith by the time I
located Brother Bartholomew. The sleeves of his cassock
rolled back from his brawny arms, his tonsured pate glistening with perspiration, he was hard at work hoeing in the
vegetable gardens to the rear of the abbey.

A beam of welcome lighting his features, Brother
Bartholomew laid down his hoe and wiped the sweat from
his brow with his forearm. Hitching up his cassock, he
seated himself on the low fieldstone wall bordering the
garden.

"I'd heard you'd returned, my son," he said affably.
"What brings you here at this early hour?"

"I come seeking information. Where is the closest preceptory of the Order of the Poor Knights of Christ?"

The monk's smile vanished. "The Knights Templar!
They maintain a commandery two day's ride from here . . .
at Moorsedge Castle. Why do you ask?"

"I'm of a mind to join the order."

Brother Bartholomew's eyebrows drew together in a frown. "What prompted this insanity?" he snapped.

I was taken aback. I'd expected the good monk to approve of my decision to join a militant religious order. "Recently," I replied stiffly, "the preceptor and some of the knights from the Hounslowe Preceptory visited Oxford bent on recruitment. A number of upperclassmen and some of the undergraduates . . . several of them from Merton College . . . took vows in the order. Are you suggesting that they were crazy to do so?"

"Not necessarily. It would depend on the circumstances and prospects of the students involved. Praise be to God that *you* were not swayed by the preceptor's beguiling rhetoric. The order is not for you."

"Whyever not?" I retorted heatedly. "Are the Templars not a holy order dedicated to protecting Christian interests in the Outremer? Is that not a worthy cause?"

"Indeed it is, but one, I'm told, they now pursue with a conspicuous lack of enthusiasm. It is not, however, their delinquency in the Holy Land that makes me opposed to the Knights Templar. I decry them because they've made a mockery of their self-imposed vows of chastity, poverty, and obedience."

"In what way?"

"Their obedience is solely to their Grand Master, whose views are often at odds with the precepts of the Holy See. By papal decree the Templars are exempt from tithes and are not bound by secular laws. Taking advantage of these concessions, the order has amassed great wealth . . . in direct contravention of its vow of poverty. In consequence, though I understand it's more evident in France than here in England, they wield political power of considerable magnitude. They've become a law unto themselves, answering to neither Church nor state. As I see it, they are an abomination. They worship not Almighty God, but Mammon."

There was one noticeable omission in the monk's scathing condemnation of the Templars. "Their vow of chastity," I queried, "—do they not honor that?"

Brother Bartholomew looked at me sharply—so much so, in fact, that I wished I'd not asked the question. "On that score," Brother Bartholomew replied, "I've no first-hand knowledge, but I have it on good authority that many of the knights treat that sacred oath with the same contempt they reserve for their vow of poverty. It is, however, the vow of chastity that is our principal concern. It's why you should have entertained no thought of joining the Templars."

I was shaken. What did Brother Bartholomew know—or suspect? Was my guilt so readily discernible?

Noting my discomfiture, Brother Bartholomew smiled faintly. "I know you well, my son. By neither temperament nor inclination are you suited to such a discipline. But that's not why I am against your joining the Templars . . . or *any* religious order imposing vows of celibacy. Think on it, Edmund. One day you'll inherit your father's earldom and barony. It will entail grave responsibilities . . . not the least of which will be your provision, God willing, of a legitimate son and heir to bear your proud name and who will, in turn, inherit your lands and title. You mustn't lose sight of the fact that you are an only son. Your father would be as strongly opposed to your entering a religious order as I am."

I must confess it was an aspect I hadn't considered until the monk pointed it out to me. Shamefacedly I nodded. "I hadn't thought of it in that light," I said contritely.

Brother Bartholomew's expression softened. "I gather," he said, "that your return to Ravenscrest was prompted by a burning desire to take the cross, and not finding your father here to bestow knighthood on you, you hit upon the idea of joining the Knights Templar as an attractive alternative. Is that correct?''

"Yes."

''Commendable crusading zeal, but needless impatience. Preparations for a campaign such as this are lengthy. It will be many months before the knights and men-at-arms are assembled, supplies procured, and transport arranged. Have no fear, Prince Edward will not leave without you.''

"But," I protested, "I've grown rusty with sword and mace. I need practice at the archery butts. Above all I need to enter tourneys against experienced knights.''

The corners of the monk's eyes crinkled in amusement. ''Such burning passion for the fray. Well, then, if you can't brook delay of a few weeks, I suggest you join your father at Windsor and be invested at the royal court. I'm sure your father will have no difficulty in making the necessary arrangements.''

I knew Brother Bartholomew was right. I really had no alternative but to join my father at Windsor. Reluctant though I was to face him, I would have to do so sooner or later. It might as well be sooner and have done with it.

I returned to the castle and packed a few belongings in my saddlebags. I advised no one of my intended departure. I did not take leave of my stepmother lest I falter in my resolve. Well before midday I was riding toward Windsor.

I arrived at Windsor Castle only to find that the court had departed and was temporarily located at Nottingham. I proceeded there with all haste.

Brother Bartholomew had been correct. My father, who

was delighted that I'd decided to take the cross, arranged for my investiture. Prince Edward had need of knights.

The evening before the solemn ceremony, I was subjected to a ceremonial bath and kept an all-night solitary vigil in the chapel. I prayed fervently that I would be worthy of knighthood—and that I might be forgiven my past transgressions.

Together with fourteen other aspirants I was knighted by the king himself. It was one of the proudest moments of my life when, garbed in ceremonial robe, I knelt before the king and swore to protect the weak and the oppressed, and to give unswerving loyalty to the royal house and England. It was my father who girded me with sword and affixed the spurs to my boots. From his hands I received my shield emblazoned with the de Beauchamps heraldic device, my shining new hood and hauberk of chain mail, and a tabard and surcoat on which the family coat of arms had been embroidered with skill and loving care.

My father's estate claims had been satisfactorily settled in his favor and he was free to return to Ravenscrest. He stayed on for a few more days to see me joust in a royal tournament.

My first official joust. It was a momentous moment, and though I strove to maintain an outward calm, I must confess I was exceedingly nervous. My war-horse, a present from my father, was a magnificent black stallion I had whimsically named Saracen. I was attended by my father's squire, John of Coombs. My armor, fresh from the foundry, gleamed brightly. A feathered plume, dyed a golden hue, was attached to the crown of my helmet. Saracen was fitted with a chamfron to protect his head and was enveloped to his shanks by a silken trapper of gold lavishly embroidered with the sable ravens of our family arms. It was almost a decade since last our insignia had put in an appearance in tourney lists. My father had spared no expense. I prayed inwardly that I would bring honor to the de Beauchamps name and colors.

In our pavilion John of Coombs helped me settle a quilted garment over my shirt of mail, then looked to encasing me in the articulated plates of my armor. He adjusted the helmet over my link-mailed coif, then patted me reassuringly on the shoulder. He led me outside the pavilion to where two retainers held my caparisoned steed and assisted me to mount. Then he handed me up my shield and an iron-tipped battle lance from which fluttered two golden pennants edged with black. All was in readiness. We awaited but the herald's summons.

From where I sat astride Saracen, I could not view the royal pavilion or the lists, but I could hear the trumpets blare, the thunder of shod hooves, the crash of lance on armor, and the shouts of the spectators. I closed my ears to the din and prayed silently for strength and courage. I was, in fact, so absorbed in silent supplication that I didn't hear our cue. Not so John of Coombs. The first intimation I had that the moment had come at last was when the retainers started to lead Saracen around the shielding pavilion onto the tourney field. Hastily I dropped my visor and socketed my lance in the upright position. In some way the excitement of the moment communicated itself to Saracen. He snorted through flared nostrils and tossed his head haughtily as we approached the list.

I heard the herald announce in ringing tones, "Edmund, Viscount de Beauchamps." A thrill of pride went through me. When we reached our position, John of Coombs took my lance and handed me up an oaken blunt-headed tourney lance. The retainers released Saracen's head and stepped back. He pawed the turf impatiently while I held him tightly in check. Through the slits of my visor I looked the length of the field to view my worthy opponent. I had not heard him named by the herald. Then my heart skipped a beat. The shield I saw bore a crimson lion rampant on a field of gold. God's teeth! In my first tournament I was pitted against none other than the prince himself, the redoubtable Edward Longshanks.

The trumpets shrilled. I set spur to Saracen and lowered my lance to the "in rest" position—and was very nearly jolted from the saddle as Saracen leaped forward as though shot from a catapult. I steadied into a forward crouch and concentrated on everything I had been taught as our steeds thundered toward each other. The distance between us narrowed rapidly. I held my lance aimed slightly toward the outside of the prince's shield. Steady! Steady! Now! I shifted my aim toward the inside edge of his shield, twisted slightly in my saddle, and braced myself for the impact.

Crash! His lance struck my shield—and glanced off harmlessly. Not so my lance. It must have made solid contact. The jolt nearly tore my arm from its socket. As from a great distance I was aware of a sustained roar from the spectators.

Sawing on the reins to slow Saracen's headlong charge, I was carried down the length of the field, before wheeling and reining Saracen to a stop. I raised my lance and lifted my visor. What I saw was the prince's war-horse, empty of saddle, at the far end of the field. On the trampled sward, about halfway down the field, the prince was struggling to his feet, the weight of his armor causing him difficulty. Sweet Mother of Jesus, I'd won the day in my first official joust.

Had this been other than a sporting event, I would have had to return, dismount, and fight my antagonist with sword or mace until one of us dropped from exhaustion, or loss of blood—or death from his wounds. This, however, was to be my only joust of the day. I cantered toward the royal pavilion to pay homage to King Henry. I swear that Saracen knew we had emerged victorious. He held his head high, with his neck arched, and pranced like a dancer as we covered the distance.

Chapter Four

Though my defeat of Prince Edward at the joust truly was
due more to luck than skill, both father and I were prideful
of the triumph. He left for Ravenscrest the day following
the tournament, happy that the family honor had been
upheld against one of the finest tourneyers in the realm. I
took a somewhat different view of the victory. To me it
seemed an augury, a sign that boded well for me in
particular and the crusade in general. What I should have
borne in mind was that while the Fates had favored me,
they had frowned on Edward Longshanks—and he, not I,
would direct our fortunes in the field of combat.

What I quickly learned was that Brother Bartholomew
had spoken nothing but the bald truth. The road between
taking the cross and actually embarking on a crusade was a
long and bumpy one.

I concentrated my efforts in recruitment to our estates in
Yorkshire, Lancashire, and Cheshire, leaving to my father's
devices a similar task in those fiefs of his barony closer to
Ravenscrest, those situated in Hereford and Worcester.

Since he was loth to travel far, this was an arrangement suited to his physical capabilities. For me, it also served to explain why I avoided Ravenscrest, since I could always say that I was fully occupied in the northern and northeastern shires. I'm sure that my father accepted that as the reason they saw naught of me at Ravenscrest. I'm equally certain that Ethelwyn of Hebb was not taken in by that excuse.

While all of the knights bound to my father by blood ties or sworn allegiance were loud in their support of the noble cause, they displayed a marked reluctance to come forward and take the cross. In my entire life I have yet to hear such a variety of excuses why most of those approached could not possibly leave their lands or whatever else it was that made pressing demands upon them. Later, certainly, but they couldn't possibly abandon their responsibilities just at the moment.

From the villains who owed us military service, and the serfs who had no choice in the matter, I received resigned acceptance. Fortunately, I must have been more eloquent than I thought because a fair number of freemen rallied to the cause.

By early November the company of knights under my command numbered fifteen. The squires, foot soldiers, and retainers swelled our ranks to well over four hundred. The de Beauchamps contribution to the holy cause was a substantial one. Others among the king's barons were less receptive to his call to arms.

All during my travels during that period of mustering support, I'd been accompanied by John of Coombs. I'd just taken it for granted that he would be my squire as he'd been my father's before me. I was surprised, therefore, when he advised me that he considered himself too old to campaign in foreign lands. In his place he selected and trained a young Lancashire lad named Hugh *fitz* William. I refer to Hugh as a young lad, despite the fact he was but three months my junior. He was, however, so slight of build and fresh of face that I always thought of him as being younger than his years.

Thus it was that when, in early February of 1270, the first wave of our forces crossed the Channel to Calais, Hugh *fitz* William was my squire.

In France our preparations were far from at an end. While we waited for the balance of our forces to join us, there was much to occupy our time. Additional war-horses had to be procured from France and the Lowlands. We had to lay in stocks of wine, grain, kine, hogs, sheep, and poultry. Our stocks of crossbow quarrels, arrows, pikes, and lances had to be added to. Siege engines such as petraries and mangonels had to be built and tested. Ships to transport us across the Mediterranean had to be chartered and assembled at Marseilles to await our embarkation. And, betimes, we had to hone our skills in archery, swordplay, and horsemanship.

In order that we might not be too much of a burden on any one district or community, our forces were spread through several provinces. My knights and men-at-arms, together with those of Baldric of Suffolk and Guy de Valois, were billeted near Lyon. Time did not hang heavy on our hands. When not engaged in procurement negotiations, or military drills, we'd ample time to sample the delights of the wineshops and the all-too-willing lissome ladies of Lyon. I was much taken by a vivacious cocotte named Cecile. While she was no match for Ethelwyn of Hebb, Cecile was an entertaining diversion who served to shift my fevered thoughts away from fantasizing about my stepmother.

Finally, in August, some fourteen months after I had

taken vows for this Pilgrimage of the Cross, our force was assembled and all was in readiness. From the various provinces in which we'd been billeted we converged on Marseilles, where French and Venetian vessels awaited us.

My knights, retainers, and men-at-arms were divided between two vessels, one French and one Venetian. When the war-horses were stabled in the holds and the loading ports caulked to make them watertight, the ships' captains called the crews and passengers to prayers before unfurling the sails. At last, at long last, as the coast of France dwindled and dissolved into the mist astern of us, we were embarked on our holy cause in earnest.

I doubt that there has ever been an endeavor as ill-starred and inconclusive as the Eighth Crusade. There were times, many times, in the dreary and terrible months that lay ahead, when my faith wavered, when I thought that God had deserted not alone Prince Edward and his English knights, but me specifically.

The first intimation I had of God's disfavor came on our second day at sea. A violent storm beset us. We were so battered by mountainous waves that the ship's planking creaked and groaned and opened at the seams. We lost our mast. Our hold filled with water. Many of the crew and passengers were swept over the side into the roiling sea and never seen again. God alone knows why we didn't founder with the loss of all aboard. It might have been a mercy had we shared the fate of our war-horses, all of which—including my beloved Saracen—were drowned.

Somehow we rode out the full fury of the storm, and three days later the widely scattered fleet continued on its southerly course.

The French knights, under the leadership of their pious king, Louis IX, had started to prepare for this crusade much more than a year before the English had agreed to join forces with them. They'd taken the field well ahead of us—but not in the Holy Land. Louis had been persuaded by his brother Charles, the Duke d'Anjou and now the king of Sicily, to launch the crusade with a campaign directed against the Moors of Carthage.

We finally joined the French forces engaged in besieging Tunis in the waning days of August. To our dismay we learned that King Louis had died of enteric fever. The French knights were preparing to return homeward bearing with them the mortal remains of their beloved monarch.

Edward could see little profit to be gained in furthering the ambitions of Charles of Sicily by continuing the siege of Tunis. We were all of a mind that the objective of the crusade should be to wrest Jerusalem from Moslem thralldom. In consequence our stay in Carthage was brief. We sailed eastward on the long voyage to the Outremer.

A formidable task confronted us. Over the years of the past century the Christian-held Outremer—which once stretched from the County of Edessa in the north to the southern limits of the Kingdom of Jerusalem at the head of the Gulf of Aqaba—had shrunk to two small enclaves, the heavily fortified coastal ports of Tripoli and Acre. It was toward the latter, the closest to Jerusalem, that we pointed the prows of our Venetian transports.

With the French knights removed from the picture, we were a relatively small force. Nonetheless we were confident that once we reached Acre and made our purpose known, the knights of the barons of the Outremer and those of the militant religious orders—the Knights of the Order of Saint John of Jerusalem, better known as the Hospitalers, and the Knights Templar—would rally to our cause and swell our numbers.

In this sanguine hope we were sadly mistaken.

We arrived in Acre to find that the barons of the Outremer, for the most part, had long ago withdrawn to their fiefdoms on the island of Cyprus. Both the Hospitalers and the Templars were much reduced in strength and displayed little enthusiasm for a crusade against the well-entrenched Turks. In fact, longtime bitter rivals, the Hospitalers and the Templars seemed more intent on vying with each other to consolidate their positions of wealth than on taking up arms for the cross. This had been Brother Bartholomew's interpretation which, until confronted with this proof, I'd doubted.

Despite his keen disappointment, Prince Edward didn't abandon his objective of freeing Jerusalem. He sent Richard de Tourville to Cyprus to enlist the support of the Lusignan king, the barons, and the Templars. To the islands of Rhodes and Malta he sent as his emissary Walter, Earl of Dunshire, to treat with the Hospitalers in similar fashion.

While these negotiations were in progress there was nothing for us to do but wait impatiently in Acre.

My knights and I were quartered in dismal accommodations off the Street of Jaforia, just inside the inner fortifications and not far from the Franciscan monastery. The hovels were rat-infested and swarmed with flies and roaches. In that section of the inner city, the farthest removed from any cooling breeze that might have found its way inland from the harbor, it was insufferably hot and humid. Moreover, there was a shortage of potable water. The sweltering city reeled in the heat and was afflicted by an intolerable stench. To further add to our misery, the wine in many of the casks had weathered the passage poorly and had soured to vinegar.

There was little to relieve the boredom other than to

drink and gamble to excess and to frequent one or more of
the drab houses of prostitution boasted by the port. Tem-
pers grew increasingly short. Minor differences were magnified into violent quarrels. Brawls were not uncommon. It
became more and more frustrating as the days of inaction
dragged on. Discipline was becoming more and more difficult to maintain.

In desperation I sought out the prince and requested
permission to lead a probing foray into the enemy-controlled
countryside. My entreaty fell on deaf ears. Edward advised
me that he'd opened negotiations with the emirates and the
sultan of Damascus aimed at guaranteeing that pilgrims
could journey to and from Jerusalem without let or
hindrance. Any hostile acts on our part—unless, or until,
we were in a position to move in strength on Jerusalem—
would nullify his diplomatic initiative.

My visit to Prince Edward, while it did nothing to
ameliorate the conditions under which my knights and
men-at-arms were chafing, had a positive result with respect to me. Edward requested that I journey to Cyprus to
convey an urgent message to Richard de Tourville. I was
happy to accept this commission. Turning over my command to my cousin, Roger de Montclair, I set sail for
Cyprus accompanied by my squire.

Had I known what the future held, I would have rejected
the mission out of hand.

I was well received in Cyprus and enjoyed the hospitality and entertaining company of knights and their ladies.
Still, I found Cyprus almost as frustrating as Acre, albeit
in a different way.

De Tourville was having no easy time of it in his
ongoing negotiations. The supplies he sought were readily
forthcoming, but not the sorely needed knights and men-at-

arms. His pleas were not met with outright refusals, but the promises he received were hedged with all manner of excuses giving rise to no firm commitments. In all the months he'd been in Cyprus he had succeeded in recruiting only four knights to our cause. I hardly could blame him for being discouraged.

When I was due to return to Acre, I was prevented from leaving by illness. I was stricken with a quartan fever and was abed for some weeks. Finally, when I'd effected a recovery, de Tourville asked me to journey first to Rhodes to ascertain how well, or badly, the Earl of Dunshire was faring in his negotiations with the Hospitalers. Thus it was that, in the spring of 1271, my squire and I found ourselves aboard a small Genoese vessel bound for the island of Rhodes.

We were not long at Rhodes. The Earl of Dunshire was faring no better than was de Tourville in Cyprus. It was when we were returning to Cyprus to communicate this dismal news to de Tourville that disaster struck.

Chapter Five

We rounded the northeastern headland and were making for the Cypriot harbor of Famagusta when, without warning, the storm struck. The cape faded from view as we were blown eastward. Throughout the afternoon and night we battled mountainous seas. In the half-light of predawn we heard the crashing thunder of breaking waves. Then we were smashed onto a rocky foreshore.

It was a miracle that any of us survived. I was swept from the heaving deck into the sea and tumbled by rolling breakers. When I had all but abandoned hope, my feet found purchase and I waded onto a pebbled shoreline. A few moments later, to my astonishment, I saw my squire and a Genoese seaman struggling toward the beach bearing between them the oaken chest in which I had stored my armor, shield, sword, and trappings.

As daylight strengthened, I sat on my beached chest and watched the remains of our small ship being battered to kindling wood on the offshore rocks. I was soaked to the skin and thoroughly miserable, yet thankful to be alive.

"I wonder," I said absently, "where we are?"

Hugh *fitz* William, seated close to me, glanced up. "I overheard the captain say that we were blown almost due eastward. He thinks we're somewhere on the Syrian coast not far from Latakia, sire."

"Comforting," I said bleakly. "With the exception of Tripoli, all Syria is in Saracen hands. We find ourselves cast up among our enemies. Since escape to seaward is denied us, we must perforce strike south for Tripoli afoot."

"How far is that, sire?"

"At a guess, I'd say twenty-five or thirty leagues."

"Can . . . can we make it?"

"God's bonnet, I know not. We can but try. But one thing I *do* know . . . this chest stays here. We couldn't make it far burdened with its bulk and weight."

"But, sire—"

"But nothing," I interjected curtly. "The Genoese might not come to harm among the Saracen, but the same does not apply to us. If we want to see England again, we'd best get started."

Without more ado we set out at a goodly pace. We did not even clear the beach. We had gone no more than two hundred paces when we found our path barred by Turkish soldiers.

We were escorted to Latakia, where we were questioned in halting Greek. Our captors must have examined the contents of my chest and concluded that I was a crusading knight, a captive worthy of ransom.

Under guard we were conducted to Antioch for further questioning. From the line of questioning, this time in passable French, I deduced the interrogation was aimed at determining what ransom could be demanded for my safe return. I was not apprised of the sum arrived at, nor the means by which the demand would be conveyed to

Ravenscrest. I was ordered simply to pen a message stating that I was held captive by the sultan of Damascus but would be released safe and sound on the receipt of the amount demanded.

We were kept confined in Antioch for a week, then, closely guarded, were conducted inland to the fortified city of Aleppo. I languished in that ancient fortress city for some sixteen months before word came from England.

During our lengthy confinement at Aleppo my squire and I were shown every courtesy and consideration. Our quarters were spacious and comfortable. Food was ample. There was a pool in which we could bathe and a walled garden in which we could enjoy sun and fresh air. From time to time we were even provided with nubile and enchanting bed companions.

We were not closely guarded. As time wore on, we were allowed to wander during daylight hours more or less at will throughout the walled city. In short, we were treated more like guests than prisoners. We lacked but one essential ingredient—freedom.

Time did not hang heavily on my hands. I was tutored in Greek by a Turko-Greek slave and instructed in both Turkic and Arabic by imams. Many a fascinating hour was whiled away playing chess or tables with Hugh, or engaging in absorbing discussions with the scholars and imams who visited me on a regular basis. No, I was not idle. Though I often fretted and was sometimes low in spirits, I put most of my time to good use.

We were not entirely cut off from news beyond the confines of Aleppo. It didn't come as a surprise to me that Prince Edward had been unable to muster support in either Cyprus, Rhodes, or Malta and, in consequence, had abandoned all thought of conquering Jerusalem. He contented himself with negotiating an agreement whereby Christian pilgrims could go to and return from Jerusalem unmolested. Then, in the summer of 1272, a particularly disturbing piece of news reached my ears. Henry III had died and Edward, accompanied by his English knights and men-at-arms, had returned to England.

Was I the only English knight of Edward's company remaining in the Outremer? What of the honor and glory I had hoped to earn on the field of combat? In three years what had I achieved? Nothing! I had neither tilted my lance nor raised my sword against either Moorish or Turkish foe. On my missions to Cyprus and Rhodes I had been nothing but a glorified messenger boy. And now! Now I was a prisoner of the Turks, abandoned by my countrymen.

In January of 1273 I received word from England. Written in Latin, it came not from Ravenscrest but from Brother Bartholomew. It was given into my hand by an imam. How it came into *his* possession I never discovered.

When I broke the seal and digested the contents of the monk's communication, my heart sank. I had indeed been cruelly abandoned.

Brother Bartholomew made no attempt to spare my feelings. He stated bluntly that my father had been killed in a hunting accident in the early autumn of 1271—about the time I'd been taken prisoner.

On my father's demise I should have become the eighth Earl of Hartleigh and inherited the estates of the barony. That hadn't happened. Word had reached Ravenscrest that I had been lost at sea. On the strength of this news, my two-year-old half-brother, Thomas de Beauchamps, had inherited the title and estates. The trouble was, until this moment, I hadn't known I *had* a half-brother.

In the spring of 1272 a letter purported to be from me,

and a separate demand for ransom, had reached Ravenscrest. Brother Bartholomew had been called upon to verify my handwriting. Though he had confirmed that the letter was from my hand, my stepmother had declared the missive to be a forgery and had refused to countenance the demand for ransom. As far as Ethelwyn was concerned, I was dead.

Appreciating that the fact I had a half-brother might come as a surprise to me, Brother Bartholomew enlarged upon the revelation. The child had been born in February of 1270—some five weeks ahead of the expected date. Despite a premature delivery, the blue-eyed, blond-haired infant had been perfectly formed and in robust health.

In closing, Brother Bartholomew stated baldly that my stepmother was betrothed to Simon de Broulay. They were to be wed in October—which meant that they were, by this time, man and wife. That would make young Thomas not only the Earl of Hartleigh, but stepson to the Earl of Croftshire.

My initial reaction to the monk's communication was cold fury. I had been robbed of my inheritance by my scheming stepmother. When my anger cooled, I tried to place myself in Ethelwyn's position. It was only natural, finding herself a widow at the age of twenty-three, that her first concern would be security for herself and her infant son. She had seized on news of my presumed death as a means to that end. Then she had learned of my present predicament, but had chosen to ignore it. If she had ever borne me affection, it had long since curdled in her breast. Her interests would take precedence over my plight. It was equally logical that she should seek to remarry before her beauty faded. She had done well. Countess of Croftshire was a prestigious title and de Broulay was a powerful and wealthy protector.

The odd thing about Brother Bartholomew's letter was that while he had stuck to bald facts with respect to what had transpired, he had dwelt at some length on the circumstances surrounding the birth of my half-brother. I had read the letter through a second time before a possible explanation for this apparent inconsistency struck me.

The child had been born in *February*—exactly nine months after Ethelwyn and I had coupled. Had she claimed premature delivery to support the myth that my father had conceived the child? Brother Bartholomew had stressed the point that the premature child had been healthy and perfectly formed—*and that it had blue eyes and blond hair*. God in Heaven, the implication was crystal clear. There was every likelihood that Thomas de Beauchamps was my natural son!

Such was Ethelwyn's nature that surely others had enjoyed her favors, but whether I had sired her child was not the point at issue. To have my lands and title restored to me I would have to petition King Edward. I could hardly do so while a prisoner in Aleppo, where, patently, my stepmother intended me to rot out the remainder of my days. Confined in fortress Aleppo, I posed no threat to her—or to her bastard son.

I informed Hugh *fitz* William about Brother Bartholomew's letter as it pertained to our predicament. Hugh, I fear, did not fully appreciate the gravity of the situation.

"Couldn't the monk get the king's ear, sire?" Hugh questioned. "Wouldn't the king intercede on your behalf?"

"If convinced I still lived, undoubtedly he would . . . but who will convince him? It would be the monk's word against that of a peer of the realm. Simon de Broulay would support my stepmother's contention that my letter is a forgery."

"Do you think, sire, that the emir knows the ransom demand has been rejected?"

"Manifestly not. Undoubtedly my stepmother's reply to the ransom demand has lagged behind Brother Bartholomew's communication. Her formal reply will go to the sultan at Damascus before being relayed here to the emir. But I would venture to say that it will not be long before the emir learns of that negative response."

Hugh gnawed his lower lip contemplatively. "Wh—what then befalls us?"

"Our status changes dramatically. No longer will we be treated as guests. Beyond that I can only speculate. If a Turkish officer or important official is being held captive in Acre or Tripoli, an exchange of prisoners might be effected. Failing that, should a prominent personage or foreign realm have need of a knight-at-arms, my services could be sold to the highest bidder. However, if our hosts can see no way of turning my continuing presence into profit, I fear they'll simply dispose of me."

Hugh's face wore a worried frown, but I didn't think that he'd grasped the significance of what I'd just told him. What I had outlined applied to knights. It didn't extend to squires. When the Turks learned that no ransom would be forthcoming, the chances were that Hugh faced immediate execution.

"Well, Hugh," I continued, "that's it in an acorn. Our prospects look anything but promising. It is indeed fortunate that we've been forewarned. While we still enjoy a measure of freedom, we must make good an escape. We've not a moment to lose."

"Escape! How? Where can we go?"

"We'll strike out for Tripoli. As for *how* we go about this, listen carefully."

Chapter Six

We left the emir's palace half an hour apart. Hugh went directly to the market to purchase most of the items we would require. I proceeded to the bazaar by a different route and bought a stout staff and a pair of oxhide sandals.

We rendezvoused in the rear of a souk operated by an Arab rug trader. I didn't trust the Arab but I'd exchanged most of my gold bezants through him during the months of our confinement. He wouldn't want those illicit monetary dealings exposed. Fear guaranteed his cooperation.

In the shadowed interior we disrobed quickly. I applied black dye to my beard. Since my head would be covered, I left my hair undyed. Hugh, who was dark-complected, could pass for a Syrian without cosmetic application. Next we donned the rough cowled robes he had bought, then slipped our feet into sandals.

Lifting the rear flap, we left the souk together. In appearance we were but two pilgrims. I hunched forward over my staff to make me seem of shorter stature. None of the passersby paid us heed as we shuffled toward the city gates. As we neared the gates, my heart was in my mouth. If we were stopped and questioned by the soldiers on guard duty, all was lost.

I kept my eyes downcast and didn't see the guard until we were almost upon him. My heart stood still. Then, with an impatient grunt, the guard stepped out of our path and allowed us to pass unchallenged.

Once the city was some distance behind us, we faced south and lengthened our stride.

There was much I hadn't disclosed to Hugh. He hadn't questioned me concerning the distance to Tripoli, which was, as near as I could calculate, about fifty leagues. It would take us about a week to make the journey on foot—even if all went well. In the cloth bags suspended from our shoulders we carried food sufficient for no more than four days if we ate sparingly. More important than food was water. We would have to refill our flasks at village wells along the way.

We could not avoid contact with villagers, if not at wells, when it became necessary to buy or beg food. Since, of the two of us, I was the most conspicuous, I would keep in the background as much as possible. Hugh's Arabic was not as fluent as mine but it should prove adequate to meet our needs.

I entertained no doubt whatsoever that, once our defection was discovered, we would be pursued with utmost vigor. That we had escaped his custody would be more than an embarrassment to the emir. It would reflect adversely on his competence as an administrator. It would be an affront he could not tolerate.

The odds against our making good an escape were far from being in our favor, yet I didn't think it to be a hopeless proposition. We had passed unnoticed through the city gates well before noon. We shouldn't be missed until late evening. In all likelihood the search would not get under way in earnest before morning. Initially it would be confined to the city. With luck we could be two and a half days ahead of our pursuers ere a widening search embraced the countryside.

Undoubtedly our southwesterly direction of flight would be guessed. Accordingly it behooved us to take evasive action. Just before dusk we turned our faces eastward. On the second day, moving along cart tracks and footpaths, we held to a southeasterly course, keeping well clear of villages we chanced upon. This looping arc would add appreciably to our journey, but if it threw trackers off the scent it was a subterfuge well worth the effort.

I hadn't discussed this diversionary tactic with Hugh. I doubt he even knew in which direction we were traveling. Trusting me implicitly, he plodded along at my side without a murmur of complaint.

On the fourth day of our flight, when I was becoming cautiously optimistic, luck deserted us.

It was midmorning when I noticed a plume of dust some distance to the northwest. Shortly thereafter the sound of distant hoofbeats was borne to us on the desert wind. Alas, concealment was denied us. On either hand a bleak and treeless plain stretched uninvitingly toward distant hills. There was nothing for it but to trudge along at the side of the road with cowls pulled down and heads bowed and hope that the approaching horsemen would pass us by without displaying interest in the presence of two dust-laden mendicants.

When the horsemen drew alongside us they slowed to a walk. Why were they pacing us? Did they suspect we were other than the pilgrims we appeared to be? I dared not glance sideways to satisfy my curiosity. My heart like a leaden lump in my chest, I kept my gaze fixed on the ground.

Then I could advance no farther. Directly in front of me was the sweat-streaked neck of a horse. A hand reached down and pulled back my cowl. The point of a scimitar pricked me beneath the chin, forcing me to look up into the grinning, spade-bearded face of a Saracen cavalry officer.

"Allah be praised," he said jovially. "In His infinite wisdom, He has led us to the Christian dogs we seek."

"We are," I said in Turkish with all the dignity I could muster, "pilgrims bound for Jerusalem. We come in peace. By treaty terms we are not to be molested."

The officer threw back his head and laughed. "You *were* on your way to Jerusalem, whelp of a fornicating Frank. You are no longer. By betraying the trust placed in you by my emir, you and your miserable turd of a servant have forfeited any rights that might have extended to you." He added something in rapid Turkish that I didn't understand but which caused his troopers to laugh uproariously.

The mounted troop was ten in number. Hugh and I were ringed by horses. At a command from the officer we were herded away from the cart track across the barren wasteland like stray goats. When we reached a boulder-strewn gully some distance from the roadway, the officer called a halt.

The troopers dismounted, seized us roughly, and stripped us of our cloaks in search of concealed weapons or valuables. Suspended from a cord around my neck was a leather pouch containing my few remaining bezants. A trooper sliced the cord and handed the pouch to the officer. He emptied its contents into his palm and scowled darkly. Treating me to scornful scrutiny, he barked a terse command.

Our undergarments were ripped from us. Belly down, we were spread-eagled over two of the larger boulders. Only then, in horrified dismay, did I realize what they had in mind.

With troopers holding us pinned to the rocks, Hugh and I were sodomized. Brutally! Repeatedly!

The agonizing pain of the anal penetration was not the worst feature of the debasing experience. Far worse was the humiliation. It was degrading, an unconscionable affront to both pride and person.

I had sinned, but did my transgressions merit punishment of such severity? Why was this mortification being visited upon me? Apart from serving me faithfully, what had my squire done to warrant such abasement?

Eventually the troopers must tire of their cruel sport. We would be abandoned here in this desolate gully, naked, and as good as dead. No one would come to succor us. We would die unshriven, our rotting remains denied Christian burial. Our bones would be picked clean by the scavengers of this godforsaken wilderness. Was it for this I'd taken solemn vows to do God's work? Why had He deserted me?

Immersed in self-pity, I'd all but forgotten that Hugh shared my plight. Now a sharp cry from him caused me to twist my head, to be presented with a gruesome spectacle.

Until now Hugh had endured the sexual assault in silence. Hugh's buttocks and flanks were streaked with blood. He looked more dead than alive. What had wrenched a cry from his lips was that a trooper, naked from the waist down, the bulbous head of his flaccid circumcised penis flopping against his inner thigh, had grasped Hugh by the hair and was holding his head extended. Why? What new refinement of torture was intended?

The Saracen officer, bared scimitar in hand, stepped into my range of vision. The scimitar flashed in the sun as he raised it high, then it arced downward, shearing Hugh's head from his body.

The stump of Hugh's neck spurted blood like a crimson fountain. The trooper, holding the severed head by the hair, stepped back quickly to avoid being sprayed by the pumping blood. With casual disdain the trooper dropped the head in the dust and kicked it to one side. Hugh's body twitched spasmodically, then went limp.

Bellowing with rage, I shook off the grip of the troopers holding me and struggled to a kneeling position. My resistance was short-lived. Something struck me at the base of the skull.

A shower of sparks swirled before my glazing eyes. Then, mercifully, darkness enveloped me.

Chapter Seven

I struggled back to consciousness in total darkness. My head ached excruciatingly. My rectum was swollen and pained me sorely. Gingerly I explored my naked body with trembling fingers, wincing as I touched areas where the flesh was scraped raw on my chest, belly, and abdomen. A throbbing lump at the base of my skull was tender to the touch. My rump and flanks were encrusted with what I assumed to be dried blood.

Unbidden, memory returned with a sickening rush. Hugh and I had been savagely sodomized. Although I tried to push it from my thoughts, the image of my squire's last moments kept intruding. I saw again with chilling clarity the flash of the descending blade, the spurting blood, the purplish phallus of the trooper who had briefly held Hugh's severed head. It was all jumbled together like some hellish nightmare.

I forced my thoughts onto another tack. Dwelling on what was done would serve no purpose. More to the point, why had I not shared the fate meted out to my squire? In

God's Holy Name, where *was* I? Surely this Stygian darkness was not the gloom of night. Had the blow on my head robbed me of sight?

I groped about me and concluded that I lay on coarse straw. It stank of urine and fecal matter. With a grimace of disgust I acknowledged that the stench probably was due to my own incontinence. How long I had lain there wallowing in my excrement I had no way of knowing.

When I stretched my legs out my feet scraped against an unyielding obstruction. Reaching out in the opposite direction, my fingers met with what I presumed was rough-hewn stone. Painfully I shifted my position to bring my back against the stonework. My knees clasped to my chest, I sat sunk in abject misery.

After a time—I know not whether hours or dragging minutes—I became aware of a subtle change. I could dimly see my knees and hands. It was *some* consolation to know I wasn't blind.

The light source was from above. It was a wavering ruddy glow that grew stronger as I watched, and as it strengthened, I was vouchsafed an appreciation of my surroundings. I was in a circular pit no more than eight feet in diameter. Some twenty-five to thirty feet above me the walls narrowed to an aperture about three feet across. This opening was sealed by a grating of crisscrossed iron bars. With a plummeting heart I recognized my prison for what it was—an oubliette.

At Ravenscrest Castle there were two such dungeons hewn from native rock deep beneath the western battlement. They might have seen use at one time, but not to my knowledge.

The source of illumination was not, as I'd initially thought, awakening dawn. It was a flaming torch, as I came to appreciate when the heavy grating above me was hauled to one side and the turbaned head of a guard, his face but partially visible in the wavering torchlight, appeared in the opening.

A cord slithered downward. Suspended from a hook at its end was a wooden bucket containing an earthenware pot and a clay jug. The pot was partly filled with swill-like mush. The jug contained brackish water.

As soon as I'd unhooked the bucket, the unburdened cord snaked upward. The grating was replaced and the torchlight faded as the guard departed. I was left once more in darkness to grope my way to food and drink.

I wot not how much time elapsed ere the guard returned to lower a laden cord into the oubliette and to retrieve the now empty jug and pot—together with a bucketful of my bodily wastes.

That became the pattern of my days—or nights—a brief moment of wavering torchlight, a mute and indistinctly seen turbaned guard, and a descending and ascending cord.

I knew not night from day and had no way to measure the passage of time. I thought the guard's visits were at irregular intervals. As I became more and more disoriented, I ceased to care.

Broken in spirit and sick in mind and body I became convinced that the sentence imposed on me was one of lingering death, yet I could not wittingly hasten the process. Some compulsion made me cling tenaciously to life even when death seemed infinitely preferable.

I wasn't alone in my confinement. For unwelcome companions I had cockroaches, ticks, and fleas. At first these intruders drove me to distraction. As time wore on I came to accept their presence as mere annoyance.

Fever and despondency weakened me to a point where I no longer could think coherently. Eventually even the instinctive will to live deserted me. I stopped eating, and when moments of clarity were upon me, I prayed that God in His mercy would release me from my suffering. The end was drawing near.

Afterward, I couldn't recall the manner of my deliverance from that stinking hellhole. As close to death as I was, I could neither have walked nor crawled. They must have carried me. I had a moment of brief awareness when the unaccustomed motion compelled me to open my eyes. I was greeted by daylight of such searing intensity that I immediately closed my lids tightly. In my befogged mind the blazing light lingered until I lapsed again into unconsciousness.

I learned later that I had been imprisoned in the Syrian town of Hama. On my release from the confines of the oubliette I had been transported twenty-five leagues north to Aleppo. I recalled nothing of that journey.

When my senses returned I found, to my astonishment, that I was once more in the palace quarters from which I'd fled. Had the emir had a change of heart? Had someone come forward to pay my ransom? What did it all mean? My addled brain was awhirl with unanswered questions. However, such was my weakened condition, I had difficulty concentrating on any subject for more than a few minutes at a stretch. It was enough to know that I'd been delivered up from grim durance without concerning myself about the reasons behind that deliverance.

The first question I put to the Greek physician attending me concerned the date. His answer was that it lacked but a few days to the spring equinox. That was a surprise. Had I been imprisoned in the oubliette a mere two and a half months? I found that hard to credit. To me it had seemed an eternity.

Ten weeks of incarceration under the conditions I had endured had taken a considerable toll. I was reduced to nothing but skin and bones. The flesh on my legs had turned a leathery brown flecked with black spots. My body was covered with festering bites. My teeth were loose in gums that were tender and bleeding. My vision was blurred and my hearing impaired. I was in a sorry state indeed.

The physician applied soothing ointment to the infected bites, kept my quarters darkened, and fed me nourishing broths until I could handle more robust fare. He told me that I suffered from an ailment common to seamen deprived of fresh fruit and vegetables for extended periods. He stated confidently that the symptoms I found so depressing would disappear if I partook of citrus fruits. He added that the damage done would right itself quickly thanks to my youth and resiliency. All that was required was proper food and rest. To my delight his prognosis proved accurate.

I questioned the Greek concerning the purpose of my rehabilitation. He offered nothing by way of explanation. He knew only that he had been instructed to restore me to health and vigor in as short a time as possible.

Although I knew it not at the time, restoring me to physical health was but a part of his mandate. He had to make me well in mind as well as body.

When imams who formerly had been friendly began to visit me I was much pleased. I thought they did so of their own accord. Forsooth, I believe some did; however, as I later learned, many did so at the Greek's bidding.

They drew me out. Soon I found myself railing against my squire's untimely demise and discussing with some bitterness the indignity of my incarceration. The imams to whom I vouchsafed this information nodded sympathetically but pointed out that, since Hugh was of low station, it was his kismet to die. They suggested that his swift death had been a kindness. Could he have survived the ordeal to which I'd been exposed? The imams thought not and argued convincingly that Hugh's death could be interpreted as benevolence on the part of Allah, the Compassionate, the Merciful. As for me, I had been tested by Allah—even to the doors of death—and had not been found wanting. When I pointed out sourly that I had been thrown into a dungeon on the emir's orders, the imams reminded me that it also had been on his orders that I had been released. After all, they said blandly, the emir was but the instrument of Allah's will.

In the third week of my convalescence the physician stated that prolonged continence could be harmful. He suggested that female companionship would speed my recovery by restoring my juices and self-assurance. He voiced surprise that I had not requested the company of a woman and asked if I had any particular preference in that regard.

In the waning months of the preceding year I had enjoyed the company and uninhibited sexual responses of a sixteen-year-old slave girl named Fatima. Now that the physician had broached the subject, I experienced a stirring in my loins. Hesitantly I named Fatima as my choice. The Greek smiled broadly. That very evening Fatima, laughing delightedly, appeared in my quarters.

During an interlude of postcoital dalliance, when Fatima was stroking the inside of my thigh, she suddenly inserted her finger in my rectum. A wave of repugnance swept over me. Angrily I pushed her hand aside.

Fatima's face instantly registered concern. "What is wrong, effendi? Have I done something to offend you? Did I cause you pain?"

"No. It wasn't that. You caused no hurt."

Since she continued to look contrite—and puzzled—I felt I owed her an explanation. I finally brought myself to talk about how my squire and I had endured buggery, something I hadn't been able to discuss with either the Greek physician or the imams who had visited me. I fully expected Fatima to be shocked and horrified by the account, but such was not the case. Unabashedly naked, she sat cross-legged on the divan regarding me solemnly.

"You should not judge them harshly," she said evenly. "They only did what was natural in their eyes."

"Natural!" I exclaimed heatedly. "It was a depraved and bestial act."

"Not to them, effendi. Not at all. As you must know, we of the Islamic faith set great store by maidenly virginity."

"God's teeth . . . what has that to do with sodomy?"

"Everything. Since coupling with young girls is denied him, a boy's introduction to sex is generally through copulation with others of his sex . . . or with beasts of the field. Did you not know that?"

I *had* been told by veteran knights of the Outremer that Moslems were much given to buggery, but no explanation, such as the one Fatima now presented, had ever been advanced with respect to the aberration. "No," I replied, "I didn't know that."

Fatima smiled faintly. "I'm told that coupling between males gives great pleasure. Most of our boys grow to manhood firm in the belief that women are for bearing children—and that young boys are for sexual gratification."

There had been nothing even remotely pleasurable in the savage penetration I'd experienced. Not wishing to pursue that line of discussion, I changed the subject. "If Moslems hold virginity in such esteem, what will become of you? For you is marriage now out of the question?"

"Not at all. I have been betrothed to a man of our

village since childhood. The marriage will take place next year. He will not know that I come to the nuptial bed deflowered.''

"How can you deceive him?'' I questioned incredulously.

Fatima laughed delightedly. "In our society girls learn at an early age to preserve the appearance, if not the reality, of chastity. My husband will display with pride my nuptial shift suitably spotted with virginal blood and will believe that he alone bears responsibility for rupturing my hymen. Thereafter I will be a faithful wife and devoted mother to his children.''

"How will you explain that?'' I asked, glancing meaningfully at the hairless lips of her vulva.

She laughed. "Once I leave off plucking it, the pubic hair will grow back quickly.'' Then, sobering, she queried, "Do not your women practice deceits to accommodate themselves to local prejudice? Are they paragons of virtue?''

I bethought guiltily of a not uncommon practice, the imposition of chastity belts on wives by husbands who expected to be absent for extended periods. My father would have displayed wisdom had he employed that device. Had not Ethelwyn resorted to deceit to hide from my father the fact that her son was illegitimate? Such promiscuity hardly could be considered an isolated case. The prevalence of the bend sinister attested to widespread profligacy. "No,'' I admitted grudgingly, "they are not above deception. They differ only in the wiles employed.''

Fatima reached down and gently stroked my penis. "Our customs differ from yours in many ways, effendi. For example, you are uncircumcised. Is leaving the foreskin intact a common practice among Franks?''

"Circumcision is not a Christian practice.''

"But does it not detract from your pleasure?''

"Not as far as I know . . . but, then, I'm hardly in a position to judge. Does it detract from yours?"

Fatima giggled. "Not in the slightest."

Soon after my disclosures to Fatima concerning the traumatic experience I'd had with the Turkish troopers, the Greek physician visited me in my quarters. During the course of his routine physical examination, he made casual reference to the degrading incident. I was deeply offended, feeling that Fatima had betrayed my confidence.

The Greek had been watching me closely and must have divined my thoughts. "Come, now," he said amiably. "She has spoken of this to no one but me . . . even though we all knew what must have befallen you. I found it passing strange that you made no mention of the experience either to me or to any of the imams who have conversed with you during your recovery. Consequently I asked Fatima to work the conversation around to sodomy. It was for your own good. Locked in your innermost thoughts it would have been detrimental to your peace of mind. It had to be brought into the open and viewed rationally."

"How can such actions be viewed rationally?" I retorted hotly.

"I thought Fatima explained that to you. Rape of prisoners is the rule, not the exception. It is a matter of attitude and custom. Once you removed yourself from the emir's protection by effecting an escape, your knighthood no longer conferred on you immunity from rape or torture. I would have been very much surprised had you *not* been raped."

Anger ebbed from me. "She tried to explain, but I found such bestiality difficult to credit, let alone believe."

The Greek smiled tolerantly. "As you gain experience,

you'll find it easier to accept." Then his smile broadened as he added, "You don't need my services any longer. I can report to the emir that you've made a satisfactory recovery. He will be delighted to learn that you are restored to health."

Just why this news should delight the emir escaped me.

Chapter Eight

I was sunning myself in the enclosed garden. The morning sun felt good. Looking forward to a noontime visit from Fatima, I was in excellent spirits.

An odd scraping noise caught my attention. I knotted my loincloth and lifted onto one elbow to ascertain the source of the unaccustomed sound. It came, I saw, from a large object two servants were pushing along the walkway leading to my quarters. Suddenly recognizing the object, I sat bolt upright. What they were pushing was the oaken trunk I'd last seen some two years ago reposing on a strip of pebbled beach.

I'd long ago dismissed the trunk and its contents from my mind, thinking I'd seen the last of it. Yet here it was. Did this mean that my ransom *had* been paid? Was I about to be released?

I followed the servants into my quarters. When they departed, I stood looking down at the trunk in disbelief. I was so preoccupied with speculation concerning its presence that I had not heard anyone approach. The first intimation that I had that I was not alone was a voice breaking into my thoughts. What added to my startled response was that I was being addressed in French, a tongue I hadn't heard spoken for some time.

"It is your property, is it not?"

I whirled and beheld a stranger standing in the doorway. He was dressed, incongruously, in European garb. Despite the warmth of the day he wore a calf-length cloak trimmed with miniver. On his head he wore a circular cap edged with white fur that matched the trim of his cloak. His legs were encased in leather boots. As far as I could see, he carried no weapon.

His long-nosed face was hollow-cheeked. The hair that curled beneath his cap and his beard was dark. His brown-irised eyes bulged from their sockets, lending him a fishlike appearance.

I stared at him for a moment before answering his question. "Yes, it's my trunk."

"Then you are the Saxon knight, Edmund de Beauchamps?"

"I am Edmund, *Viscount* de Beauchamps."

"And you *do* speak Greek, as I've been told?" he queried, ignoring the pointed reference to my nobility.

I liked not his questions. "Passably," I replied curtly.

"Good. I feared they might have lied. What does the trunk contain?"

I considered his question impertinent, but answered tersely, "Chain mail, plate armor, shield and sword, and sundry articles of clothing. At least that is what it contained two years ago when it was taken from me."

"Check its contents to make sure that nothing has been stolen."

Whatever it contained, the trunk's contents were none of

his concern. "I'll examine it at my leisure," I said irritably. "Now, if you'll excuse me, I'm expecting a visi—"

"Check it now," the stranger snapped brusquely.

"Look," I flared, "by what right do you intrude on my privacy? I suggest you leave now before I—"

He stopped me with an impatient gesture. "You haven't been told? The emir said that was so, but I did not believe the lying heathen. I am Count Leonardo Orsini. I have paid far too large a sum in *livres tournois* for your release. I allowed myself to be cheated only because I have a pressing need for a man of military skills to command the Greek ruffians who form my escort."

I drew myself up and glared down at the count. "My services aren't for sale."

Orsini's eyebrows inched upward. "You don't seem to understand your position. You have no say in the matter. I *bought* you. I *own* you. Check your trunk and be dressed for travel and ready to leave, *with* the trunk, within the hour. We are camped outside the north gate." With an imperious wave of dismissal Orsini turned and stalked out without a backward glance. In gape-mouthed stupefaction I watched his retreating back.

God in Heaven! I'd been sold into bondage! No wonder the emir had been anxious to restore me to health. The transaction with Orsini must have been concluded through an agent while I'd lain rotting away in Hama.

The choice was simple; either I put in an appearance at the count's encampment within the hour, or I faced execution. It really wasn't much of a choice.

Resignedly, I donned a *jallabah,* shrugged into a burnoose, wrapped a turban around my head, and pushed my feet into pointed upturned slippers.

I then addressed myself to a cursory inspection of the trunk's interior. Its contents reeked of must but seemed to be intact. I added to the contents a change of undergarments and a spare *jallabah*, then lowered the lid. I was as ready as I'd ever be to undertake a journey.

It was only then that an encouraging aspect of my predicament occurred to me. That I knew neither the purpose nor the destination of Orsini's undertaking was of small moment. Sooner or later it would take me outside the limits of Damascene authority and present me with an avenue for escape. Of a truth, bondage could be a blessing in disguise.

Two slaves carrying my trunk preceding me, I exited the city by the northern gate. I gazed back on the stone ramparts with mixed feelings. Fortress Aleppo had been a prison, yet at the same time it had been a sanctuary. Within its confines I had learned much, not the least of which had been to come to terms with myself. I owed the city a debt of gratitude if for no other reason than that the female companionship provided me had served as an effective antidote to the virulent poison introduced into my bloodstream by Ethelwyn of Hebb.

I found it difficult to get answers to the questions I posed. The Bedouins loading the camels knew only that the caravan was heading eastward along an ancient trade route that would take us through the Syrian hinterland into the Zagros Mountains and from thence across the Persian desert. They knew not our ultimate destination, having been hired to guide the caravan only as far as the Turkestan city of Merv.

When I questioned them concerning distances, the answers were confusing. They did not speak in terms of leagues or miles but equated distance to the time involved. To reach Merv should take us four to five months depending on what weather we encountered. Another factor we would have to consider was that Persia was a land of bitter conflict between the Moslem forces of the Mamelukes of Egypt and the fierce horsemen from beyond the eastern ranges, the dreaded Mongols. I assumed they were referring to the Tartars with whom Louis IX had tried to form an anti-Moslem alliance during the Seventh Crusade.

On one point the Bedouins were agreed. We were embarking on a perilous journey through hostile terrain.

Other than that they thought him to be a Venetian, the Bedouins could tell me nothing about Count Orsini. I sought out his retainers in order to learn something about the Venetian nobleman. The information I garnered was not encouraging.

True, the count was of Venetian extraction, but his family had ruled as feudal lords on the Ionian island of Kefallinia for close to two centuries. Leonardo was the youngest son of the present ruler of the island domain, Duke Adolfo Orsini. From all accounts Leonardo had led a sheltered existence. Prior to his present odyssey he had ventured no farther afield than Venice—and that but rarely. He had no experience in the world of commerce. What in Heaven's name, I wondered, had prompted him to undertake this hazardous expedition?

The armed escort were Greek-speaking Ionians, farmers and fishermen owing allegiance to the Venetian duke. The retainers in Orsini's entourage were, with one exception, Italian-speaking Lombards from the Ionian islands.

The exception was a Venetian merchant named Lorenzo Roccenti. He had lived some years in Acre. He alone, of all that company, had any previous experience in trade. He had a superficial knowledge of the Outremer and spoke halting Arabic. It was he who had retained the services of the Arab guide, camel drivers, and camels. And it was he who had advised the count of the presence of an English knight at Aleppo.

The impression I got from talking to Orsini's retinue was that while they had a healthy respect for his father, the duke, the same did not apply to his youngest son. For the most part they appeared to hold Leonardo in thinly veiled contempt.

To my way of thinking one would be hard put to assemble a less likely company of adventurers.

We did not leave within the hour. It was closer to three hours before Orsini, accompanied by a fresh-faced youth, emerged from his pavilion and signaled for the tent to be struck. He had exchanged his fur-trimmed cap for a woolen beret and had buckled on a sword. Otherwise his garb was unchanged.

He looked around until his gaze settled on me. His eyebrows drew down as his bulging eyes fixed on me coldly. "Why are you dressed like a camel driver?" he rasped. "As my military commander I expect you to go armed . . . and suitably attired . . . at all times."

I had no wish to antagonize him at the outset of our relationship. "My apologies," I answered deferentially. I nodded toward one of the loaded camels. "My trunk is there. It will take but a moment to don mail and arm myself."

"Not now," Orsini snapped impatiently. "The hour grows late. Select a mount and ride behind me. But tomorrow I shall expect you at least to *look* the part of a military commander."

I seethed inwardly, yet held my tongue in check. His petulant reprimand was unjustified, an arrogant attempt to gain stature in the eyes of his retainers at my expense.

* * *

In the early part of the afternoon we forded the Euphrates River. The camels would not be hurried. They ambled along at a sedate pace. By sunset of that first day I doubt we had covered as much as three leagues.

On the second day I was up with the dawn. If it was an English knight Orsini wanted, it would be an English knight he'd get. I donned trousers, boots, quilted vest, and hauberk and coif of chain mail. Over the mail shirt I wore my tabard boldly embroidered with the de Beauchamps escutcheon. I belted my sword at my waist and contrived saddle loops to hold my battle-ax. Fixing spurs to my boots, I slung my shield over my shoulder.

If one didn't look too closely, I presented a most impressive figure. Unfortunately the blades of my battle-ax and the links of my chain mail were liberally flecked with rust, and my tabard and sword scabbard were mildewed. A day in the sun should rid my tabard of its musty smell, but the chain mail and ax blades would need to be brushed vigorously and lightly oiled. As I rubbed the mold from my scabbard, I thought ruefully of how dependent a knight was on something he took for granted—the menial services provided by a squire.

The aroma of brewing coffee reached my nostrils. I walked over to the campfire around which the Bedouins squatted. Settling on my haunches, I joined the circle. The guide, his face creased by a grin, handed me a bowl of mutton and rice. "Imposing, effendi," he said, "but garb, I fear, ill-suited to what lies ahead."

I poured thick coffee into a small brass cup and grinned in response. "I don't intend to wear it long. What *does* lie ahead?"

The Bedouin inclined his head toward a nearby grove of palms. "Regard them well, effendi; they're the last trees we'll see for some days. By midmorning we will start into the desert. It is three days' journey to the first oasis.''

When Count Orsini emerged from his pavilion, he found me mounted and waiting patiently. He regarded me fixedly, then swung his gaze to the escort standing beside their horses. A puzzled frown clouding his features, Orsini hesitated, then strode to his horse and swung himself into the saddle. "Well, Saxon," he snapped peevishly, "what are you waiting for?"

In Greek I barked out, "Mount!" When they were all mounted, I gave a second command, "Fo-orm flanking line!" Without waiting to watch the milling confusion that was bound to result from my second command, I wheeled my steed and fell in behind Orsini. The camel drivers, ill-concealed amusement on their faces, prodded their stubborn charges to their feet and coaxed them into swaying motion.

About an hour later I dropped back and rode beside the escort's sergeant-at-arms, quietly explaining what I wanted of him. He was to divide the escort into two columns, allocating each man a place in his respective column. On the command to form flanking line, they would divide and position themselves on each flank of the line of camels at a distance of about twenty paces. They would then move forward in single file matching the speed of advance of the camels. I left it to the discretion of the sergeant-at-arms to determine the distance between horses.

The sergeant-at-arms listened attentively and nodded his understanding. "Yes, sire." Then he added by way of an apology, "None of us has had military training."

I chuckled. "It has not escaped my attention."

Spurring my steed, I resumed my station to the rear of Orsini. I was plagued by disturbing thoughts.

Donning knightly trappings appeared to have altered my status. The Bedouin guide had addressed me deferentially as "effendi." The sergeant-at-arms had used "sire" respectfully. Even Orsini had seemed to be nonplused in his reaction. I feared I might be placing myself in an anomalous position from which there was no retreat. Would the entire company look to me for leadership in time of peril? If I was the only one trained in the use of arms, that might prove to be the case. Yet I was untried in battle— and it would mean I would be assuming authority right-fully belonging to Count Orsini. How would Orsini react in that event? I could ill afford to incur his jealous wrath when he held my fate in his hands.

I would have to walk a fine line. A very fine line.

Chapter Nine

Syria's arid wasteland was child's play to the Bedouins. To us, unaccustomed to desert travel, it seemed like purgatory. From a cloudless blue-white sky the sun blazed down with cruel intensity on a parched landscape of hard-baked rock-strewn earth totally devoid of vegetation.

Well before noon I had divested myself of tabard, coif, hauberk, and undervest, shrugged into a burnoose, and pulled up the hood to protect the back of my neck from the sun's rays and to shield my eyes from the fierce glare. Our Bedouin guide smiled knowingly. Orsini scowled but said nothing. He, too, was suffering and soon replaced his cloak with a garment of lighter material.

By evening, when we made camp, most of our party were feverish from overexposure to the direct and reflected sunlight. As soon as the tents were pitched, Orsini retired to his pavilion. My intention had been to devote an hour or two to instructing my charges in swordsmanship. I abandoned the idea as impractical.

I partook of an evening meal, then took the spare *jallabah* from my trunk and tore the cotton garment into strips that would make do as turbans for the escort. It was while I was absorbed in this task that the Bedouin guide approached me and spoke his mind.

"Effendi, your people lack desert experience."

"As do I."

"You know how to protect yourself from the sun and drink sparingly. They *must* learn these things if they hope to survive. In Persia we face a much more formidable desert, the Dasht-e-Kavir. Not only must we conserve water, but we must make earlier starts if we are not to be forced into travel by night. That, effendi, I don't recommend. The desert *djinn* prowl the dark hours and exact a fearsome toll."

I suppressed an involuntary shiver. "Thank you. I will relay your advice to the Venetian count."

I sought out Roccenti. Accustomed to the clime, if not the desert, he had fared better than most of his companions. "Have you spoken with the guide?" I questioned.

Roccenti looked uncomfortable. "No. My command of Arabic is limited . . . which, I suppose, is why I was excluded from the negotiations effecting your release. I've only just learned that you were sold into bondage by your Turkish captors. I'm sorry, sire."

I didn't believe Roccenti's protestation of innocence. I shrugged. "It's too late to lament the transaction, but it puts me in an awkward position. I can't approach Orsini directly. I presume you can."

Roccenti smiled wryly. "I have his ear."

"Then, tell him that the guide recommends we make better time by starting off each day before dawn. He also urges strongly that we make every effort to conserve water and guard against sunstroke by keeping the back of the neck covered. Those are instructions Orsini should issue if he wishes his party to survive.''

I turned from Roccenti, then paused and turned back to face him. ''Do *you* know our destination?''

''I—ah—haven't been told . . . but I can guess it. I know in whose footsteps we follow.''

''But it isn't Merv?''

''No. Much farther east. At Merv we are to be met by a Nestorian monk who will guide us to our final destination.''

I didn't press Roccenti for more information. I had the distinct impression that there was little more he *could* tell me. Turning from him, I walked away deep in thought.

Every step eastward took me that much farther from England. I seriously considered stealing a horse and striking out for Tripoli, or Acre. Reluctantly I put that idea behind me. We were still in Syria. If I fled the caravan on a stolen horse, I would be labeled a thief—as well as an escaping slave—and hunted relentlessly.

No, I concluded sourly, if I wanted to live to see England again, I had no choice but to accept things as they were and make the best of it. Ultimately Orsini *must* return to Lombardy, or Kefallinia. But when? I wondered morosely.

Day after day, from one oasis to the next, the camels plodded on, seemingly impervious to thirst and heat. In spite of our precautions two of the mounted escort and three of our horses died on that first short leg of our journey. The men we buried in shallow graves. The horses were left lying where they dropped, to be picked clean by hyenas and vultures.

In the cool of the evenings I instructed the escort in weaponry and tactics. They were willing enough but progress was painfully slow. Still, after several weeks, I was confident that they would give a good account of themselves if we came under attack. There was, however, little likelihood of that happening in this remote region.

The only people we encountered were a few goatherds and their families at oases in our path. Our guide was sorely puzzled by the absence of other caravans.

We forded the Tigris and threaded our way into a range of mountains. When we reached the mountain town of Hamadān, we learned the reason behind the lack of caravan traffic.

The guide had gone to the marketplace to buy three replacement mounts. He returned without having concluded his business. When he came to see me, he was in a highly agitated state.

"Effendi, we have seen no caravans because all Persia is ravaged by war. We must go no farther."

"Who is warring?" I questioned.

"The realm is held by Abaqa Khan, son of the fearsome Hulagu Khan, but his authority is being challenged by armies of the caliph of Cairo and by Mongol forces from the khanates to the east and north. There is scarcely a town or village untouched by conflict. Marauding armies are everywhere."

"How did you learn of this?"

"In the bazaar they talk of little else. It is said that Qom, some four days' journey from here, was sacked by a Mameluke army three months ago. Qom was to be our next replenishment stop, effendi. It now is rumored that Abaqa Khan rides against Bokhara."

"Is that in our path?"

"No . . . but it lies close to Merv."

I stroked my beard meditatively. The tough old Bedouin would not give undue weight to mere rumor. Still, if the forces of Abaqa Khan were campaigning at a distant location, that should mean we faced no immediate danger. I voiced that supposition.

The Bedouin inclined his head in agreement. "True, effendi, but when armies ebb and flow who can tell where conflict will erupt tomorrow? All Persia is in chaos. In disturbed times caravans are looked upon as legitimate prey. We should turn back while there is yet time to do so."

Turn back! What the Bedouin recommended represented safety for Orsini's party. For me, it well could mean salvation. If we returned to Acre, or Tripoli, surely I would find *some* means by which I could obtain my freedom. Hope surged anew within my breast.

Taking care not to show elation, I said gravely, "I'll alert Count Orsini to the acute danger facing us and do my best to persuade him to return to Acre."

It was not a matter I could entrust to Roccenti. I'd have to accept the risks involved in approaching Orsini directly. Striding to his pavilion, I pushed aside the flap and stepped within. I couldn't have chosen a more inappropriate moment.

Completely naked, Orsini's youthful companion lay sprawled on a disarray of cushions. The count, a silken robe accentuating rather than concealing his nudity, was pouring wine into a goblet. Distracted by my entrance, he spilled wine on the carpet as he turned to face me. When he recognized me, his protruding eyes glazed with fury.

"You!" he shrilled. "How *dare* you come here unbidden!"

"I would not have intruded," I said coldly, "had I not had news of utmost urgency." Glancing pointedly at the youth, I added, "For your ears alone."

Orsini's mouth worked convulsively. "You . . . you— this will cost you your life, Saxon!"

"If you don't listen to what I have to say, and act quickly on it, all our lives could be forfeit."

Orsini's gaze wavered. By now the youth had scrambled into a robe and was edging past us. Following the lad's unceremonious exit, Orsini made an effort to recover his dignity and assert his authority. "Explain yourself," he grated.

Stressing the grave nature of the threat facing Orsini and his party, and the possible theft of the caravan's trade goods, I recounted what the guide had told me, and the course of action he advocated.

"But we can't turn back!" Orsini exclaimed.

"If the guide and camel drivers leave, what choice do you have?"

"They wouldn't do that. They contracted to take us as far as Merv. I won't release them from that commitment."

"You won't have much say in the matter. Rather than face robbery and death, they'll simply disregard their commitment and leave."

"No, no!" Orsini protested. He searched through a heap of clothing until he located what he was looking for. He held up a metal plaque. "This ensures our safety."

I thought he had taken leave of his senses. "How?"

He handed me the plaque. It was incised with strange markings. At its bottom was an engraved circle containing what looked to be a replica of a falcon. "How can this protect us?" I asked. "Has it magical properties?"

His confidence returning, Orsini smiled. "No. It's an imperial edict guaranteeing safe conduct through all domains under Tartar control. The bird you see is a gyrfalcon . . . the personal seal of the mighty Kubilai Khan. Persia is but one of his satrapies. So you see, Saxon, to turn back would be unthinkable. We have nothing to fear from the forces of Abaqa Khan. You can assure the Arabs on that score.''

"They fear equally the Moslem mercenaries of the caliph of Cairo,'' I pointed out.

"If Abaqa Khan, as you say, is now campaigning far to the northeast, does that not mean that he has subdued the Mameluke forces in this region?''

That had been my deduction. It surprised me that Orsini had arrived at the same conclusion. Whatever else he might be, the count was no fool. "Perhaps,'' I conceded.

"Although I foresee no danger, you may tell the Arabs that I will double the agreed-upon price for their services. That should still their fears.''

"It should,'' I observed, "but what about your retainers and men-at-arms? Fear is contagious. They know naught of this talisman you claim guarantees safe conduct. They have been kept completely in the dark, knowing neither the ultimate purpose nor the destination of your expedition. I can assure you, they grow restive. It would require but little for them to desert you.''

Orsini's face registered concern. For the moment his hostility toward me seemed to have evaporated. He regarded me contemplatively, as though weighing a decision. When, finally, he spoke, he did so as though thinking aloud.

"Those disclosures I wanted to withhold as long as possible. Till the Nestorian joined us at Merv. Even later, if possible. But the time may be at hand. Yes, if there is danger of their deserting me, they must be told.'' Turning his eyes to me, he said in a firmer voice, "You seem to enjoy their confidence. You can tell them.''

It was an incredible tale.

Since childhood Leonardo Orsini had been afflicted with

a respiratory ailment. His father had heard of a learned doctor in Venice who claimed success in alleviating the symptoms of this condition. In the autumn of 1270 Leonardo went to Venice to be attended by this physician.

During his sojourn in Venice Leonardo met Niccolò and Maffeo Polo, Venetian merchants but recently returned from a country they claimed to be fabulously wealthy. This realm they called Cathay. It was ruled by a Mongol overlord, Kubilai Khan, grandson of the infamous Genghis Khan whose Tartar hordes had swept out of the east to the very gates of Europe. The Polos claimed that Kubilai Khan held sway over an empire so vast that the time taken to cross it from west to east was measured not in months, but in *years*.

Kubilai Khan had evidenced an interest in Christianity. Accordingly the Polos had a twofold mandate: to establish trade links, and to petition the pope to send one hundred theologians to Cathay to instruct the khan and his court in the ways of the Cross.

It long had been a dream of Christendom to make common cause with the Tartars in order to stem and turn back the flood of Islam. To the trade-minded Venetians, the Polos looked to be a godsend. They represented a means whereby the long-sought alliance could be wedded profitably to commercial interests.

Circumstances played neatly into Leonardo's hands. Due to squabbling among the cardinals, the papal seat had remained empty since the death of Pope Clement IV in 1268. The Polos, therefore, were prevented from presenting their petition directly to the pope. The Doge of Venice, fearing the golden opportunity might be exploited by outside interests, acted to forestall that eventuality. He ordered the Polos to return immediately to Cathay by way of Acre, where they could petition the papal legate, Teobaldo

Visconti, on the khan's behalf. The doge wrote a letter to Visconti requesting that the Polos be given every assistance, then speeded on their way.

The Polos had intended to return to Cathay laden with trade goods. Compliance with the doge's instructions didn't allow them time to assemble the goods. Alerted to this contretemps, Leonardo approached the Polos with a suggestion. He proposed to purchase the required items, with his father's financial assistance, and follow behind the Polos with a trade caravan. Since the Orsini name was synonymous with probity, the Polos seized on Leonardo's offer with alacrity.

The Polos gave Leonardo explicit instructions concerning what goods to buy, and in what amounts. They turned over to him the khan's metal plaque with the assurance that it would see him and his caravan safely through Tartar domains. Nonetheless they cautioned him that he must be accompanied by an armed party to guard against attack by bandits in isolated regions. When all was in readiness, he was to proceed to Acre, where he would be contacted by a Venetian merchant, Lorenzo Roccenti, who would see to the hiring of camels, camel drivers, and someone qualified to guide them on the first leg of their journey, to Merv. At Merv he would be contacted by a Nestorian friar, Brother Demetrios. The Nestorian would take care of necessary arrangements and guide them on their onward journey.

As he'd presented it, Count Orsini's story was plausible, but I had the feeling he was concealing something.

"I take it that the Polos have a share in the caravan?" I queried.

"A one-quarter share in its profit."

"When did they leave Venice?"

"They set sail for Acre early in 1271. They were a small party . . . Maffeo, Niccolò, Niccolò's young son

Marco, and three retainers. I understand from Roccenti that, while they were in Acre, Visconti was elected to the papacy as Pope Gregory X. He bestowed papal blessing on the Polos and gave them a written message to be delivered to Kubilai Khan. He entrusted them with valuable religious objects to be delivered to the khan and attached two learned theologians to the Polos' party.''

"Two! It's far short of the hundred requested.''

"I presume that the pope promised more to follow.''

"I see. Yet you have no theologians among your retainers. How were they to get to Cathay?'' Then another question sprang to mind. "When did the Polos leave Acre?''

"In the spring of 1271.''

"Why has it taken you two years to follow them?''

Evidently it was a question not to Orsini's liking. He dwelt a lengthy pause before answering. When he did so, his voice was tinged with bitterness. "My father is a conservative man. To his way of thinking the Polo brothers were charlatans who had hoodwinked the doge. Firmly opposed to such an expedition, my father refused to finance the purchase of trade goods. He was convinced that a journey such as I described would lead us to the edge of the world—and death and damnation. My brothers, Guillermo and Andreas, sided with my father.''

"How did you overcome their opposition?''

There was no humor in Orsini's smile. "My mother intervened on my behalf. The Franciscan abbot at San Georgio lent his support. My offer to forgo any inheritance altered the stance taken by my brothers. Eventually, albeit reluctantly, my father yielded to the pressure. Then I ran into another difficulty. It took a good deal of persuasion to put together the motley group I now have with me. Had they suspected the distance and hardships lying ahead of us, I doubt that I could have enticed more than one or two to join me. The delays, Saxon, were extremely vexing.''

"So you hid the truth from them. Other than those we've encountered to date, what hardships face us? What *is* the distance you speak of?''

Orsini bridled. "I know only what the Polos told me. We face deserts and mountains that defy description. I've been told we will face extremes of heat and cold undreamed of in our experience. The Polos estimate the distance from Acre to Cambulac—the khan's capital in Cathay—to be six thousand miles.''

I whistled soundlessly. Translated into leagues, a measurement of distance with which I was more familiar, I arrived at the incredible figure of *two thousand leagues*. No wonder the Polos had stated that the journey should be looked upon in terms of years. Suddenly I did not blame Orsini for having withheld this information.

Chapter Ten

The Bedouin guide, once assured that he had naught to fear from the Tartars, and that the agreed-upon price for his services would be doubled, agreed to continue the journey.

We reached Qom, and the dry-baked alkali marshes marking the beginning of the Dasht-e-Kavir, early in July. The Bedouin's information had been accurate. The town lay in ruins. Most of the population had fled. Those who remained were apprehensive and suspicious of our presence. At considerable cost we partially replenished our supplies.

Our waterskins filled to overflowing, we set off to the northeast. Within hours our camels and horses were slowed by the loose sand of the desert dunes. On our left barren foothills rose to equally barren peaks we could see but indistinctly through a shimmering haze. Ahead of us, and as far as we could see to our right, the endless dunes of yellow sand stretched to a wavering horizon.

Day after day, week after week, we slogged through that blistering inferno. Unrelenting glare assaulted our eyes.

The air seared our parched throats. If the Syrian desert had seemed like purgatory, the Dasht-e-Kavir was as Hell itself.

Still, the Syrian desert had served a useful purpose. It had taught us to conserve both our strength and our supply of precious water. In that long trek around the rim of the Persian desert, we lost two horses, but only one man.

That war had passed this way was much in evidence. Scarcely a day went by that we did not stumble upon bleached skeletal remains of humans, horses, or camels. Most of the villages along our route were deserted. Some looked to have been abandoned long ago. Others, where charred beams and lintels indicated they had been put to the torch, had been emptied of life but recently. In the latter case we encountered skulls and heaps of bones on the outskirts of the villages, grisly detritus of wanton slaughter.

One long-abandoned village proved to be our salvation. To be buffeted by hot winds laden with abrasive sand was by no means uncommon, but that morning was different. The sky took on a brassy sheen. Not a breath of air fanned our faces. Our guide's leathery face reflected concern. He altered our line of advance toward the foothills. Call it kismet, if you will. We came upon the shell of a deserted village just before the sandstorm struck.

For the better part of two days we huddled against shielding walls of mud and brick, our faces shrouded in unwound turbans, while the wind shrieked and sand swirled and eddied around us. Had it not been for the protection afforded by those crumbling walls, we would have been buried alive.

In early September we left the desert sands behind us, climbed onto firmer ground, threaded our way through a range of scrub-mantled hills, and descended into a fertile plain. It was mid-September when we filed wearily into Merv.

We understood now why we had encountered so few people and no marauding armies in our path. We appreciated why the fighting had shifted to the northern region. No military commander in his right mind would commit his forces to the Dasht-e-Kavir during the summer months.

Fatuously we believed that the worst part of our journey lay behind us.

Brother Demetrios was not on hand to meet us. I made inquiries, but no one knew the whereabouts of the Nestorian friar. He was well-known in the community but had not been seen in his usual haunts for many months. When I reported this to Orsini, he flew into a rage.

The camels of our caravan were unloaded and the bales and boxes stored in a *makhzan*. Our erstwhile Bedouin guide and camel drivers were paid off and dismissed. Our reduced party put up at two inns. Orsini and his retainers were quartered at a comfortable inn. I and my men-at-arms were billeted in meaner quarters.

In spite of Orsini's fretting and fuming there was little that could be done about the absence of the Nestorian. We dared venture no farther without the services of a competent guide. My efforts to procure a suitable substitute came to naught. No one seemed willing to take on the responsibility. I was told, in fact, that the mountains to the east soon would be impassable due to the onset of winter. Since we were barely into autumn, this seemed to me a flimsy pretext.

I found Merv fascinating, a bustling cosmopolitan hub of commerce. Apart from Persians, it sheltered Armenians, Jews, Greeks, Arabs, Turks, and assorted tribespeople too numerous to mention. Its Tartar overlords, swaggering through the bazaars and narrow streets with bandy-legged arrogance, were much in evidence. Among themselves they were given to loud talk and shrill laughter. Rarely did they deign to acknowledge the presence of those not of their race.

This was my first exposure to the much-feared Asiatic conquerors. They were a villainous-looking lot. Stocky and well-muscled, they were bronze-complected with broad, high-cheekboned faces and hooded, almond-shaped eyes. They were as alien a breed as I had yet encountered.

Their military trapping intrigued me. On their heads they wore caplike helms of bronze with a spikelike projection on the crown. The helms were fitted with leather flaps to afford protection to the ears and neck. There were some among them who boasted horsetail adornments attached to their helm spikes. Those I assumed to be of superior rank, since they wore, in addition to a sort of breastplate fashioned of hard leather, overlapping vertically curved plates of bronze affording protection to the shoulders much as did the pauldrons of my plate armor. Their unadorned shields were circular and of steel.

Their weapons, too, were of unfamiliar pattern. The swords they wore appeared to be little like my broadsword, but looked to be broader and heavier than the Saracen scimitar. The strangest feature, however, was the fact that *every* Tartar, regardless of rank, was equipped with a bow and one or two quivers of arrows. No English, French, or Teutonic knight, regardless of how adept he might be with a bow, carried one into battle. With the Tartars it appeared to be their weapon of choice. Their bows were vastly different from the English longbow. They appeared to be a good deal shorter and of curious shape in that they curved outward at the tips. They carried these strung bows in a tooled leather case something like a half-scabbard.

How was it possible, I thought wonderingly, for these short-statured warriors to have wreaked such havoc among their neighboring states?

Roccenti had dropped by my quarters for a visit. We were in a quiet corner of the drinking room absorbed in a game of chess. I had not heard anyone approach, but suddenly sensed an alien presence. Glancing up, I beheld a rotund figure clad in a grubby cassock standing a few feet from our table. He was staring at me intently, and when my gaze locked with his, a broad smile lit up his features. "I was told," he said in heavily accented Greek, "that a foreigner with hair and beard the color of ripened grain was seeking me. Perchance you are that man?"

I countered with a question of my own. "Are you Brother Demetrios?"

"In flesh and spirit . . . but why do you seek me?"

"I sought you on behalf of Count Leonardo Orsini."

The friar looked nonplused. "Why? Who is this nobleman of whom you speak?"

"Orsini! Count Orsini," I repeated. "The Polo brothers must have told you he was coming. They volunteered your services as a guide from here to Cathay."

"Uncommonly accommodating of the Polos," the friar observed dryly. "They might have advised *me*. This is the first I've heard of any such arrangement."

It was my turn to be nonplused. "Surely they arranged this with you when they passed this way en route to Cambulac two years ago."

The friar scratched his chin. "I've not seen the good merchants for well over five years. On that occasion they were westward, not eastward, bound. They made no mention of this Count Orsini. There is some mystery here, my lad. May I join you? Over a bowl of wine we might find the answers we seek.''

I moved over to make a place for the friar. Roccenti signaled the innkeeper and ordered another bowl and another flagon of wine. Turning to Brother Demetrios, Roccenti said earnestly, ''There is indeed a mystery. The Polos left Acre bound for Merv in the spring of 1271. Their stated purpose was to seek your assistance for Count Orsini.''

Since we had never discoursed in the tongue, it came as a surprise to me that Roccenti spoke Greek. The friar turned toward Roccenti and responded solemnly. ''I don't doubt you, but I can assure you they did not pass this way. Had they done so, even had I been absent, I would have learned of their visit. Had they sought my assistance, they would have left some message.''

''Could they have journeyed eastward by another route?'' I asked.

''It's possible, though highly unlikely. However, I've just returned from Yarkand and Kashgar by way of Samarkand. There's no word of the Polos having visited *any* of those places within the last six years . . . yet they would have to have stopped in at least one of those communities regardless of the route they took. The Polos are resourceful men, but Persia has been ravaged by war for more than two years. If nothing has been heard from them in all this time, I fear the worst.''

I took Brother Demetrios to see Orsini. What the friar had to relate could hardly have been what the count wanted to hear. Nevertheless, to my surprise, Orsini was all for pressing on with the journey.

''Since the Polos wished it,'' Brother Demetrios said

gravely, "I'll be happy to guide you thither, but I'm afraid you'll have to wait here until spring."

Orsini scowled. "Why? Have you a prior commitment?"

"It's now October. Before this month is out the passes will be choked with snow. We call those towering mountain ranges the 'Roof of the World.' You have no conception of what the mountains are like, even in summer. To enter them before the spring thaw sets in is to commit suicide."

"If we have no choice," Orsini responded dejectedly, "we'll have to accept the delay. In the meantime we'll visit Bokhara, which is, I'm told, the place to barter linens for carpets."

"True," Brother Demetrios responded, "but out of the question. Leaving Samarkand, I had to bypass Bokhara. Though Abaqa Khan has taken the city, he's hard-pressed to hold it. It's not safe anywhere in the vicinity of that beleaguered city at this time."

We saw out the winter at Merv, a city not lacking in distractions. Brother Demetrios introduced Roccenti and me to pleasurable establishments where, as the spirit moved us, we could eat, drink, gamble, and besport ourselves with a seemingly inexhaustible supply of doxies. If, as is said, variety is the spice of life, Roccenti and I partook of well-seasoned fare.

The friar was a great favorite in the taverns and tea-houses we frequented. I began to suspect that his interests lay more along temporal than spiritual lines.

Despite his faltering command of the tongue, Brother Demetrios claimed to be Greek e'en though his cheek-bones and heavy-lidded eyes betokened Asiatic heritage. As I learned later, his father was a Byzantine Greek hailing from Constantinople who had settled in the oasis of

Turfan and married a Uighur Tartar. Demetrios had been the only issue of that union.

A gifted storyteller, the friar regaled Roccenti and me with spellbinding tales of his travels and adventures. At first I believed most of his stories to be grossly exaggerated. Later, as I gained experience in the lands lying to the east, I came to appreciate that he had strayed but little from unadorned fact.

Probably because he considered me abysmally ignorant, Brother Demetrios took it upon himself to further my education. Initially this took the form of disabusing me of a number of misconceptions. For example, as most crusading knights were wont to do, I applied the term "Tartar" to all peoples from the distant east opposed to the Islamic faith. The friar pointed out that Moslems, be they Egyptians, Arabs, Turks, or Moors, referred to Europeans collectively as "Franks." In using the collective term "Tartars," I erred in similar fashion by not differentiating between Tartars and Mongols.

The Tartars embraced a bewildering number of tribal groups, yet all spoke some variation of the Turkic tongue which imparted loose but definable cultural ties. The Mongols, on the other hand, were nomadic herdsmen from the boundless grasslands of Central Asia who spoke a different tongue. Until united under the leadership of Genghis Khan, the Mongols had been vassals of a Tartar prince of the Kerait kingdom, himself a vassal of the Jürched Tartars.

Under Genghis Khan the Mongols had thrown off the yoke of Tartar thralldom. They'd surged forth from their native steppes, laying waste to everything in their path. Their fury had been directed first against the Tangut kingdom of Hsi Hsai. But one man in ten of that hapless realm had been left among the living.

Next Genghis Khan had turned his attention to the Jürched Tartars, who, as the Chin Dynasty, held sway in northern Cathay—or, as the friar referred to it, "China." The khan had abandoned that assault in response to an affront handed him by Mohammed-Shah, the Moslem king of Khorassan. Mohammed-Shah paid dearly for that insult. Genghis Khan turned westward, pushed through the mountains, and descended on Bokhara. After conquering Turkestan, he had divided his Mongol hordes, sending them scything northward to the Dnieper River and southward to Baghdad.

The conquest of China hadn't been forgotten, merely postponed. Following the death of Genghis Khan his son Ogadei, and then his grandsons Mangu and Kubilai, moved against the realm. In South China the conquest was still in progress.

Brother Demetrios dispelled another myth. We crusaders held fast to a belief that there was a Christian kingdom far to the east ruled by a king named Prestor John. When I mentioned this, the friar chuckled. He stated flatly that no such kingdom existed but added that the myth might have originated from the fact that Genghis Khan had been a convert to the Nestorian faith.

"He was a *Christian*!" I exclaimed in disbelief.

"So he professed, yet I've been told he continued to rely on shamans, seers, and astrologers for guidance."

As winter waned, I assisted Brother Demetrios in the procurement of additional horses and the purchases of additional equipment, stores, and provisions that would be needed for the resumption of our delayed journey. The friar supervised the hiring of a string of two-humped Bactrian camels together with the Tartar drivers to tend the ugly, ill-tempered beasts.

By the third week in March we had taken our trade

goods out of storage, loaded the camels, and were ready to proceed. Word reached us that the region near Bokhara was still in turmoil, so we filed out of Merv heading almost due east on the somewhat shorter, but more difficult, southern caravan route.

The going was easy. We made good time. I estimated we were averaging close to ten leagues a day. The terrain was relatively level. The trees were greening and new grass carpeted the rolling hills. Spring flowers added bright splashes of yellow, scarlet, and delicate mauve. To our right and left blue mountain ranges reared in the far and middle distance. The distant snow-crowned peaks formed a scenic backdrop of theatrical magnificence. I commented about this to Brother Demetrios, voicing a suspicion that he'd exaggerated the perils facing us in order to prolong his stay in Merv.

"They don't look as formidable as you intimated," I observed.

He laughed. "Not yet, my impatient young friend, but each day they'll grow closer and look more forbidding."

He was right. The valley narrowed and our progress slowed as the ascent grew steeper. The character of the country through which we passed changed. The mixed forest gradually gave way to the brooding blue-black of conifers. Patches of snow appeared between the trees and the trail was wet with meltwater. We slogged through mud, then slush, and finally ice-crusted snow. The mountains closed around us and took on a menacing aspect as they soared skyward in glacier-mantled splendor.

It was mid-May before we entered the weathered, snow-dusted, icicle-festooned town of Balkh.

Chapter Eleven

We stayed in Balkh just long enough to trade our horses for shaggy ponies, exchange the camels for a packtrain of surefooted mules, and replenish our supplies.

As replacements for the camel drivers Brother Demetrios hired stocky, deep-chested muleteers. They were a taciturn lot bundled in wraparound fur-lined hooded coats with fur-lined mitts attached to the sleeves by leather thongs. Their feet were encased in thick-soled felt boots; on their heads they wore fur-lined hats with earflaps that tied above the crown. The friar purchased similar coats, hats, and boots for our party. The protective clothing I could understand, but the bales of hay and bundles of firewood with which many of our pack animals were laden puzzled me.

The summer months were harrowing beyond belief.

Soon after we left Balkh we began a steep and tortuous ascent. The pine forest thinned, then dwindled to stunted shrubs and tufted grass. When, eventually, the ground leveled somewhat into a high plateau ringed by towering peaks, there was no vegetation whatsoever, just barren soil, bare rock, and ridges of crusted snow. It became apparent why we'd brought the hay and firewood.

The air was thin. Fires burned with a low flame that gave off little heat. The breathing both of men and beasts became labored. We tired easily and even thinking taxed our benumbed brains. We now averaged no more than two to three leagues a day.

When the sun beat down from a cloudless sky and was reflected off snowbanks and glacial ice, we sweltered, but such days were rare. More often than not clouds wrapped us in a chilling embrace or blizzards lashed at us. The nights, without exception, were bitterly cold. I awoke each morning with my moustache rimed with frost.

Five of our number suffered severe frostbite. One man lost three fingers of his right hand. Another had to have his left leg amputated when gangrene resulting from frostbite threatened his life. It was Brother Demetrios, assisted by the head muleteer, who performed the crude surgery.

The hazards were many. In places the trail narrowed to laboriously hacked ledges snaking along the faces of sheer cliffs. They seemed as though suspended between heaven and hell. One misstep meant hurtling to certain death in the mist-shrouded gorges thousands of feet below. At other times we found our progress blocked by raging torrents plunging down rock-filled chasms. We crossed these by means of swaying rope suspension bridges, taking with us lead ropes so that our ponies and pack animals, strung together like living necklaces, could be hauled across the roiling waters to safety. We negotiated passes so high that they left us gasping for breath. But our greatest fear was that the summer-softened snows perched precariously above us would come crashing down in avalanches that could obliterate our entire caravan. This was no empty threat, as a close brush with annihilation demonstrated.

Our head muleteer signaled a halt in the nick of time. Ahead, beyond an outcropping, we saw curtains of falling snow, then heard an ominous rumbling followed by a mighty roar as countless tons of snow thundered downward. It took us the better part of two days to flounder our way around the gigantic snowpile that filled the shallow valley to overflowing.

We did not come through these trials unscathed. In all, six pack-laden mules, three ponies, four of our mounted escort, a muleteer, and one of Orsini's retainers either plunged to their deaths or died by drowning in the roiling streams. It was a heavy price to pay. We'd left Aleppo with a mounted escort numbering sixteen men-at-arms. We now were reduced to half that number.

By the friar's reckoning the distance from Balkh to Yarkand was three thousand li. That worked out to about three hundred thirty leagues. At the rate we were going, we'd be lucky to be quit of these mountains before being overtaken by the snows of autumn, if *any* of us survived to see that day.

In the third week of August there came a day when we crested a saddle between two sentinel peaks. On the eastern side of that pass our descent was gradual, but consistently downward. In the days that followed, the temperature grew appreciably warmer and the thin air richer in substance. Brother Demetrios remarked offhandedly that our mountain ordeal was at an end. To a man our spirits lifted.

Early one morning we topped a rise and gazed down at a narrow valley. The near end of this valley was carpeted with coarse grass. The far end was screened from view by a thin mantle of evergreens.

Trees! It was all I could do to suppress a shout of glee. I'd almost forgotten what a tree looked like.

As we started a cautious descent of the rock-strewn trail, Brother Demetrios rode ahead to confer with the head muleteer. When I drew abreast of them I pulled off the trail and joined them.

"What is it?" I asked Brother Demetrios.

"Haven't you seen the beasts grazing yonder?"

"I see them. They look like long-haired oxen."

"They're yaks . . . a beast common to the Tibetan highlands. We suspect from their numbers that it's a domestic herd. But, if that is so, why do we see no herdsmen?"

"They could be hidden from view by those rocky outcroppings."

"Perhaps, but until we can confirm that fact, or that it's a wild herd, the caravan should go no farther. In particular it should keep well clear of yon narrow defile."

"What have we to fear from herdsmen?"

"From herdsmen, nothing. What we fear are Tibetan bandits. That twisting defile up ahead is an ideal place to set an ambush. Tell the count to hold the caravan where it is until we've had a chance to scout the rocks up ahead. Bring two troopers back with you and we'll move along the ridge to get a clear view. If there are bandits there, we should be able to flush them into the open."

I delivered the friar's warning and returned with two of the mounted escort. In single file we set out along the face of the slope, scrutinizing the outcropping for signs of life.

We had proceeded some distance when, to my horror, I looked back and saw the caravan moving downward into the defile. A few moments later the bandits erupted from their places of concealment.

Wheeling our mounts and yelling at the top of our lungs, we galloped full tilt down the precipitous slope to join the fray. As I slid from the saddle, I unhooked my battle-ax and thrust it into the friar's hands.

Powerless to prevent it, I witnessed Orsini's death. Ashen-faced, sword in hand, he stood with his back to a rock. A Tibetan bandit deftly sidestepped Orsini's futile thrust, then stepped in to lay the count open from neck to breastbone.

The bandit did not have time to savor his victory. Bellowing in anger, his bald pate glistening with sweat, Brother Demetrios swung the battle-ax in an arc that sheared the bandit's head from his shoulders.

I saw no more of that encounter. I was too busy defending myself against two bandits who rushed me in unison.

The sharp encounter was quickly at an end. Our arrival on the scene had turned the tide of battle in our favor. The bandits fled, making off with three of our pack mules.

At a point where a waterfall feathered downward into a pool of icy water, Roccenti and I bathed and dressed our wounds. Mine was nothing serious, a swordthrust in my left thigh. Seated on a rock at the pool's edge, Roccenti wrapped a bandage around a jagged gash in his forearm.

"A costly victory," I observed tartly.

Roccenti inspected his handiwork critically. Apparently satisfied, he responded, "It was that. Three dead, two badly injured."

"Why? What in God's name made Orsini ignore the friar's warning?"

Roccenti shrugged eloquently. "Pride. It looked as though you had given him an order. I guess he wanted to assert his authority. You and the friar were scarcely out of earshot before he gave the command to move forward."

"An error," I said wryly, "that cost him his life."

Roccenti grinned. "And gave you your freedom."

In truth, until Roccenti gave voice to it, that thought had not crossed my mind. "Yes," I said gravely, "so it did."

When Roccenti walked off toward the cooking fire, I remained by the pool some moments longer. I gave thought to Orsini. He had not been a brave man, yet he'd refused to abandon the expedition even when the Bedouins had wanted him to turn back. He'd lived in fear, yet he had endured the desert heat, a sandstorm, and the terror of our harrowing passage through the mountains without voicing complaint. Why? What had driven him? I thought I knew the answer, but now that he was dead I'd never know for sure.

From all accounts Leonardo had been a sickly and solitary child. The youngest son, he had known the dukedom to be beyond his reach unless some miracle should remove two older brothers from the picture. He had grown to manhood in the shadow of his brothers and an autocratic father. His only ally appeared to have been his mother. Then he'd met Maffeo and Niccolò Polo and seen an opportunity to step from the shadows by proving to himself, his brothers, his father, and the world, that he was made of heroic stuff. He'd felt strongly enough about it that he had renounced his inheritance to finance the undertaking. He *could not* abandon the venture. To have done so would have been to admit that he was nothing. Less than nothing.

I had disliked him intensely. Was part of that due to his homosexuality? Perhaps. Still, in some strange way his death saddened me more than I would have believed possible. He'd made a valiant effort to rise above himself. I felt he had deserved to win.

There was yet another fact I could not easily brush

aside. Had it not been for Orsini's purchase of me, in all likelihood I'd have perished in the oubliette. Whether I liked it or not, I owed my very life to the late Count Orsini.

The following morning we buried our dead and, at the friar's insistence, the four corpses of the Tibetan bandits.

Following that brief ceremony Roccenti, Brother Demetrios, and I went through Orsini's personal effects. In one of his saddlebags we found the plaque supposedly assuring us of safe passage through Mongol-held domains, and a metal box containing the count's store of gold coins. We were relieved to find that there appeared to be ample funding to take care of our immediate and foreseeable needs.

With Orsini's passing much had changed. I called a meeting of all but the muleteers. It was agreed that the surviving members of the party, including Brother Demetrios, would share equally in whatever profits the remaining trade goods might bring. We were also in full accord with the friar's suggestion that the muleteers had served us well and should be given a bonus when it came time to dispense with their services. As the final order of business we addressed ourselves to the question of leadership.

I was about to advance the suggestion that Brother Demetrios, since he alone knew what dangers lay ahead of us, was admirably suited to assume the leadership. I was forestalled by the sergeant-at-arms. He stated bluntly that, since Aleppo, he and his men had looked not to the count but to me for leadership and saw no reason to alter that state of affairs. That sentiment was heartily endorsed by Roccenti and, with no dissenting voice, I was proclaimed leader of the expedition.

*   *   *

There came a morning early in September when we emerged from a foothill valley and were greeted by an all-too-familiar spectacle—a static sea of yellow sand stretching to the far horizon. A bloodred disc of sun was struggling to free itself from clutching dunes. Even at this hour the air was heavy with promise of blistering heat to come.

Frigidarium to solarium, I thought wryly. In this godforsaken part of the world was there no such thing as a happy medium? Wistfully I thought of England's gentle autumns.

I thrust England from my thoughts. I had a commitment to fulfill before I could think in terms of directing my footsteps toward England—and Ravenscrest.

Ahead and to the left lay the palm-fringed oasis that sheltered and sustained the ancient town of Yarkand. According to Brother Demetrios, Yarkand but marked the midpoint in our journey from the Outremer to Cambulac.

Chapter Twelve

When he brought the brown-robed Tibetan monk into my presence, Brother Demetrios was beside himself with excitement. "It defies reason. I'd given them up for dead. Not so! This heathen cleric has news of them. He claims to have spoken with them. It's a miracle."

I laughed. "I'm happy to hear it, but with whom has the monk conversed so miraculously?"

"The Polos . . . Niccolò, Maffeo, and young Marco."

I stared at Brother Demetrios in stunned disbelief. I, too, had thought them dead. "Where? When?"

"In Srinagar, not more than six months gone. They were waiting for summer before challenging the Karakoram passes."

"How? How could Orsini's party start out two years behind the Polos, yet reach here ahead of them?"

Brother Demetrios spread his hands in a gesture of uncertainty. "Faith, I know not. The Tibetan spoke of illness in their party. For them to be in the Kashmir, they must have swung far to the south by way of India. We'll not know what route they followed till we've had a chance to talk with them.''

I looked at the Tibetan monk, who smiled at me hesitantly. It was obvious he'd not understood a word of my conversation with Brother Demetrios. "How did *he* get here?" I asked the friar.

"By yak, and on foot. He left Srinagar about the same time we left Merv."

"And when did the Polos leave Srinagar?"

"He knows not. They were still in Srinagar when he embarked on his journey."

"Then he doesn't know if the Polos actually left."

"No-oo. That's true. It's an assumption on my part, but, knowing the Polos, I think it a safe one."

Brother Demetrios was against our staying in Yarkand to see if the Polos put in an appearance. He argued convincingly that when they *did* arrive, they would learn that we had passed this way ahead of them. They would learn, in terms of time, how far ahead we were and, not slowed as we were by a caravan, should have no difficulty overtaking us.

We exchanged our mules for Bactrian camels and our ponies for tough little horses of the eastern plains. With hired drivers handling their shambling Bactrian charges, we set off to the northeast, our immediate destination, Kashgar, the foothill town that was a vital link in the trade route. At this nexus we would exchange woolen and linen textiles for carpets and jadestone, items that would command excellent prices in Cathay.

One thing puzzled me. Brother Demetrios had insisted we bring with us the fur-lined garments on which we had depended for survival in the mountains. Pulling my horse alongside his, I smiled inwardly at the picture of dejection he presented. He'd imbibed overly much the evening before in Yarkand and now was paying the price. Sweating profusely, he rode hunched forward in the saddle. When I questioned him about the fur-lined clothing, he belched loudly and turned a baleful eye on me.

"You'll know when winter comes," he answered curtly.

I gazed at the serried ranks of dunes, some of which rose to heights that must have exceeded three hundred feet. "I can't picture this desert blanketed wth snow."

"It never is, though it's cold enough for snow in the winter months. No rain falls here—ever. The encircling mountain ranges trap and hold all moisture. Yet in the winter, when winds blow down from glacial peaks, it's brutally cold here. Many have frozen to death in their tents, and some even in their saddles. Believe me, ere many weeks have passed you'll welcome the warmth of furs."

"This doesn't look like the Persian desert," I observed.

"It isn't. It's worse. I doubt that there are deserts anywhere on earth like this, or the Lop desert east of here. This is called Taklamakan. In Turkic that means, 'Go in and you won't come out.' It is no exaggeration. Entire caravans, even whole armies, have ventured into these deserts never to be seen or heard of again. The Chinese call this desert *Liu Sha*—'moving sands.' "

I grinned. "The dunes look reasonably steady."

"They aren't. They are ceaselessly in motion, stirred by the constant desert winds. If, for any reason, an oasis or village is abandoned, it is soon swallowed by the relentless march of the dunes. The sands are never still. If you listen, you can hear the 'music of the dunes'—the mournful sighing of the wind and the murmur of restless sand in motion."

I strained my ears, but all *I* heard was the whisper of a

faint breeze. It brought to mind a threat I'd all but forgotten.
"Is this desert plagued with sandstorms?"

The friar grimaced. "If God is kind, He'll not inflict on
us a *kara-buran*—'black hurricane.' If He's *not* kind—"
Leaving the sentence unfinished, he groped for his waterskin,
gulped greedily, wiped his mouth with the back of his
hand, then belched. "Please, Edmund, no more questions.
For some reason I don't feel at all well this morning."

Having concluded our trading, we left Kashgar in early
October. As we moved northeastward along the desert rim,
the days stretched into weeks, the weeks into months.
Between oases, spaced no more than two days' travel
apart, we encountered few people. At one point we passed
a westbound caravan. On two occasions we were stopped
and questioned by Mongol military patrols.

Both times we were stopped I produced the metal plaque
for inspection. In each case the reactions were markedly
similar. The examining officer frowned darkly, subjected
me to sharp scrutiny, then passed us with every show of
reluctance. I remarked on this to Brother Demetrios.

The friar chuckled. "You're right. They have no choice
but to let us pass . . . but they like it not, especially here
in Turkestan."

"Why? Why here especially?"

"The empire's khanates are ruled by *yarlik*—mandates
issued by Kubilai conferring authority on the regional
khans to govern in his name. Some khans have exceeded
that authority rebelliously. Here, Kaidu, allied with Kubilai's
distant cousin, Barak Khan, is a troublemaker. It was
Barak Khan who, in defiance of Kubilai, attacked his
cousin, Abaqa Khan, in Persia. These disputes, however,
are but family squabbles. Regardless of rivalries, the trade

routes are vital to the wealth and well-being of the empire as a whole and must be kept open to commercial traffic. Our safe conduct *had* to be honored."

The morning dawned ominously still. Brother Demetrios scanned the sky anxiously. Suspecting what lay in store for us, he instructed us concerning the precautions to take if a *kara-buran* overtook us. The camels would be made to recline and the horses lie flat. We were to wrap ourselves in our felt tents and shelter behind our horses.

Shortly before noon the sky darkened. We scarcely had time to comply with the friar's instructions before the storm struck with frightening ferocity. It was like a preview of hell. Sand and pebbles were sucked aloft, then hurled down upon us with terrific force. The wind shrieked like a thousand tortured demons. With our tents wrapped tightly around us we trembled helplessly while the storm lashed us relentlessly, and fiends from the underworld did their best to strip us of protective cover.

The voice of the storm became less strident. Then, almost as quickly as it had come upon us, the storm abated. We emerged from our felt cocoons to be greeted by bright sunshine and little more than a vagrant breeze. The horses, sensing they were no longer in danger, struggled upright, snorting and shaking sand from their bruised hides.

The *kara-buran* had moved away from us toward the southeast. It was an awesome spectacle. A wavering inverted cone rose skyward from a billowing mass of swirling sand. At its apex this dark funnel mushroomed into a cloud that spread like a black stain across the sky.

Brother Demetrios watched the retreating storm some minutes before turning toward me. "In His infinite wisdom, God has seen fit to spare us," he said solemnly. "The storm merely brushed us in passing."

* * *

On the ninth day of December we reached the oasis of Turfan. Even though Brother Demetrios had described his birthplace, I was ill-prepared for its reality. Frankly, I'd dismissed much that he'd said as fanciful embellishment. Imagine my surprise to find that, if anything, he had understated the case.

We approached the town through an expanse of fertile, well-tended fields, vineyards, orchards, and majestic groves of oil and date palms. It was a garden spot holding the desolation of the surrounding countryside at bay by the ingenious employment of irrigation ditches and canals. It was the stockade-protected town itself, however, which occasioned my greatest amazement.

Like Merv, Turfan was a crossroads of commerce. A melting pot of humanity, it had attracted migrants from Cathay, India, Persia, the realms of the Outremer, and the kingdoms of Eastern Europe. Now, it even boasted one transient Englishman.

A babel of tongues resounded in the bazaars, though people of different races gravitated toward separate quarters where they lived and worshiped according to individual customs and faiths. In various parts of town I encountered Moslem mosques, Buddhist temples, Confucian and Shamanist shrines, Jewish synagogues, and Christian churches. Esoteric religions I'd never heard of, such as Manichaeism and Zoroastrianism, commanded modest followings. In its polyglot mixture of races and its hodgepodge of customs and beliefs, I have never, before or since, encountered anything quite like Turfan.

We were quartered in the Nestorian Christian enclave, wherein lived a motley collection of Greeks, Armenians, Bulgars, Tartars, and various mixtures thereof. Since there dwelt in that neighborhood some fair-haired Greeks, I was not looked upon as an oddity.

We lingered in Turfan for more than two weeks, enjoying the openhanded hospitality of the townspeople. We frequented myriad wineshops and houses of pleasure. Betimes we engaged profitably in trade, acquiring goods such as dried fruit, casks of wine, saffron, and Tibetan musk, commodities much in demand in Cambulac.

One incident stands out vividly in my memory. Brother Demetrios and I were walking near the town gates when we came upon a number of two-wheeled wagons with canopies of felt from which were suspended colored silken panels that effectively screened the interior of the vehicles from view. Yoked oxen, harnessed to the whiffletrees, stood listlessly in the traces of the stationary wagons.

As the friar and I approached, a group of girls and young women, cloaked warmly for traveling, emerged from a side street. Escorted by Mongol soldiers, the women moved as a body toward the parked wagons. As the group neared the wagons an officer divided them into smaller groups alongside individual vehicles.

We were fairly close when an errant breeze lifted the head covering from a girl waiting her turn to get into the aftermost wagon. As she reached up to readjust her shawl, the girl turned toward me. I stopped in benumbed astonishment. For a fleeting moment I could have sworn I was looking at Ethelwyn of Hebb.

Except for her creamy complexion and fineness of features, the girl was not really that much like Ethelwyn. The girl's hair wasn't dark red, but black as a raven's wing and her eyes were a deep shade of violet. For a brief moment the girl caught my eye and looked directly at me.

Her lips parted in a timid smile before her readjustment of the shawl hid her face.

Brother Demetrios tugged at my sleeve. His voice betraying concern, he said, "Come away from here, Edmund, lad, before you get us into serious trouble."

Still bemused by the encounter, I stood as though rooted to the cobblestones. Exerting firm pressure on my elbow, the friar got me moving and steered away from the loading wagons.

"The soldiers belong to the Imperial Guard," the friar explained. "Those young women have been honored by being selected to grace the khan's harem as concubines. They're now Kubilai's personal property. It's forbidden to have any contact with them . . . even to gaze on them is considered a crime. It is just as well that the officer was otherwise occupied and didn't notice your obvious interest."

"I'm sorry," I mumbled apologetically. "She reminded me of someone I knew some years ago."

"Well, you can put her from your mind. She's as much out of your reach as though she were in another world. In fact, she *is* about to enter another world—a world of idle luxury and total isolation."

"But how," I asked, "can the khan hope to service all of them?"

Brother Demetrios snorted good-humoredly. "They're but a small portion of his harem. The selection here, and in other oases, is an annual event. It's a form of tribute. Kubilai has a taste for variety. He *might* get around to servicing one or two of them. He might bed none of them. Their fate is not your concern. Bear in mind that he exercises the power of life and death over them . . . and over every man, woman, and child in his domain."

*　　*　　*

When the Polos hadn't put in an appearance by the last week in December, our decision was to move on. The idea of wintering in Turfan was tempting, but with the possible exception of Brother Demetrios, there was not a man in our party not anxious to see an end to the journey.

We left Turfan two days after Christmas. When we made camp the first night out of Turfan, Brother Demetrios came to my tent carrying a lacquered box. When he'd settled himself comfortably and accepted a bowl of wine, my curiosity got the best of me. "What's that?" I asked, pointing to the box he was holding in his lap.

Brother Demetrios grinned. "A belated Christmas present." He opened the box, displaying to view a wooden cup filled with brushes, a stoppered flask, a shallow covered dish, a flat object that looked like a whetstone, and several short lengths of a substance resembling jet. "Over the past year, in the time at our disposal, you have made gratifying strides in attaining a measure of fluency in spoken Chinese—at least insofar as the Mandarin dialect is concerned. Now it's time I introduced you to the mysteries of the written language. This," he said, holding up one of the black objects, "is an inkstick."

We traveled eastward, keeping to the northern fringes of the Lop and Gobi deserts, until we reached the foothills town of Hami, then turned to the southeast. The giant dunes that had characterized the Taklamakan and Lop deserts now gave way to rocky ground, winter-browned scrub foliage, and sere grass. Now well into winter, we were thankful indeed for the warmth of our fur-lined garments, sleeping furs, and the heat provided by charcoal braziers in our tents.

On the twentieth of January we reached Tun-huang. Since it was a point of convergence of three caravan routes, I would have thought it to be a bustling cosmopolitan community. Not at all. It offered little by way of trade goods or diversions to tempt the wayfarer. We passed through the squalid village with barely a pause.

We now traveled eastward into gently undulating terrain carpeted with brittle, snow-dusted grass. Brother Demetrios informed us that these were the steppes that had provided grazing land for a bewildering array of nomadic herdsmen since the dawn of time. All, he claimed, were quarrelsome breeds who had visited death and destruction on their neighbors. Praise be to God, he added, that the steppes were but sparsely populated.

The grasslands stretched as far as the eye could see. I questioned the friar concerning their extent. His answer was that he knew no man who could testify to the actual limits of the steppes. He'd been told that one could journey for a full year in any direction yet still be within the confines of the grassy tableland.

That the steppes indeed were sparsely populated soon became only too evident. We traveled the better part of a week without encountering a living soul.

On the evening of the sixth day we came to the lip of a shallow depression and gazed down upon a group of white circular tents clustered on the bank of an ice-glazed stream. Smoke rose lazily from holes in the tops of the tents. Slightly removed from the cluster of squat tents was a larger one erected on a flat-bedded wagon. Sheep, cattle, and horses grazed near the tents. Horsemen, carrying long poles with loops of rope attached to their ends, moved among the livestock.

"Odd-looking tents," I remarked to Brother Demetrios.

"They're called *yurts*. Lime-washed felt stretched over a framework of poles. The frame can be disassembled and the yurt folded for transporting. The big one belongs to the tribal chieftain. When *he* moves, they hitch bullocks to the wagon and haul the whole thing off to the new campsite.''

''Who are they?''

''Mongols . . . in their natural state. This is how they've lived for thousands of years—until some of them got it into their heads that their destiny was to conquer the world.''

Chapter Thirteen

Three horsemen detached themselves from their fellow tribesmen and galloped toward us.

"What do you suppose they want?" I asked the friar.

"Undoubtedly to invite us to spend the night and join in the festivities. When they aren't intent on killing you, the Mongols are hospitable folk."

"What festivities?"

"Tonight we'll be treated to wrestling bouts . . . and filled to the eyeballs with *kumiss*, a potent drink made from fermented mare's milk. Tomorrow morning they will indulge in competitive feats of horsemanship expressly for our benefit. No one can match the Mongols in equestrian skills, and like children, they love to show off."

We were twenty days out of Tun-huang when we encountered something Brother Demetrios had not seen fit to mention previously. Rising up from the morning mist I saw what I took to be the battlements of a castle. As we drew closer, I realized that the crenelated rampart was no ordinary battlement. From the bastioned gate that loomed in front of us the fortification stretched eastward in an unbroken line as far as the eye could see. Reinforced at intervals with watchtowers, it followed the contour of the land, snaking over hills and low mountains until it faded from view in the far distance.

I waited until Brother Demetrios drew abreast of me.

"In God's name," I questioned, "what is it?"

"The Great Wall. It extends from here to the Eastern Sea. Fortifications designed to protect China from the incursions of barbarians."

"God's teeth!" I exclaimed wonderingly "How far is it to the Eastern Sea?"

"About sixty-five hundred li."

God in Heaven! It staggered the imagination. *Seven hundred leagues!*

The friar watched my face mirror astonishment and disbelief. He chuckled. "I'm not lying to you. You're going to find many things in China that will leave you awestruck, but this wall undoubtedly surpasses most of China's wonders. It is, by the way, an ancient structure falling into disrepair."

"How old is it?"

"It was built during the reign of the First Emperor, Shih Huang-ti, some two centuries before the birth of Christ."

"Fifteen hundred years ago!"

"Give or take a few decades . . . but parts of the wall are much older. The First Emperor joined together fortifications built centuries earlier to protect smaller kingdoms than that of the Chin Dynasty founded by Huang-ti."

I rode forward in silence, digesting what I'd been told. When we were almost within the wall's shadow, I ventured comment. "It's massive."

"About twenty-five feet in width at the base. Fifteen

feet at the top. It varies in height between twenty and fifty feet.''

"I don't see any guards at the gate, nor soldiers manning the watchtowers.''

"Nor will you. It fell into disuse centuries ago. I don't think it ever proved very effective against determined attackers. Invasion after invasion has swept over the wall. The Mongols are but the latest in a long list of conquerors.''

We filed through the yawning gate in the Great Wall at Shanhai Pass and entered fabled Cathay. Our journey, I felt, was almost at an end. Or was it? A realm that boasted a fortified northern frontier of five hundred leagues had to be a domain of fantastic size. Just where within its borders lay the imperial capital?

For the remainder of our first day in Cathay we traveled southeastward. Rugged snow-mantled mountains rose steeply on our right. To our left the brooding wall was constantly in sight. If I'd expected to be greeted by prosperous towns and villages, I was sadly mistaken. The countryside was as empty of populace and habitation as it had been north of the Great Wall.

When we made camp that evening, I questioned Brother Demetrios. "How long,'' I asked innocently, "should it take us to reach Cambulac from here?''

"Mmmm. It's now mid-February.'' The friar's brow furrowed in concentration. "We should reach Lanchow by the end of the month—in time to celebrate the lunar New Year. From there to Ch'ang-an, where we'll pick up fresh mounts, will take about three weeks. From there on, we should make better time. The road is considerably better, and spring will be upon us. Then Loyang, Kaifeng, and north to Cambulac. If we encounter no unforeseen delays, we should reach Cambulac no later than the end of May.''

Any hope that I'd harbored about an early end to our journey was rudely dashed.

It was shortly before our arrival at Lanchow that Brother Demetrios gave me sound advice. "To the Chinese," he said seriously, "you are a *man-tze*—a 'barbarian.' I suggest you profess ignorance of their tongue until you've been here some time. Instead of being pleased that you can converse with them, they well could be offended. This applies doubly to the small skills you've acquired in the written language. Literacy is reserved for the mandarin class. It sets them apart from the uneducated masses. Mandarins would look with suspicion on any barbarian who had attained such skills."

"*Barbarian!*" I exclaimed indignantly. "I'm a knight of noble birth."

Brother Demetrios smiled indulgently. "You could be Edward of England, yet still considered a barbarian by the Chinese. Even the lowliest peasant in this realm thinks of himself as 'civilized' and all from beyond the borders of the Middle Kingdom as inferior barbarians."

"Do they include their Mongol emperor in that category?" I queried sarcastically.

His answer surprised me. "Indeed they do . . . despite the fact that Kubilai was raised in China. And the ironic thing is that his own people consider him more Chinese than Mongol."

"I don't think," I said dolefully, "I'll ever fathom the workings of the Asiatic mind."

Brother Demetrios chuckled. "You will, Edmund, lad, you will. If a desert-born Greek like me can master its subtleties, an English nobleman should not find it trying. All you have to do is keep your eyes and ears open . . . and your mouth shut."

I smiled inwardly. By then I'd come to appreciate that

Brother Demetrios *did* think of himself as Byzantine Greek, e'en though he'd yet to set foot in Byzantium. It wasn't that he repudiated his Uighur heritage—he just did not give it thought. Of course he understood the workings of the Asiatic mind. He was born to it. Whether he admitted it or not, it was part of his heritage. His approach to a problem lacked the logic I'd come to associate with Greek philosophers. Often I'd found the good friar's reasoning distressingly oblique.

Of a truth I found the friar's values were slanted more toward the Orient than the Occident. If, eventually, I gained a moderate grasp of Asiatic thought processes it was more from having to cope with the instinctive dissembling of Brother Demetrios than from exposure to any other influence.

Yet, withal, he truly thought of himself as a "desert-born Greek" applying Hellenistic logic to any problem that confronted him. I never disputed this harmless conceit.

We arrived at Lanchow, as the friar had predicted, in time for the lunar New Year. For most of us it was a novel experience.

The Chinese were bidding farewell to the Year of the Dog and welcoming in the Year of the Boar. Although we stayed but three days, the festivities went on for an entire week with rituals honoring the family ancestors, visits between relatives and friends, exchanges of gifts, and much feasting.

Promptly at midnight on the first day of the festivities, a frightful din scared me half out of my wits. What I had thought to be but colorful decorations hanging from eaves and lintels turned out to be something else entirely. These strings of small cylinders made of heavy layers of paper were sealed at one end and had a twisted strip of paper protruding from the other end. The cylindrical tubes were filled with an explosive mixture called "black powder." When the protruding strips of paper were intertwined, the result was a long string of these small cylinders.

If a glowing stick ignited the twisted paper protrusions, a rippling chain of explosions followed—loud bangs, flashes of flame, and a thin cloud of acrid smoke. It was startling, to say the least.

I first thought that these exploding devices were a form of nocturnal entertainment. Everyone appeared to enjoy the noise and fiery display immensely. I learned, however, that the primary purpose was less frivolous. The explosions were designed to frighten away demons and evil spirits attempting to effect entry into a household by accompanying the spirits of the ancestors who returned at midnight to preside over the New Year's festivities.

We arrived at Ch'ang-an at the end of the third week in March. It was a teeming city of great antiquity. It had been, in fact, the ancient capital of the Han dynasty and, in those long-gone days, had been the eastern terminus of the caravan routes. Although the metropolis offered much in the way of pleasures, we stopped just long enough to procure fresh mounts.

From Ch'ang-an we moved on via Loyang and Kaifeng, then almost due north through greening fields of grain. News of our coming had preceded us. We were accorded every courtesy at the inns along the way. We were treated, in fact, more like visiting dignitaries than merchant adventurers.

On the twenty-third of May—two years and one month to the day since I'd departed Aleppo—we arrived at our final destination, Cambulac. Brother Demetrios, Lorenzo

Roccenti, and I were assigned comfortable quarters within the walled compound of the Imperial City. The remainder of our party were billeted in the city proper.

Brother Demetrios underwent a remarkable transformation. He discarded his frayed cassock and scuffed sandals, replacing them with a robe of rich damask and slippers of embroidered felt. The fringe of hair that emphasized rather than mitigated his baldness he now wore neatly trimmed. In truth he now looked more like a courtier than a humble Christian cleric.

One evening shortly after our arrival in the capital he bustled into my quarters beaming broadly. "Edmund, lad, you've been summoned to appear before the khan the day after tomorrow. It's to be a private audience. A rare privilege, rare indeed."

"Why has this signal honor been bestowed on me?"

"It must have reached the king's ears that you're an English knight of noble birth. The summons refers to you as a *chün fa*—a 'warlord.' It makes mention of the fact that you put to flight the Tibetan bandits."

"*I* put them to flight? How could that have come to his ears? We came late upon the scene and played but a minor part in the encounter."

"It was you who trained our escort in fighting skills, was it not?"

"Yes, but—"

"Well, there you are," the friar interjected. "If you didn't rout the bandits personally, the credit for our victory is yet yours."

It was specious reasoning, but I let it pass. "*Why* has he summoned me to this private audience?"

"I know not. However, since I'm to accompany you as an interpreter, I'll learn when you do. You will, however, have little need of me. Your discussion with the khan—at his request—will be conducted in Mandarin.''

God's teeth! My command of the dialect still left much to be desired. "I'll have need of you, little father, rest assured of that." Then another thought sprang to mind. "How should I be garbed for the occasion?"

"Though I've yet to view them, I'm told you possess knightly trappings. I suggest you wear military attire. Have you any more questions?"

"None that come to mind at the moment."

"Good. We mustn't be late for the appointment. I'll come by to fetch you the day after tomorrow shortly before the hours of the dragon."

"The hours of *what*?"

Brother Demetrios grinned apologetically. "Forgive me. The hours of the dragon are from eight to ten in the morning. Your audience is scheduled for nine o'clock."

Brother Demetrios started to leave, then paused at the doorway and turned back to face me. "Oh, I almost forgot. Word has reached the capital that the Polos have reached Ch'ang-an. They should be here ere long."

It wasn't until some minutes after his departure that a disquieting thought came to me. While many of our party knew that Brother Demetrios had been tutoring me in Chinese, I'd not spoken the tongue in public. The only way the khan could have known I was able to converse in Mandarin *must* have come through information supplied him by the friar. In fact, *everything* Kubilai knew about me must have come from the same source. Why, and when, had Brother Demetrios talked to the khan about me?

My trunk had remained untouched for more than two years. I didn't expect to find its contents in good condition, but I wasn't prepared for what greeted me.

The plate armor was so rusted that none of its articulated parts would function. Probably the helmet and breastplate could be salvaged, but little else. My immediate concern, however, was the chain mail, surcoat, boots, and leather gauntlets. They as well were in a sorry state.

I spread those items on the Bokhara rug, added my sword belt, scabbard, and spurs, then summoned a manservant. For his benefit I pantomimed what I wanted done. His face impassive, he nodded his understanding, gathered everything up, and departed.

I wouldn't have believed it possible. The next morning he returned my accoutrements almost as good as new. The hauberk and coif had been brushed free of rust and buffed until they shone. My surcoat had been laundered and ironed. The boots and gauntlets had been cleaned of the green mold that had furred them, the boots polished to a high gloss and light oil worked into the gauntlets to soften the leather. My spurs had been scraped clean and polished, my sword belt and scabbard rubbed with darkened oil.

I was much pleased with the miraculous transformation.

Chapter Fourteen

Brother Demetrios subjected me to critical appraisal. "Impressive, but there's one thing I should have mentioned. No guards will be present during the audience. You must not go into his presence armed. The belt and scabbard are acceptable but you'll have to leave your sword with an attendant."

"Any more instructions?" I questioned testily.

"Two more. When you come into his presence you're expected to kowtow. Take your cue from me and do as I do. On leaving, your back must never face him. Back away from his presence . . . and be sure you don't trip over your scabbard."

When I rose to my feet after prostrating myself demeaningly in the obligatory kowtow, my confidence left me. The opulence of the audience chamber and the richness of the khan's attire made me feel like a country bumpkin.

The throne on which he sat dwarfed him. It was of ornately carved wood inlaid with gemstones and mother-of-pearl. Four marble steps, divided in the center and bounded on the sides by intricately carved balustrades, led up to the platform on which his throne was mounted. Twenty-foot hanging panels of yellow silk formed a backdrop for the dais.

On his head the khan wore a close-fitting cap of black silk edged with scarlet velvet. His robe was voluminous, with a high collar and upward-flaring wings at the shoulders. Of scarlet silk trimmed with black, the robe was heavily brocaded in gold and encrusted with glittering jewels. It was an impressive—almost overpowering—display of riches.

I'd been told by Brother Demetrios that Kubilai was in his fifty-ninth year. I found that difficult to credit. His broad face was unlined. There was no trace of gray in the moustache that curved downward at each side of his mouth, or in his sparse beard. On either side of his flat-bridged nose his droop-lidded eyes regarded me unblinkingly. His face was devoid of expression.

Finally he broke the lengthening silence with a question that took me by surprise. "Are you familiar with Mongol weaponry?"

"No, sire. I have had neither the chance to examine Mongol weapons nor the opportunity to see them put to use."

"That will be remedied. Tell me, would that cloak of metal you wear beneath your tunic turn aside an arrow?"

"Not a direct hit sped from close range, sire."

"I understand that crusading knights wear heavier armor. Would *it* be proof against arrows?"

"Yes, sire."

"Do you possess such armor?"

"I do, sire, but so rusted through disuse I fear it is beyond repair."

"Then have it copied by our metalsmiths."

"That, my lord, would resolve but half of the dilemma. An armored knight must go mounted into battle. I have seen no horses in your realm capable of supporting such weight over an extended period."

"Be not deceived by appearances. Our horses are bred for speed, but are a good deal stronger than they look. However, should a sturdier breed be required, we have some in the Imperial Stables. I will issue instructions that you be allowed to select a horse more suited to your needs."

"Thank you, sire."

Kubilai regarded me steadily for a moment, then abruptly changed the thrust of his questioning. "I am told that you were captured by Muslims. Why were you not executed?"

"They hoped to profit, my lord, through ransom."

"Was the ransom paid?"

I was certain that Kubilai knew the answers to these questions. Was he baiting me? "No, sire, yet profit was forthcoming through the sale of my services to a Venetian merchant."

"For whom you trained and commanded his armed escort. Yet, if my information is correct, you harbored neither respect nor affection for the Venetian. Still, when the caravan was attacked by Tibetan bandits, you risked your life to save his. Why?"

"In vain, sire. The Venetian lost his life."

"So I have been told, but why should you lift your hand to defend a man you evidently disliked intensely?"

"It was my duty, sire," I replied stiffly.

"Ah, yes. Duty." Kubilai lapsed into silence. His eyes stayed focused fixedly on me. Finally he inclined his head slightly as though arriving at a decision. "The empress has gone with my sons to the Summer Palace in Shangtu. I join them a week hence. You will accompany my party.

At Shangtu you will be instructed in Mongol tactics and the use of our weapons." He paused, then added as an afterthought, "The birds embroidered on your tunic. What birds are they? What do they signify?"

"They are ravens, sire. A bird common in England. The device is that of my family—the de Beauchamps coat of arms."

Swinging his gaze from me to Brother Demetrios, Kubilai addressed him at some length in the Mongol tongue. Brother Demetrios listened intently and responded deferentially.

Following that exchange the khan dismissed us with a curt nod. We backed from his presence.

When I'd collected my sword, the friar and I left the palace by a side portal. I must confess to both confusion and uneasiness.

"Why did he display such interest in me?"

The friar rubbed his jaw in a gesture of bewilderment. "Faith, I know not. I thought the sole reason for the audience was to satisfy his curiosity."

"You left little curiosity to satisfy," I retorted acidly. "It *was* you, was it not, who told him of my capture by the Saracens, and the events that followed?"

"What would you have me do?" Brother Demetrios said defensively. "He is, after all, the *khaghan*—the 'supreme ruler,' the khan of khans. His spies are everywhere. For the most part he but seeks verification of facts already known to him. When he questioned me about you, I answered in all frankness."

"What sort of questions?"

"Oh, your status as both knight and nobleman. What sort of training you gave our men-at-arms. How those Greek islanders responded to your authority. How it came to pass, following Orsini's death, that you were chosen to lead the expedition. Questions of that nature."

"He made no mention of the military training he has in mind for me?"

"Not a word. That came as a complete surprise."

"At the end of the audience, what was it he said to you in his native tongue?"

Brother Demetrios hesitated. He looked decidedly uncomfortable. "I was ordered to accompany you to Shangtu and . . . ah—"

"And what?" I prompted.

"He said that your ravens resemble the imperial gyrfalcon too closely. They are to be expunged from your coat of arms."

"God's blood!" I exploded. "In no wise do they resemble a sea falcon. But if he took my coat of arms as an affront, why did he not address his remarks to me? Why relay them through you?"

There was much to be done in the week prior to our departure.

With Brother Demetrios I visited the Imperial Stables. The stablemaster had been expecting me and produced a number of horses for my inspection. I had not expected to find anything like a Flemish-sired war-horse similar to Saracen, yet, to my surprise, the stablemaster brought out several spirited mounts of almost comparable size. These, he explained, derived from Ferghana bloodline—famed as the "heavenly horses" of the Han and T'ang dynasties. While I was indifferent to the fabled lineage, I was delighted by the horseflesh it had spawned. I selected a stallion that was as black as polished jet. Whimsically I named him Scimitar.

Next, together with a manservant burdened with my rust-pitted armor, we visited a metalsmith. He examined the plate armor and assured us that he could duplicate it—but not in steel, a metal in short supply reserved for shields and sword blades. We would have to content ourselves with a duplication in bronze. Additionally I needed protective armor for Scimitar. I explained what I wanted to Brother Demetrios, who, in turn, explained it to the metalworker, who measured the horse's head for a chamfron and his chest and flanks for barding. We had to accept the fact, however, that the armor would not be ready in time for our departure.

We called in a tailor to measure Scimitar for a trapper made of gold silk edged in black and two pennants of similar material for my lance.

Having nothing to serve as a model, I used charcoal to sketch on a piece of parchment a battle lance. A carpenter made one for me out of a hardwood called teak and sheathed it with an iron tip.

The last item on my list called for the services of a saddler to provide Scimitar with tack suited to his new calling as a war-horse and a saddle for me. In accordance with my instructions the saddle was fitted with a lance socket, loops for my battle-ax, and stirrups of sufficient length to meet my requirements.

Apart from these essential tasks another matter demanded my attention. I found time to confer with Roccenti. He assured me that negotiations for the disposal of our trade goods and the acquisition of silks, spices, gems, and porcelains for our return journey were proceeding satisfactorily. I cautioned him to keep a strict accounting of all transactions, reminding him of Orsini's commitment to reserve one-quarter of the profits for the Polo brothers.

"When do you think we'll be ready to embark on the return journey?" I asked.

"With luck, by summer's end. How long do you expect to be in Shangtu?"

"Forsooth, I cannot say with certitude, but I don't anticipate being gone much longer than a month. I've seen little of our party. How are they faring?"

Roccenti grinned. "Famously, despite the language barrier. There's no shortage of wine, and the local wenches are most accommodating. But they are, to a man, anxious to embark on the homeward journey."

I laughed. "I share their sentiments. It's remarkable how hardships fade into insignificance when home and hearth beckon."

On our arrival in Shangtu, Brother Demetrios was allocated comfortable quarters. If I had expected to be treated as a military observer, I was quickly disabused on that score. I was assigned to a cavalry troop and there was nothing—absolutely nothing—comfortable about the pallet of straw allotted me in the troopers' compound. The only concession made to me was that I was allowed to retain Scimitar.

I was treated as a raw recruit. Worse. The Mongol captain of the troop, an officer named Toghu, singled me out for abuse and ridicule. I accepted this humiliating treatment without rancor. I assumed that Toghu had been instructed to make life difficult for me.

One thing that compounded my difficulties was that I had to pretend ignorance of Chinese and was handicapped in that I could not discuss the happenings of the day with my Mongol and Chinese comrades in arms. Keeping my mouth shut and my ears open, as Brother Demetrios had counseled, was easier said than done. Still, I found there were advantages to this policy. Much was said in my presence that would not have been had they known I spoke their tongue. For example, I would not have known the meaning of the nickname given me. I cannot say that it was flattering, but it was appropriate. I became known as *Chin man-tze*—the "golden barbarian."

I dressed like the rest of the troopers in a leather jerkin and baggy trousers. I rapidly learned enough of the Mongol tongue to understand rudimentary commands. I went through the motions of taking instruction in the Mandarin dialect, and though I pretended slowness, I'm sure there were many who were astonished by the rapidity of my progress.

My most shattering experience came when I was first introduced to the composite bow. Compared to the English longbow, it looked to be a mere child's plaything. It was not fashioned of seasoned yew. It was of laminated construction, with horn on the inside of the belly to add rigidity and strips of gut glued and lacquered to the outside of the belly to lend resilience. It was strung by bending the bow backward against its natural curve. My first shock came when I attempted to string the bow. It took all of my strength to achieve this. Then, I drew the bow. To my amazement, when I held the bow extended with my left hand at arm's length, try as I would I could not draw the bowstring back farther than the tip of my nose.

A Chinese trooper had been watching my efforts with an amused expression on his face. He took the bow from me, fitted a notched ring of bone over his thumb, held the bowstring next to his cheekbone by means of the thumb ring, then extended the bow outward with his left hand.

With practice I soon mastered the technique. Almost without exception my arrows flew unerringly to the mark. Moreover, thanks to my strength and stature, I could achieve this accuracy at greater ranges than my fellow troopers. Wisely I resisted the temptation to demonstrate this ability.

When it came to archery from horseback, I found that Scimitar was more of a liability than an asset. The hardy little horses from the steppes were smooth-gaited and astonishingly swift. Scimitar could not match their speed and agility, which put me at a disadvantage.

At full gallop the Mongol and Chinese cavalrymen stood upright in their stirrups winging arrows with deadly accuracy. I found I could not match their performance when mounted.

And in swordsmanship I had difficulty. There is not much finesse involved with a broadsword. The chief requirement is brute strength. The Mongol single-edged sword demanded much more deftness. By dint of much practice I improved my performance with the Mongol weapon but I failed to attain the skill at swordplay exhibited by most of my fellow troopers.

I was learning, and put forth my best effort without complaint. In time this dogged tenacity earned me grudging respect, if not acceptance as an equal.

Familiarizing myself with Mongol weapons was only part of my training program. I was there, as well, to study the tactics they employed in warfare. These were deceptively simple. Their tactics had evolved from the character and capabilities of the Mongol people.

The horse was an integral part of a Mongol's life. He learned to ride almost before he was weaned from mother's milk to mare's milk. He could stay in the saddle, even sleeping while mounted, for up to seventy-two hours at a stretch. He subsisted on meager rations he carried with him in a leather pouch—milk curd and air-cured meat—for weeks on end. He obeyed orders without question, knew no fear, and neither asked nor gave quarter. Couple those features with the incredible capabilities of their composite bow and the answer to their phenomenal success in battle emerges. The key to their success was mobility. They had developed the most effective cavalry the world had yet seen.

They favored a two-columned attack, advancing with lightninglike speed to achieve maximum surprise. Before moving on to a new objective, they laid waste to what already had been conquered, leaving none alive who could possibly oppose them in battle. Such annihilation did not appear to be prompted by cruelty. It was a practical consideration.

Yet in their very strength lay the seeds of their weakness. Essentially mobile forces, they didn't adapt readily to siege tactics and protracted warfare. Oh, they *had* adapted, but it struck me that they weren't at all comfortable in their role as Cathay's overlords.

The conquest of Cathay begun by Genghis Khan was not yet completed. Lin-an, the capital of the Southern Sung Dynasty, had fallen to Mongol forces only last year, and pockets of Sung resistance still held out in Southwest China. The Mongols were not in sufficient numbers to sustain campaigns of such magnitude. Therefore, while the generalship was chiefly Mongol, an increasing number of junior officers and the majority of the foot soldiers were Chinese conscripts or mercenaries. The cavalry, however, was an elite force that remained predominantly Mongol.

There was a good deal of competitive rivalry between cavalry units. The Seventh Troop of the Cavalry of the Silver Fox Banner—the troop to which I was attached for indoctrination—considered itself without equal. This position of self-appointed preeminence was subjected to almost constant challenge.

It was this continuing contest which led me, unwittingly, to the brink of disaster.

Chapter Fifteen

The challenge was presented by the Eleventh Troop, commanded by a Turkoman reputed to be something of a martinet. Our commanding officer, Captain Toghu, accepted with alacrity.

Appreciating I'd be no asset in events involving horsemanship or swordplay, Toghu did not list me as a competitor in those categories. He must, however, have observed me practicing archery from a standing position. I found myself entered in the long-range marksmanship event.

In the early stages of the event I easily held my own. Eventually the field narrowed to two, me and a Mongol marksman from the Eleventh Troop.

At a range of eighty paces I hit the ground-driven peg with all three of my arrows. My opponent missed on his third try, which should have eliminated him from competition. The Turkoman claimed that his contestant had been distracted by noise and insisted that we shoot again.

Vanity was my undoing. I had the mark moved out to one hundred paces. My first arrow cleanly hit the peg. The

Mongol missed the mark by a good two feet. A cheer went up from my fellow troopers.

Scowling darkly, the Turkoman strode over and snatched the bow from my hand. He examined it critically. Turning to Toghu, he snarled, "This dog turd of a foreign devil is using a heavier bow than those of normal issue."

Seething with anger, I reached out and wrenched the bow from his grasp. His face registered disbelief, then reddened in anger. Lashing out with his clenched fist he struck me in the face. As he started to unsheath his sword, Toghu, his face pale, stepped in and pinned the Turkoman's arms to his side.

My rash act constituted insubordination, an offense punishable by death. On the other hand, by striking a subordinate, the Turkoman had violated an unwritten code of officers' conduct. And, though I believed the only one of the troop who knew of this was Toghu, the issue was further complicated by the fact that I enjoyed special status.

I was confined to the troopers' compound while the matter was referred to the khan. It was Toghu who apprised me of the khan's decision.

Since I was a knight, and therefore had officer status, the incident was considered an affair of honor to be resolved through trial by combat. In view of the fact that I was the one who'd been struck, the choice of time, place, and weapons was mine.

Brother Demetrios did his best to talk me out of it. "A tournament! The Turkoman knows naught of tourneys. You've not restricted him in the use of weapons. By your own admission your link armor is no proof against his arrows. You're mad, Edmund. This is no game. The rules of chivalry don't apply. Your life is at stake."

I gestured impatiently. "I've helm and shield to fend off arrows. The Turkoman has yet to face an English battle lance. I intend to spit him on the first charge."

Brave words to mask my lack of confidence. In truth I knew no other way to fight him. In hand-to-hand combat I was not at all sure my broadsword or battle-ax would prove effective against a lighter blade in the hand of an experienced swordsman. I *had* to rely on my lance—and the solid weight Scimitar would lend to the thrust.

But Brother Demetrios was wrong. It was a game. A deadly game. Kubilai Khan had chosen to make it so, if only for his own amusement.

A pavilion had been erected to the right of the field. It shielded the khan and members of his court from the hot July sun. The khan, enthroned at a level slightly above his attending courtiers, gazed on the scene with no display of emotion. If, from that distance, he could see the ravens emblazoned on my shield and embroidered in the coat of arms on my tabard, he gave no sign of recognition.

Through the visor slit of my helmet I looked down the field to where the mounted Turkoman awaited the clash of cymbals that would set us in motion.

He was too distant for me to read any expression on his face but I could well imagine that my helmet must be causing him confusion. I doubted that he'd ever faced an opponent whose head was encased in steel. It was my hope that he'd find the spectacle unnerving.

The clang of cymbals rang out clearly. I dug spurs into Scimitar, thankful that I'd not bedecked him with a trapper for this encounter. Had the trapper flapped around his shanks, he might have bolted. I waited until he stretched his neck forward as he settled into his pounding stride before lowering my iron-tipped lance.

At the far end of the field the Turkoman came toward me at full gallop, bow in hand. He rose in his stirrups and in one fluid motion fitted an arrow and drew the bow as he waited for the range to lessen.

The gap narrowed. Three arrows reached me in rapid succession. One clanged as it was deflected by my shield. A second tugged at my tabard in passing. One found its mark, sending a searing pain shooting up my left side, but I was concentrating too hard on my growing target to pay it heed.

As I closed him, I expected him to take up shield. He made no attempt to cover himself. Then, at the last second, he swayed outward and swung sideways with all the grace of a Gypsy dancer. The point of my lance slid by him.

I'd *missed*. For a fraction of a second that fact didn't register fully. The momentary pause very nearly cost me my life. He must have let fly an arrow before he'd fully recovered his balance. It glanced harmlessly off my right shoulder as I was in the very act of shifting my shield to protect my back. In all likelihood his next shaft, which *did* hit my shield, would have caught me squarely between the shoulder blades.

At the end of the field I wheeled and reined in. I was shaken by the fact that I'd failed to unseat the Turkoman. He must have been equally unnerved by the fact that I'd withstood a hail of arrows. As I watched, he handed his sheathed bow and quiver of arrows to the trooper attending him and took from him a slender cavalry spear. Reaching down, the Turkoman unhooked his round Mongol shield from his saddle.

I debated what to do in the face of these changed tactics. My chain mail afforded no more protection against the thrust of a cavalry spear than it did against a squarely shot arrow. Should I switch to sword or battle-ax? I opted to go again with my lance.

From tip to hand guard my lance was of approximately the same length as a fully extended cavalry spear. If, at the moment just before contact, I could shift from the normal "in rest" position (with the butt pulled back and tucked in firmly to lend steadiness to the shaft) to a forward thrust, this would give me an advantage of about a foot in added length. The Turkoman, gauging his response to the tactics I'd used on the initial charge, shouldn't anticipate the modification I now intended.

I waited until the Turkoman set his steed in motion before touching spurs to Scimitar. He shot forward like a bolt from a crossbow. Lowering my lance, I settled into a crouch as I anxiously watched the distance shrink with each thudding hoofbeat.

Closer! Not yet! Closer! *Now!*

Taking the weight of the butt on my forearm, I extended the lance by about a foot. The point struck his leather breastplate where the pauldronlike shoulder plates ended. The handgrip of my lance was rammed backward into the crook of my arm with such force that I thought my shoulder had been dislocated. Then, at that instant, the shaft of my lance shattered.

Hauling on the reins, I brought Scimitar to a skidding stop. Even before he'd lost his forward momentum, I'd tossed aside the butt of my lance and drawn my sword. I slid from the saddle and hit the ground sword in hand.

The Turkoman lay sprawled on the trampled grass. He lay on his back. He tried to rise as I strode toward him, but his right arm was useless. His shoulder and clavicle must have been mangled to a pulp. Blood seeped from beneath his shoulder armor. From neck to waist the right hand side of his breastplate was stained crimson. Defenseless, he stoically awaited my coup de grace.

Had this been England I'd have spared the life of my vanquished foe. This wasn't England. Where the code dictated that quarter was neither asked nor given, mercy would be interpreted as mawkish timidity. Holding my sword point-down, I raised it above my head with both hands, then thrust down forcefully. The point penetrated the breastplate as though it were gauze. The Turkoman emitted a gurgling cough, then lay still. A thin trickle of blood oozed downward from one corner of his gaping mouth.

My sword held high, I turned to face the pavilion.

I sat on the low stool in the quarters now allocated to me in the imperial compound. The Chinese physician removed the glowing iron from a charcoal brazier and walked toward me. I gritted my teeth. As the smoking iron cauterized the jagged wound beneath my rib cage, I winced and choked back a gasp of pain.

Brother Demetrios watched the surgical ministration, a worried frown on his face. It was not only my wound that had him so concerned. His gaze settled briefly on my torn, bloodstained tabard lying in a heap on the floor, then swung to the surcoat draped across my oak chest. "The ravens," he said accusingly.

"I know," I said tersely.

"But the khan explicitly ordered their removal."

"Had it been a command, he would have directed it to me. I chose to look upon it as a suggestion. It was a humiliation I don't believe he expected me to accept. I think he was putting me to some sort of test. In any event, it's too late now. He can't have missed seeing them on my shield and tabard."

The friar took a deep breath, then exhaled slowly. "God help us if you're wrong."

There was no turning back. The moment I'd put in an appearance on the field of honor displaying my family coat of arms on shield and tabard, the die had been irrevocably cast. "We'll know soon enough," I said curtly. "Our audience is within the hour."

The throne room was crowded with richly gowned courtiers, uniformed officers, and saffron-robed clerics. The khan, ringed by halberd-bearing guards, sat enthroned on a dais. On a smaller throne, attended by ladies-in-waiting, the Empress Chabi sat decorously.

When our names were called, Brother Demetrios and I stepped forward and kowtowed. Thanks to my wound I did so awkwardly and rose stiffly to my feet.

I felt that the khan's gaze was fixed on the coat of arms embroidered boldly on my surcoat. A chill gripped my bowels.

Kubilai addressed me directly in Mandarin. "You have brought honor on the birds you display so proudly, *Chin man-tze*. Let us hope you continue to do so in the months ahead."

My spirits lifted. Two sentences—yet they contained a world of information. Kubilai had not expected me to expunge the ravens from my heraldic device. I got the distinct impression that I would have lowered myself in his estimation had I done so. That he'd used the sobriquet bestowed on me by the cavalry troopers, *Chin man-tze*, indicated that he'd been kept well-informed of my progress while in training. As for his reference to the months ahead, I took that to be an expression of his approval.

Switching to the Mongol tongue, he spoke at some length with Brother Demetrios.

When we'd been dismissed and were walking back to our quarters, Brother Demetrios was unaccountably quiet.

Growing impatient, I queried, "Well? What had he to say to you?"

"We were discussing your military future. He's seen fit to confer on you the temporary rank of cavalry commander. A new cavalry *touman* is being raised. You are to be its commanding officer."

I was speechless. A *touman* was a Mongol military unit of indeterminate size. It could be as small as one thousand in strength or embrace as many as ten thousand men-at-arms. By English standards a *touman* of even medium size constituted an army. Its size, however, was irrelevant. What mattered was that Kubilai was placing me, a foreign officer of questionable qualifications, in command. It struck me as being the height of folly.

"It makes no sense," I protested weakly.

"It does to him," Brother Demetrios said flatly. "He used his native tongue not as a means to exclude you from the conversation. While few of his courtiers speak the Mongol tongue, all of his military commanders do so. The khan's pronouncement was for their benefit."

"Have I no choice? Can I not respectfully decline the honor?"

"I fear not, Edmund, lad. This is something you can't interpret as a suggestion."

"What of you? Do you fit into this picture?"

Brother Demetrios sighed heavily. "I'm afraid so. I'm to be attached to the *touman* as your interpreter."

There was much I didn't even begin to understand. Events were moving too swiftly. Patently I was being used by Kubilai, but to what purpose?

In the light of this new development a suspicion grew on

me that there had been nothing remotely accidental about the Turkoman's actions. He must have been instructed to provoke me into challenging his authority. That meant but one thing. The trial by combat had been prearranged. That I had emerged the victor had established, at least insofar as Kubilai was concerned, my credentials as a cavalry commander.

Had that been the *real* test—a grimly final graduation exercise?

Chapter Sixteen

The question uppermost in my mind was, how long did Kubilai intend that I remain attached to the cavalry *touman*? Now that summer was nearing an end, Roccenti should soon be in a position to start the return journey. My situation had been radically altered. I could see no way that I could accompany the homebound caravan.

I'd planned to visit Cambulac to collect the bronze armor. When I did so, I'd acquaint Roccenti with the dubious honor I'd had thrust upon me. If there was no way of persuading him to delay the departure, the caravan would have to leave without me.

My meeting with Roccenti came sooner than I'd expected. To my surprise he called on me in my quarters at Shangtu. He explained that the Polos had journeyed to Shangtu to pay their respects to the khan, following which they wanted to meet with me.

I asked Roccenti why it had taken the Polos close to four and a half years to complete a journey that had taken us but two years? The answer was relatively simple.

Not slowed by camels or the necessity to barter trade goods, the Polos struck out from Acre intending to stop but briefly at Merv to contact Brother Demetrios, then proceed to Kashgar by way of Samarkand. Since they'd left Acre early in the year, their hope was that they could effect the mountain crossing before the onset of winter. It was a hope that was rudely shattered before many months had passed.

When crossing the Persian desert, they'd heard rumors of war and seen signs of recent fighting but hadn't encountered any actual conflict. As they neared Neyshabur, that changed dramatically. Fierce fighting erupted directly in their path. They had, in fact, been forced to flee for their lives. The two Dominican monks with the party pleaded illness and turned back. The Polos, now reduced to five in their party, headed south on a grueling trek to Hormuz at the southern extremity of the Persian Gulf. Knowing that Arab seafarers traded with ports in Southwest China, the Polos hoped now to secure sea passage to Cathay.

On reaching Hormuz, to their consternation they found the region plague-ridden and no sea transport available. They continued overland following the coastline to the east. Reaching the Indus River delta they moved inland in a northeasterly direction. Eventually they reached Kashmir in the foothills of the majestic Himalayas.

In Srinagar young Marco Polo was afflicted with a grave illness. It wasn't until the late summer of 1273 that Marco had recovered sufficiently for the party to make an attempt to brave the passes and stark uplands of the Karakoram Range. Blinding snowstorms and an avalanche had sealed off the Karakoram Pass, forcing them to return to Leh and from thence to Srinagar. The following summer they'd ventured the crossing a second time—this time meeting with success.

When they reached Yarkand, they learned of Orsini's death, and that our caravan was less than two months ahead of them. But the chilling winds of winter were too close for comfort. The Polos wintered at Kashgar before resuming their long odyssey.

I found that meeting the Polos was a letdown. Perhaps I'd expected too much of them. Oh, I don't mean to detract from their feats. No one could question their bravery. What I found disillusioning was the discovery that they were motivated more by avarice than a spirit of adventure. That shouldn't have come as such a surprise. They were, after all, merchants, not soldiers of fortune.

No matter where the conversation started it quickly turned to the question of profit. Where could they obtain silk of the best quality, and at what price? What effects were the continuing hostilities in southern Cathay likely to have on the availability of raw silk and cinnamon? Could the khan be persuaded to decree increased production of porcelain from the Imperial Kilns? Even references to their recent harrowing experiences were slanted toward trade. They'd brought with them samples of yak hair, and musk from Tibetan gazelles. They debated whether or not these commodities could be obtained in commercially viable quantities. Everything they discussed was equated to profit and loss.

Was Marco, two and a half years my junior, cast in the same mold? He was, but with the saving graces of intelligence, insatiable curiosity, and a retentive memory. On the debit side was his absence of a sense of humor. Even at the age of twenty-one, when first we met, he was serious beyond his years. He disapproved strongly of swearing and looked upon gambling as an invention of the devil—both sins of which I must confess myself guilty.

Yet, withal, I found Marco infinitely preferable to either his father or uncle.

If no close bond of friendship ever developed between me and Marco, the fault, I fear, was largely mine. As a nobleman and knight-at-arms I'd been raised to think of mercantile activities as beneath my dignity. The almost continual harping on the commercial aspects of any given situation engaged in by the Polos, including young Marco, soon palled on me.

Pouring another cup of wine for Brother Demetrios, I observed caustically, "They bore me. Even Roccenti. He's changed a great deal since his exposure to the Polos."

The friar grinned. "I, too, find them dull beyond belief. As for Lorenzo, he hasn't changed, simply reverted to type. I fear, Edmund, that you and I aren't cut out to be rich men."

I bridled. "I'm heir to a sizable fortune."

"You *were* heir to estates and high station. From what you've told me, you've been stripped of those benefits."

"They can be restored to me. I've written a letter to someone I can trust, a Dominican monk, to intercede on my behalf."

Brother Demetrios regarded me skeptically. "How will you get the letter to England? Have you considered how long it would take to get a reply?"

"Lorenzo will take the letter when he leaves and turn it over to the Dominicans in Acre for onward dispatch to England. I don't expect a reply. Armed with the letter Brother Bartholomew can enlist the support of a sympathetic peer of the realm to prove to King Edward that I'm alive and well. Once the king is convinced on that score, the restoration of my lands and title should be a mere formality."

"Hmmm. I hope you're right. But in the meantime we've other matters to occupy our attention. The *touman* should keep you busy, especially now that we've been notified we're to join the Army of the Blue Dragon in South China."

I grimaced. "You know better than that. Toghu has been promoted to serve as my second in command. Mangatei, a distant relative of the khan, has been placed in tactical command with equal rank to mine. My authority is purely nominal. I'm nothing but a figurehead."

"But you do have command. The overall responsibility is yours. It will be different when we leave Shangtu. Have you been advised when that's to be?"

"Next month. . . . Oh, I forgot to tell you. I'm journeying to Cambulac next week. I'd like you to come along to act as interpreter."

"I knew of the trip. Marco is coming with us."

"What for?"

"Kubilai wants the lad exposed to local customs and traditions. I imagine I'll be spending most of my time acting as *his* interpreter."

"The Polos seem to stand high in Kubilai's favor."

"With good reason. He wants to encourage trade with the western kingdoms. The Polos are the only merchants to have negotiated the caravan route in its entirety."

"So did we," I observed sourly.

"True, but Orsini's interest was sparked by the Polos. Indirectly the Polos are responsible for our presence in China. But there's more to it than a simple matter of an expansion of trade. Kubilai wants to establish closer ties with the Christian world."

"The Polos weren't helpful in that regard. They didn't even manage to get here with the two theologians attached to their party. At that rate it will be a long time before Cathay is converted to Christianity."

"Oh," Brother Demetrios said mildly, "I don't think Kubilai is interested in converting either himself or his domain to Christianity. Had that interest been close to his heart he could have called on the Nestorian Patriarch for assistance. He's never done so, even though the patriarch is now under the protection of Abaqa Khan."

"Then why in the name of heaven did he commission the Polos to petition the pope to send one hundred Catholic priests to Cathay? Other than spreading the faith, what purpose could they serve?"

The friar smiled thinly. "Now that you've some idea of the population density and immensity of China, I think you would agree that it would take a far greater number than a mere one hundred priests to convert this realm to Christianity. But they *could* serve another purpose. Bear in mind that Kubilai is both devious and politically astute. He has had to rely heavily on Chinese mandarins and the Buddhist priesthood to perform the administrative functions of government. In particular the Buddhist clerics wield great influence. Placing Catholic priests in sensitive administrative posts would act as an effective counterbalance to the growing political power of the Buddhist priesthood. Of course, that's purely speculative on my part, but it provides a logical explanation for the khan's sudden interest in Christian clergy."

"Couldn't he achieve that aim with Nestorian clerics?"

"Too close to home. They'd be too easily influenced by court interests."

"Well," I commented, wiping perspiration from my brow, "the Buddhists are the khan's worry. I'll be happy to head south and bid farewell to the Polos, and the corruption and intrigue of life at court."

Brother Demetrios drained his wine cup and chuckled as he refilled it. "You'll find just as much intrigue and corruption in the Army of the Blue Dragon, and I doubt that you'll be saying good-bye to the Polos. I've been told that Kubilai plans to send Marco, and possibly his uncle, along with us when we march south."

I groaned. "Marco I can live with, but God preserve me from that dullard Maffeo."

In Cambulac I took delivery of my armor and Scimitar's bronze barding. From the woodworker who'd supplied me with the original, I ordered a new battle lance. Those chores attended to, I took it upon myself to become acquainted with those merchants I felt had supplied the *touman* with equipment of questionable quality. While procurement wasn't my province, fighting effectiveness was. Perhaps an unexpected visit from the *touman*'s commanding officer, and an exchange of pointed pleasantries, might assist in effecting an improvement.

When he wasn't assisting me, Brother Demetrios reluctantly accompanied Marco in his frenetic exploration of the city. The friar returned to our lodgings each evening footsore and bad-tempered. In contrast Marco bubbled with enthusiasm as he recounted the day's happenings and produced various items for my inspection. Most of his finds I deemed oddities of little or no worth, but I must admit there were others which intrigued me.

One evening he produced five identical documents. These, he explained, were not hand-brushed duplicates. They'd been produced by pressing Chinese paper against inked characters of kiln-baked clay. "Think of it!" he exclaimed excitedly. "What takes us weeks to copy by hand the Chinese can do in a matter of minutes."

One discovery chanced upon by Marco excited me more

than it did him. He'd visited a foundry and been shown some ancient pieces of military hardware.

"You know those small exploding tubes used to scare away evil spirits?" Marco asked.

"Yes," I replied absently.

"At the foundry they showed us a kind of wide-mouthed bronze urn they called a mortar. They use the explosive powder to propel an iron or stone projectile weighing several hundredweight from the mortar. They also showed us a compartmented box from which they claimed that rockets with explosive heads could be aimed and fired."

My interest quickened. I turned to Brother Demetrios. "Is this true? Are such devices used in warfare?"

"I've not heard of mortars being used, but bombards and rockets are said to have been used in naval battles between Chin and Sung forces about a hundred and fifty years ago. I've not heard of them being put to use since then."

"Could a demonstration be arranged?"

"I don't see why not."

Two bullock-drawn carts brought the rocket launcher and mortar to a secluded meadow on the outskirts of the city. A charge of black powder was placed in the concave bottom of the mortar. A cloth was placed over the powder, then a large snugly fitting iron ball was hoisted up and rolled down onto the cloth. When a glowing joss stick was touched to a small powder-filled hole near the base of the mortar there followed a thunderous roar and a great cloud of white smoke. The iron projectile shot out of the mortar and, several moments later, buried itself in the hard-packed earth of an embankment at the far end of the field—a distance I judged to exceed two hundred paces.

They had only four rockets. These they fired from the

boxlike launcher at varying angles of tilt. The rockets swooshed out, leaving fiery trails behind them. At a predetermined interval each rocket exploded in the air.

In my mind's eye I pictured the effect these weapons would have on fortifications, or an advancing battle formation. Devastating! I left the demonstration determined that the *touman* would not move south without several of those awesome engines of destruction in its train.

Chapter Seventeen

On my return to Shangtu I summoned Mangatei. I stated bluntly that I had visited a number of suppliers in Cambulac and that I was far from satisfied with the quality of much of the equipment scheduled for delivery. As tactical commander of the *touman*, this should be of paramount concern to him. I suggested that he adopt whatever procedures he deemed necessary to rectify this situation.

If I had expected to learn anything from Mangatei's reaction, I was disappointed. His face was devoid of expression. He nodded curtly and turned from me without waiting for my dismissal.

I let the surly Mongol get almost to the tent flap before adding a casual statement: "I've taken the liberty of ordering additional equipment."

Mangatei stopped and turned to face me. There now was some expression—a look of annoyance. "What equipment?"

Briefly I described the mortar and rocket launcher, observing that I felt them to have tactical application in both siege warfare and field combat. To put them to a test under combat conditions I had ordered that we be supplied with two each of the mortars and launchers together with an adequate supply of black powder, projectiles, and explosive-headed rockets.

"I should have been consulted," Mangatei interjected angrily. "They are tactical weapons. *I'm* in tactical command. You should not have taken this step without my approval."

"Exactly," I said agreeably, "which is why I'm informing you before bringing it to the khan's attention."

Mangatei knew full well that I owed both my military rank and my command to Kubilai's whim. He had no way of knowing whether or not the relationship went beyond that. It was possible that I had direct access to the emperor. It wasn't something Mangatei wished to put to the test. I enjoyed the uncertainty that showed in his eyes.

Four days later I was summoned to the khan's presence. To my surprise Brother Demetrios was not included in the summons. A military escort conducted me to a small pavilion by the lake. There, informally attired in a simple robe of yellow silk, Kubilai awaited me unattended.

When the military escort withdrew, I started to kowtow. "Dispense with formalities," the khan said tersely.

I stood awkwardly a few feet from him. I'd never been with him at close quarters. Always he'd been seated at a level above me. I was surprised to find that he was at least a head shorter than I and much plumper than I had imagined.

For some moments he ignored my presence. He stood beside a low balustrade gazing out at the placid surface of the lake. His back to me, he murmured, "The willows are becoming tinged with yellow. There is a hint of autumn in the air. It is time to return to Cambulac." He turned slowly from the balustrade to face me. "Well, *Chin man-*

tze, soon you will be taking leave of us when your *touman* journeys south to join General Hsü Ch'ien's Army of the Blue Dragon. Once you reach Changsha, some surprises await you. I trust you will find them to your liking. However, some clarification is required. It will be necessary for me to review some background leading up to the predicament in which I find myself . . . and to the role I wish you to play in helping me resolve my difficulties. Bear with me, I will keep it brief.

"In the opening years of this century my illustrious grandfather, Genghis Khan, set out to subjugate the Chin, the Tartar dynasty then holding sway here in North China. He was diverted from this conquest by insults heaped upon him by the Muslims of Persia. He turned his attention westward to redress those wrongs.

"Two decades later when my grandfather died, the tribal khans gathered at Karakoram to convene the *kuriltai*— the Mongol conclave by which the *khaghanate* succession is determined. Genghis Khan's eldest son, my uncle, Ogadei Khan, was the chosen successor and became the Khaghan, the khan of khans.

"Assisted by my father, Tuli Khan, Ogadei turned his attention to the completion of the conquest of the Chin dynasty. Three years later my father died campaigning in North China.

"Ogadei died at the Mongol capital, Karakoram, nine years after my father's death. He was succeeded as the Khagan by his son, Kuyuk Khan, who ruled but two years before he, too, passed away. The succession then went to my older brother, Mangu Khan, who ruled the empire from Karakoram.

"I have spent most of my life in Cathay. My mentor was a venerable Confucian scholar and minister of the court, Yao-shi. From Cambulac I ruled in North China in

Mangu's name. My ambition was to complete the conquest of China initiated by my grandfather . . . to unify the Middle Kingdom and restore it to its former glory. By following Yao-shi's sage advice I enlisted Mangu Khan's support in this worthy endeavor.

"Leaving my younger brother, Arik-Buka, to act as regent in Karakoram in his absence, Mangu and his ablest generals joined me in my campaign against the Sung dynasty in South China. It proved to be a protracted struggle. The Sung fought stubbornly.

"In the year 1259, by your Christian calendar, Mangu was stricken with a fever of the bowels. To no avail he sought the coolness of a mountain climate. That summer he died.

"I should have succeeded to the *khaghanate* automatically, but Arik-Buka advanced a spurious claim to the leadership. Gathering my forces I marched north to meet this challenge to my rightful authority. It took me five years to reduce his forces to a point where they no longer posed a threat. Only then, when I was the undisputed Khaghan, was I free to turn my attention back to China and the recalcitrant Sung."

Kubilai paused in his account. A thin smile played briefly on his lips. "I took steps," he continued evenly, "to ensure that there would be no repetition of a disputed succession to Mongol leadership. I had already established the Yuan dynasty to supersede the Sung when their dynasty was finally subjugated in the process of the unification of China. Now, following the resolution of our family squabble, I abolished the *kuriltai* and moved the administrative seat of the Mongol Empire from Karakoram to Cambulac. Out of respect for my adopted country I took a Chinese dynastic name, Shi-tzu.

"War raged unabated in South China. It was not until

last year, the thirteenth year of my dynastic reign, that the Sung capital of Lin-an finally fell to Yuan forces. Several events led up to the fall of Lin-an. The Sung Emperor, Tu-tsung, died. The Sung succession went to his seven-year-old son, with the dowager empress acting as regent. The scheming old chief minister, Kai-se-tao, was defeated in battle. He was tried by his own people, thrown out of office, and murdered as he journeyed into banishment. Convinced that all was lost, the dowager empress surrendered the city.

"If the city had been taken in my grandfather's day, or by any of my uncles or my older brothers, it would have paid dearly for its years of defiance. I, however, have learned to temper victory with mercy. The only items removed from the former capital were its imperial treasures. None of its inhabitants were put to the sword. The city did not taste the torch. The dowager empress and her deposed son were brought to Cambulac where they live in comfort as my honored guests. I even made the former emperor a prince of the third rank.

"That should have been the end of it. Far from it. My leniency was interpreted as weakness. My generosity has been repaid by continuing resistance. A young lad of the imperial family, Shi, was persuaded to declare himself heir to the Dragon Throne. Former ministers of the Sung court, supported by Sung generals, continue the fight at Fo-kien and in the southwestern provinces. It has been a long and costly campaign which, intermittently, has continued through two generations. More than a quarter of China's population have forfeited their lives to satisfy the overweening pride of the Sung imperial house."

Kubilai eyed me intently from beneath hooded lids. He stroked his sparse beard reflectively. "Are you wondering," he questioned softly, "why I am telling you all this?"

I *was* curious—and confused by the khan's reasoning. Did he truly believe that the Sung should have handed over South China to Mongol overlordship without protest? Evidently he did. "Frankly, sire, I can't see how it relates to me."

"You will," the khan said tersely. "Many of my finest military commanders have either died in combat, or of old age. Increasingly I have had to rely on Chinese field commanders of questionable loyalty. Many of the reports I receive from the field are suspect. I need objective appraisals. You are in a position to provide an unbiased viewpoint. *That* is the service I require of you."

I was stunned. "But, sire," I protested, "what reliance can be placed on *my* views? I am not familiar with the issues involved. I have but a rudimentary grasp of your tactical and strategic concepts. In addition, as nominal commander of a cavalry *touman*, my contacts and the scope of my observations will be severely restricted."

"That will be rectified," the khan observed dryly. "Though you must make no mention of this until my decree is presented to you, on your arrival at Changsha you will be promoted to general of the third rank. General Hsü Ch'ien will find employment for you commensurate with your rank; however, your primary function will be to act as an objective observer. You will report to me directly on matters pertaining to the strength, disposition, and caliber of the Sung forces opposing us and on the deployment, employment, and morale of our Yuan forces. You are also to report in detail on the conduct of any actions in which you take part. Report what you see and hear honestly and without prejudice. I will judge concerning its merit. My one desire is to put an end to this debilitating resistance once and for all."

That I was to be promoted to banner rank I found

incredible. While I considered the implications, comment eluded me. The khan seemed not to notice my preoccupation. "I am, by the way," he continued, "sending Marco Polo with you in a civilian capacity. He has a discerning eye. He will amplify your reports by advising with respect to the economic and political conditions prevailing in the region together with his interpretation of the temper of the common people. To crush the Sung is not enough. We must reshape the economy from the ground up to restore confidence where it has been eroded by excessive abuses of conscription and taxation."

On the face of it the khan's concern for the plight of the peasantry did him credit. However, considering that the burden imposed by the Sung was largely in response to Mongol pressures, Kubilai's reasoning was specious. Tactfully I withheld comment. I waited patiently for the khan to continue. When he did so, he shifted abruptly to an unexpected and wholly unrelated subject.

The corners of his eyes crinkled in response to inner amusement. "It has been brought to my attention that you are given to visiting the bathhouses and teahouses of Cambulac."

I was taken completely by surprise. "Ah . . . er—" I stammered, stuck for a reply and coloring to the roots of my hair. The information, I was sure, could have come only from Marco Polo, who made no secret of his disapproval of my amorous activities.

The khan's lips twisted in a smile. "I understand that the singsong girls of those establishments are almost as gifted as the famed 'little flowers' of Lin-an. It is a healthy thing for a lusty young stud like you to indulge in such diversions. My one objection is that a man of your station need not resort to the ministrations of those ladies of pleasure. I feel you need a young woman more suited to your rank. I will give the matter due consideration.''

The court was in the throes of preparation to return to Cambulac. The eve of the departure of my *touman* was almost upon us. There was a good deal of last-minute confusion and it didn't help matters that Mangatei appeared to be growing more obstructive with each passing day. It was all I could do to hold my temper in check in the face of his thinly veiled insolence. I drew consolation from the fact that once we reached Changsha I would outrank him.

It had been a particularly trying day. I strode back to my tent that evening in a foul mood. My response to the grin of welcome given me by the trooper standing guard outside my tent was a surly grunt.

Inside the tent the oil lamp on the centerpole cast a circle of light. The lamp on the bench by my sleeping mat also should have been lit by my servant, Wong Sin, who was nowhere in evidence. Muttering curses, I threw my plumed helm into the corner and started to unbuckle my sword belt. I opened my mouth to call out for Wong Sin. No sound issued from my throat. At that moment a figure detached itself from the shadows and moved toward me hesitantly. My mouth hung open in stunned disbelief. It couldn't be! Was I losing my mind?

When speech returned, I stammered, "Wh—What? How? God's blood, what are *you* doing here?"

Her violet eyes mirrored bafflement. "You know me, my lord?"

"I—ah—saw you but once, and that only briefly . . . in Turfan.''

She lowered her eyes. "I recall the meeting, but I thought that you would not, my lord."

"Have you a name?"

"In Turfan, I was called Karla. Now I am known by a Chinese name, Wei Feng—'Gentle Breeze,' my lord."

"But why are you here?"

She stood with her eyes still downcast. Her voice was so low I could barely make out her words. "The eunuch in charge of the harem sent me to you. If . . . if I do not please you, my lord, you can send me back."

Chapter Eighteen

I'd taken the khan's remarks about my amatory pursuits as nothing more than mild criticism. It never entered my head that he'd present me with a woman from his harem. According to Brother Demetrios once a woman was installed in a harem she was permanently removed from all contact with the outside world.

Manifestly the friar was in error. It placed me in a quandary. To reject Gentle Breeze meant offending the khan. If I returned her to the harem, she would lose face. Worse, it was not beyond the realm of possibility that it could cost her her life. What made the situation even more perplexing was that I didn't know what acceptance of his openhanded generosity entailed. Was she meant to be a bed companion on a temporary or permanent basis? What was her status?

As I stripped off my tunic, I was struck by another thought. Was it possible that the khan knew I'd seen the girl in Turfan? I dismissed that as impossible. On what basis, then, had he singled her out as a suitable choice? I pondered this as I poured water from an urn into a bronze basin and sponged my arms and chest free of accumulated sweat and dust. When I'd toweled myself dry and donned a loose linen shirt, I turned to face the girl.

"Where is my servant?" I asked brusquely.

"Gone, my lord, to fetch food and wine."

"Mmm. Tell me; you say you recall meeting me, albeit briefly, in Turfan. Could the khan know of that meeting? Has that any bearing on why you were sent here?"

"How *could* the khan know? But it was not the khan who chose me to be your concubine. I was selected by the head eunuch because it was thought you might find me pleasing, even though, my lord, in the harem I am considered unattractive."

"Unattractive! They must be mad, or blind."

Gentle Breeze's lips trembled in a smile. "I don't conform to Asiatic standards of beauty. I'm too tall. My nose is too long and my eyes too large."

"Of course you don't conform to Asiatic standards. You aren't of Asiatic extraction."

"Oh, but I am, my lord. My father was what the Turks call a *Turcople*—a Syrian of mixed Greek and Turkish blood. My mother is a Kipchak Tartar. I'm of Asiatic stock—but must be a throwback to some Greek ancestor. I suppose I was selected for his harem because the Great Khan is said to like variety. I suppose he does, but he is strongly influenced by Chinese custom and tradition. That my feet are not bound weighs heavily against me."

Of all the Chinese customs I'd encountered I found the practice of maiming a female child through footbinding the most barbaric form of idiocy. Chinese men seemed to find this deformity erotic. They assured me that fondling the sensitive "golden lotus" feet generated heightened sexual responses in women. That well might have been true, but I found the disfigurement abhorrent.

We were prevented from continuing my probing into her background and imagined shortcomings by the arrival of Wong Sin and a young boy he'd recruited to assist him. Outside the tent they set up a large brazier to which was fitted a convex grillwork. They'd brought with them thinly sliced strips of beef and mutton and an assortment of green vegetables. Wong Sin, beaming proudly, produced a basket of rolls made from wheat flour and dusted with sesame seeds, bowls of spiced soya sauce, several kinds of wine and, last but not least, a flagon of kumiss. Into the tent he brought a table-mounted conical oil stove used in the preparation of Mongolian soup. Having set up the stove and arranged cushions around the low table, he scurried off and returned with the ingredients for a soup, a covered bowl of steaming rice and bamboo containers laden with Chinese specialties such as shredded pork cooked with ginger and mushrooms, crisply fried duck skin, and steamed crab claws.

I smiled inwardly. Wong Sin was inordinately pleased with himself, as well he should have been. On short notice he'd produced what amounted to a nuptial feast.

I had cause for amusement in another aspect of the situation. Gentle Breeze had been brought to my field tent by an escort of the imperial guard. No wonder my guard had been grinning on my return and Wong Sin had gone to such pains with respect to the evening meal. By now the entire *touman* must be aware that their commanding officer had been honored by the khan. It could not have escaped Mangatei's attention. He must be seething inwardly at this display of favor on the part of Kubilai Khan. It would do nothing to endear me to my tactical commander but it would make him think twice before defying me openly. In choosing this manner of presenting me with the gift of a concubine I was almost certain the khan had done so to enhance my image in the eyes of my troops. The guile of the emperor was almost beyond belief.

Wong Sin served the sumptuous repast. As soon as each course was finished, the boy assisting him whisked away the empty platters to make room for the next delicacy. Even though I drank sparingly, and Gentle Breeze drank not at all, Wong Sin saw to it that our jade wine cups were never empty.

To conclude the meal Wong Sin produced a pot of jasmine tea and litchi nuts in syrup. He removed the wine cups and brought wooden bowls and the flagon of kumiss. Then, grinning from ear to ear, he bowed low and said, "I will see to it, master, that you are not disturbed." Then he backed from the tent.

When the tent flap stilled following Wong Sin's departure, Gentle Breeze and I sat facing each other in embarrassed silence. Actually, we'd spoken but little during the meal. I had told her that I came from a far off land called England, but little else. From her I learned that her father had been dead for some years and that she had just turned seventeen. Since the Oriental custom is to consider a child one year old at birth, that made Gentle Breeze eight years my junior. God's blood, that made her some three years younger than my sister, Catherine.

I splashed kumiss into the bowl in front of me and looked at Gentle Breeze questioningly. She hesitated, then nodded assent. I poured a small amount of the liquid into her bowl, commenting, "It's a heady brew that quickly clouds the senses. It should be drunk with due caution."

"I know," she said softly, reaching for the bowl with a trembling hand.

*   *   *

Gentle Breeze extinguished the lamp by my sleeping mat and disrobed self-consciously in the shadows. I peeled off my clothing and turned down the coverlet on the mat with fumbling hands. Unaccountably, I was nervous. I hoped I'd not drunk too much kumiss. My penis should have been stirring in anticipation, yet it seemed strangely lifeless.

Having placed the cushions to suit me, I turned toward her. She stood shyly just outside the pool of light cast by the centerpole lamp. My breath caught in my throat and I swear that my heart skipped a few beats.

Her youthful body was as breathtakingly beautiful as her exquisite face. How, I thought wonderingly, could anyone in his right mind have thought her unattractive? Her pink-nippled breasts were small but well formed. Her waist was small. The tangled down of hair thinly veiling her pubis was the same shade as that of the hair framing her oval face and cascading downward over her creamy shoulders. From boyish hips her perfectly proportioned legs tapered downward to trim ankles and narrow feet. She was as slender and graceful as a willow sapling. She reminded me of a frightened fawn.

I reached out, took both her hands in mine, and drew her to me. Her eyes wide, her lips trembling, she looked up into my face. I held her close and kissed her tenderly to still the fear that gripped her. I need not have worried about the effect of the kumiss on my manhood. Blood surged to my loins and my phallus stiffened against the swell of her belly. A tiny gasp escaped her lips as she drew them from mine, yet she pressed her body even closer against me.

"Be patient with me, my lord," she whispered close to my ear. "I have never been with a man."

I could scarcely believe what I'd heard. How was it possible for her to have come to me from a harem, yet be a virgin?

She must have read the disbelief in my eyes. "It is true. None but the khan could touch me . . . and . . . and he did not. I'm sorry if it displeases you."

I could not suppress the laugh that sprang to my lips. "It does not displease me, little one. Nothing could please me more."

My difficulty was that patience in copulation is not one of my stronger points. Only once in my life had I coupled with a virgin. She had been the fourteen-year-old daughter of our gamekeeper. She'd been every bit as anxious to rid herself of the encumbrance of a maidenhead as I had been to oblige her in the deflowering. There had been nothing at all gentle about that encounter, nor do I recall it as having been particularly memorable. This was vastly different.

Gentle Breeze was anxious to please me. She helped me adjust a cushion beneath her hips, then spread her legs wide to receive me. Then she froze.

The lips of her vagina were dry as dust. I moistened them with saliva but she remained so tight that I could not effect an entry. I rubbed my glans slowly just within the portals of her jade gate, but it seemed to have no effect. I was beginning to think that my forbearance was to no avail when, slowly, the tension ebbed from her and her juices started to flow. I eased into her until my glans came up against the obstruction of her unruptured hymen. I paused momentarily, then lunged forward until I was fully sheathed. She cried out sharply and tensed again, but only for a second. Moaning softly, she started to move her hips beneath me and I felt her legs slide up and over my back. Gradually the tempo of my thrusting quickened. I did my best to exercise restraint, but it was hopeless. As her moans gained in volume and her hips pushed up to meet my pumping strokes I could contain myself no longer. With a strangled cry I shot my seed deep within her and, after a few more strokes, sank down upon her crushed breasts.

When my breathing steadied, I lifted from her and, on shaking legs, walked over to the basin, dampened a towel, and returned with it to my sleeping mat. I knew that I had not brought her to a full climax. I was sorry about that and vowed to exercise more control when next we coupled. Gently I mopped the perspiration from between her breasts and from her belly. Then I cleansed her matted pubic hair and the pouting lips of her vulva of sweat, juices, and her virginal blood. As I was engaged in this labor, Gentle Breeze sat up and watched me. I held the towel up for her inspection. She giggled when she saw the bloodied towel.

Reaching toward me, she pulled my face to hers and pressed her lips to mine in a lingering kiss. Then she lay back against the cushions and drew my head down onto her breasts.

She sighed contentedly. "I'm glad now, my lord, I waited. I'm happy it was you who was my first."

The friar's face reflected bewilderment. "Incredible! He's been known to present visiting dignitaries with concubines from his harem . . . but why bestow such a gift on you?"

I couldn't disclose that I was destined for banner rank, which, undoubtedly, had had bearing on the khan's magnanimous gesture. I shrugged. "She tells me she's considered unattractive in face and form. It might not be the generous gesture you imply. Of course, I can always send her back to the harem."

"No, no!" Brother Demetrios protested, his voice registering concern. "That you *cannot* do. It would be an insult to the khan. Mayhap she could have been sent back yesterday when first she came to you . . . but certainly not now when she's spent a night with you."

"What would have happened had I sent her back yesterday evening?"

"She'd have been deemed worthless and, in all probability, put to death by strangulation."

"Then it seems I'm burdened with her."

"Unless you wish her killed, I fear so."

I rubbed my beard thoughtfully. "It's perplexing. There's no parallel to concubinage in England. What is her status? Is she a slave?"

"It's difficult to relate her status to a social structure such as the one to which you're accustomed. Since she's become your legal property, essentially she falls into the category of a slave—but not quite. I suppose she falls somewhere in between a courtesan, who enjoys no legal status, and a *ying*."

"*Ying?*"

"A secondary wife. It all stems from the Confucian doctrine which teaches that the greatest sin is filial impiety. It's the duty of a wife to produce sons. Since this isn't always possible, Confucian Chinese seized on an inability to produce offsprings as a justification for polygamy. The first wife is the principal wife . . . to whom all other women in the household are subservient. Subsequent wives are called *ying*. If a man is of a mind to, and can afford them, he can add any number of concubines to his women's quarters. Except that they aren't accorded the benefit of marriage vows, concubines can be considered in the same bracket as secondary wives within the framework of the Confucian ethic."

"God's teeth! Is the only restriction the size of a man's purse?"

Brother Demetrios laughed. "That's about it. Take the khan, for example. Traditionally he's entitled to one 'great wife'—in his case, Empress Chabi—three queens of the first rank, nine of the second rank, twenty-seven of the third rank, eighty-one of the fourth rank, and an unlimited number of concubines. Of course, in his case, financial considerations are not a limiting factor."

"No," I observed wryly, "they're not. In my case it's somewhat different. Providing for just *one* woman could be a burden. Gentle Breeze won't find it easy being attached to an itinerant soldier of fortune. Four days hence, when we break camp, what am I supposed to do with her?"

"Take her with you. Had she been Chinese, it would pose a problem. A Chinese concubine would be expected to go into seclusion within the confines of your household. She would become a *nei jen*—an 'inner person.' Gentle Breeze is a daughter of the desert. She'll expect to accompany you to Changsha."

Chapter Nineteen

What amused and rather astonished me was how quickly Gentle Breeze adapted to her role as mistress of my household. It wasn't a demanding role, since my abode was naught but a field tent and my staff consisted of Wong Sin and the soldiers who guarded my tent.

One minute Gentle Breeze would be issuing a stream of imperious orders to Wong Sin. A moment or two later I was likely to find the two of them giggling together over some shared joke. Wong Sin seemed not to resent her commands in the slightest. In fact, all who came in contact with her were captivated by Gentle Breeze and would fall all over themselves to do her bidding.

The fact that she'd come to me from the khan's harem undoubtedly had something to do with the respect paid her. But the esteem in which she was held stemmed largely from other attributes. She was mercurial, but generally in bubbling good spirits. She was one of that rare breed whose moods were infectious. When she laughed, the whole world—even if clouds hung low in a leaden sky—

seemed a sunlit and happy place. When sadness claimed her, people automatically talked in hushed tones. I've never witnessed anything quite like the effect she had on those with whom she came in contact.

The shyness she'd manifested in our initial coupling disappeared along with her virginity. She had a healthy curiosity and shed her inhibitions as we indulged in sexual experimentation. The learning process wasn't on her side alone. In bringing her sexual gratification, I found I was adding new dimensions to my own enjoyment. I soon concluded again that someone in the khan's harem had erred grievously in bestowing on me this blessing.

I'd divided the *touman* into two sections. The largest of these, under my command, consisted of foot soldiers, heavy equipment, and spare mounts. We would proceed to Tientsin and there embark on an armada of sailing craft to make our way south by the famed inland waterway, the Grand Canal.

The second section, comprised of cavalry units and a baggage train of light equipment, was commanded by Mangatei. It would go overland at a pace calculated to time its arrival at Changsha to coincide with that of my waterborne section.

The Grand Canal, much of which had been constructed in pre-Christian times, rivaled the Great Wall as a feat of engineering. From Tientsin to Lin-an, at the western end of Hangchow Bay, was an almost unbelievable distance of three hundred leagues. We wouldn't go all the way to Lin-an. At Nanking we would leave the Grand Canal and head upriver on the Yangtze Kiang, a river, Brother Demetrios informed me, that originated somewhere in the Tibetan uplands and flowed on a course exceeding one thousand leagues in length.

* * *

A cabin had been constructed on the poop of the huge river junk that was the flagship of our armada of sixty craft. The cabin was living quarters for me and Gentle Breeze. It was divided into several sections by means of carved wooden screens, and bamboo curtains that could be rolled up to allow a free passage of air. We left Tientsin in the latter part of September with the trees bordering the canal tinged with the yellow of autumn and the evening breezes crisply reminding us that winter was on its way, but as we proceeded southward the weather gradually grew warmer and more humid. The lifting curtains, which I'd considered an unnecessary adjunct at the outset, proved their worth before October drew to a close.

One feature of our shipborne quarters that did not appeal to Gentle Breeze was the fact that it was compartmentalized by the wooden screens. When I entertained junior officers in my quarters, she retired into the relative seclusion of our screened-off sleeping compartment out of deference to Chinese custom. I made an exception when I entertained Brother Demetrios and Marco Polo. On those occasions she was permitted to eat with us and to converse with us as our equal. There were those aboard the flagship who looked askance at my flaunting of traditional mores, but nothing was ever said in my presence. Needless to say, Gentle Breeze was delighted, and I found myself entertaining the friar and Marco more and more often as the weeks progressed.

In North China early autumn is a season of contrary winds. When they blew at all they were predominantly from the north or northeast and filled our square batten-slatted sails. We proceeded south at a sedate but steady pace I estimated to average between six and eight leagues per day.

Twelve days out of Tientsin we angled across the Hwang Ho, the river known as "China's Sorrow." The somber nickname, Brother Demetrios informed me, derived from the fact that the meandering river often burst its diked banks and wreaked havoc by destroying crops and drowning livestock and peasants by the tens of thousands. I was no stranger to the river. We first had come across it between Lanchow and Ch'ang-an and had followed it downstream for some two hundred leagues on our initial approach to Cambulac. I had not seen it in flood, nor did its placid ochre-colored water look terribly menacing where we crossed.

Here the canal described a giant arc to keep clear of a range of hills that loomed on our left. On our right, fields of ripened grain stretched to the far horizon. The harvest, in fact, was well along, and in many places, the stubbled fields were being prepared for winter planting.

The lazy October days were pleasantly warm, the nights refreshingly cool. There was little in the way of military affairs to occupy my time. I was afforded an opportunity to learn more about my enchanting young concubine—and to tell her much about myself.

Her father had been a Muslim, but Gentle Breeze had not been reared in the Islamic faith. Her mother's family had been Buddhists and Gentle Breeze was of that persuasion.

She had not been born in Turfan but some distance to the northwest in a village named Bakhty. Many of her mother's male kinfolk had been—and, as far as she knew, still were—Tartar horsemen attached to the White Horde under the Mongol leadership of Kubilai's cousin, Orda Khan.

When she had been nine years of age the family had moved to the oasis of Turfan, where her father, until his death three years ago, had been a trader in fresh and dried fruit. It had been a small business and the family had lived on the edge of poverty. When her father died, Gentle Breeze, her two younger sisters and an infant brother, and her mother, had subsisted largely through the charity of their neighbors. That she'd been chosen by Kubilai's agents as a concubine had been not only a great honor but a financial boon to her struggling family.

In turn I told Gentle Breeze of my family background. I'm ashamed to admit that I was guilty of bragging about my noble lineage, hoping to impress her. I am not sure if I achieved that aim, since, later in my disclosures, I had to confess to having been robbed of my lands and title by my unscrupulous stepmother and to having been sold into slavery by my Turkish captors. Nobility was, after all, not something I'd earned. It had been conferred on me by an accident of birth.

I recounted certain episodes from my childhood and youth. I told her of my strict Catholic upbringing and of my respect for and admiration of Brother Bartholomew. I related some amusing incidents from my time at Oxford and told her how I'd been knighted by the king at Nottingham, had taken the cross, and had embarked on the crusade against the infidel.

In some detail I told her how Hugh *fitz* William and I had been shipwrecked off the Syrian coast and had been imprisoned in Aleppo. I told her of my stepmother's refusal to pay the ransom in order that my half-brother could retain my title and estates, of my attempt to escape, and of my recapture which led to my being sold into bondage. Since she must know of the rigors of the caravan route, I didn't dwell on that aspect of my journey but I did recount the incident wherein Count Orsini met his death, thus freeing me from obligation.

I did not tell her of my affair with Ethelwyn, nor the fact that I suspected my half-brother to be my bastard son. Though I told her of Hugh's death by beheading I made no mention of our first having been sodomized by our captors. Nor did I say anything about my cruel incarceration in the oubliette at Hama.

Gentle Breeze listened attentively to everything I told her. She asked many questions about England and a way of life she found hard to understand. At one point she asked me if the English king had as many wives and concubines as did Kubilai Khan. I explained to her that, like all Christians, the king could have but one wife and that my father, had my mother lived, could not legally have taken a second wife. Gentle Breeze expressed astonishment and wanted to know what men did when they tired of their wives—and what the wives did if they tired of their husband's advances. Those were not easy questions to answer. I told her that some husbands consorted with doxies, or indulged in extramarital affairs, but that such conduct was considered a mortal sin in the eyes of both the church and state. Gentle Breeze considered this for a moment, then declared that our customs seemed to her to be neither logical nor practical. She said bluntly that it flew in the face of nature, since the male animal always would seek gratification from a number of sexual partners and a woman would be a fool to expect any man to stick to her for life.

I guess it was talking about marriage customs in England that led Gentle Breeze into her next line of questioning. Her opening gambit was a seemingly innocuous question. She wanted to know if premarital chastity was guarded as rigorously in England as it was in China.

It was not an easy question, nor was it a fair one, since my exposure to Chinese mores along those lines was limited.

I temporized by explaining that while, in theory, virginity was a highly prized commodity, in practice its absence did not seem to generate the opprobrium one normally should expect. I added hastily that this did not hold true among the wellborn and that my sister's chastity had been jealously protected. I was not entirely sure I was on safe ground with respect to that latter positive statement.

Gentle Breeze's next question was more specific. She asked me at what age I'd had my first sexual experience with a member of the opposite sex. I sensed that I was being drawn into a trap, yet I answered her honestly.

She sprang the trap. Surely, she said, with wide-eyed innocence, I couldn't have become so expert in the art of lovemaking on the basis of a single experience. Had I not had numerous such encounters?

The tendency among men is to boast of their sexual exploits, yet instinct warned me that I should proceed with caution. Again I temporized. Without amplification I stated that I had enjoyed other experiences at Ravenscrest and that, during my student days, I'd gone awenching in Oxford town. I observed that celibacy was not a conspicuous virtue among soldiers and that I had had my fair share of sexual experiences during the crusade, both in France and in the Outremer.

She drew me out skillfully. "It must have been terrible that you were deprived of sex during the long period of your imprisonment in Aleppo."

"Oh, we weren't deprived of sex. Not entirely. From time to time we were provided with young women . . . many of whom were well versed in the art of making love."

"How so? In what way?"

"Well," I said, warming to the subject and throwing

caution to the wind, "most of them enjoyed oral and anal sex . . . and many of them had no pubic hair."

Gentle Breeze's eyes widened. "They were *that* young."

I laughed. "Not at all. It was their practice to pluck the hair from that area and to remove the stubble through frequent applications of hot wax."

"Oh. Did the lack of hair excite you?"

"With the younger ones, it did, but I must confess that I didn't find it that attractive with older women."

"Did they do anything else that was . . . well . . . unusual?"

At this point I was guilty of attributing Ethelwyn's extraordinary muscular control to Fatima. "There was one," I said, "whose name was Fatima. She exercised such control of her vaginal muscles that she could hold me entrapped after ejaculation and coax my phallus into a second, even a third, erection."

"I've read of that accomplishment in the *Kama Sutra*," Gentle Breeze said wonderingly, "but I didn't believe it possible. How did she manage to acquire that skill?"

I was getting out of my depth. "I—ah—am not sure . . . but it must have taken much practice."

"Yes," Gentle Breeze agreed musingly, "it must have."

Chapter Twenty

The wind dropped to a whisper, then died altogether. Our flotilla, sails slatting, was being poled along the canal. Taking advantage of the situation, I invited a number of officers from nearby craft to join me in a noontime meal. Prior to their arrival Gentle Breeze retired to the seclusion of our screened-off sleeping compartment.

Social commitments of this nature were becoming a chore for me. Though my command of the Mandarin dialect was improving with each passing day, paradoxically this added to rather than detracted from the prevailing communication gap. The more I understood the words the less I understood their real meaning. The Chinese penchant for dissembling was disconcerting. The Mongols, while less convoluted in their thinking, were almost as annoying in the oblique approach they took to any given topic. Why, I wondered, did the Asiatics find it impossible to come directly to the point? There were, I appreciated, two sides to that coin. Without doubt they were driven to distraction attempting to discern hidden meanings in my straightforward statements.

It was trying. I was happy to see the last of my guests being sculled on sampans toward their respective vessels. As I wended my way aft, I breathed a long sigh of relief. I now could look forward to several pleasant hours in the company of Gentle Breeze before Marco and Brother Demetrios would arrive to join us in an evening meal.

I wasn't prepared for what awaited me. As I rounded the angled end of the screen, I was absently undoing the frog fastenings of my brocaded silk gown. When I took in the spectacle that greeted me, my fingers froze on the braided toggle.

Completely naked, Gentle Breeze sat cross-legged on the sleeping mat. On her right was a bronze holder containing the stub of a gutted candle. Before her was a wooden bowl from which bronze tweezers and fragments of hair-tufted wax protruded. A frown of concentration on her face, she was examining the results of her painful handiwork.

She had done an excellent job of depilation. Her crotch and pudendum were denuded of pubic hair. The flesh was pink-flushed and the pouting portals of her jade gate were slightly swollen from the irritation occasioned by her cosmetic endeavors. I inhaled sharply in astonishment.

Gentle Breeze started and looked up. "Oh, dear!" she gasped, her hand flying to her mouth. "I wanted to surprise you."

We entered a lake which, though not of great width, stretched for a distance exceeding thirty leagues. After some days on this lake we again entered the Grand Canal. The next day we tied up at Suchow, a city of considerable size liberally laced with narrow canals.

It struck me as odd that so large a city should have grown in such a setting. I questioned Brother Demetrios as to the reason. He gave me a logical explanation. At some time in the past the city had stood at the junction of the Hwang Ho and the Grand Canal. Then, during one of its periods of flood, the river had changed its course. The city was no longer the important nexus of waterborne commerce it once had been but it was, nonetheless, large enough to serve the purpose of resupplying our diminishing supply of provisions.

I did not set foot on shore. I was inundated with a veritable flood of stores lists that needed checking and of requisitions and receipts that required the affixing of my official chop of approval. While I was thus occupied with my duties, Gentle Breeze, accompanied by Wong Sin, went into the town to do some shopping. She made a number of small purchases which she showed me on her return. One item that she did *not* show me— and which, in fact, I didn't see for some months—was a ceramic vase of peculiar shape. It didn't matter. Even had I been with her at the time of its purchase I would not have guessed the purpose for which it was intended.

Late that same evening we slipped our lines and proceeded on the final leg of our canal transit to Nanking.

I couldn't help but be impressed with the changing face of China. As we neared Nanking the yellowish loam that favored the coarse grain crops of the north gradually gave way to darker alluvial soils, a more abundant supply of irrigation water, and paddy fields undergoing preparation for a winter planting of rice. On our left, in the distance, we could see the contours of low mountains etched against the sky. All during our southward journey we'd been favored with beautiful weather, and when we reached Nanking, even though we now were well into November, the days and nights were still balmy, and flowering shrubs added color to the passing scene. What most impressed itself on me, however, were the numbers and industry of the peasantry who labored endlessly in the fertile fields that bordered the Grand Canal, or plied its waters, or crowded the towns and villages along its banks.

Everywhere I looked I saw black-clad people wearing platelike, wide-brimmed hats. Here was the real strength of China—its disciplined, hardworking peasants. They seemed more plentiful here than they had in North China, which probably was due to the fact that here they enjoyed a kinder climate. But I could see now how some of the wonders I had viewed had been achieved. With such manpower to draw upon, undertakings such as the Great Wall and the Grand Canal not only could be conceived but translated into solid accomplishments. No wonder cities such as Lin-an could boast populations running into the millions. Nor was it any wonder that the nomadic tribes from the wind-seared crags and grasslands of the steppes would gaze with covetous eyes on the more generously endowed land to the south.

Four and a half million! When that figure had been casually presented as the population of Lin-an I'd neither fully believed it nor grasped its significance. Now that I had seen something of the teeming southland, I was much more inclined to give credence to that incredible statistic. God's teeth, that almost equaled England's entire population. But I really should not have been so skeptical. The *touman* I commanded—which represented but a part of one of the khan's field armies—considerably exceeded in numbers the English crusading force commanded by Prince Edward. These were comparisons that stretched my imagination to its limits.

That a realm as populous and technically advanced as China should be so little known beyond its confines was almost beyond belief. I had to concede that the products of fabled Cathay—the silk, jade, and exotic spices—had been known in Europe since the days of the Roman Empire, yet the land itself and its people had remained a mystery to all but those on the periphery of the Middle Kingdom—those who had tasted the bitter fruits of Chinese conquest. Still, to one such as I who had followed the caravan route over its entire length, it shouldn't be that much of a mystery. Chinese were not wont to brave those haunted deserts and terrifying mountain barriers. Nor, as far as I had been able to determine, did they venture very far to seaward from their shores.

Indeed, why should they stray to distant lands? From what I had seen it appeared that the Chinese had everything they could need or want right here in their immense homeland. Then, too, they considered all those beyond their borders to be barbarians. The longer I stayed as an alien in this baffling land the stronger grew my conviction that they *could* be right in that belief.

Nanking was a scene of hectic activity for us. Our flotilla tied up along the southern bank of the Yangtze Kiang within the shadow of the walls of the ancient city. From this point we were to proceed westward through a network of rivers, lakes, and canals. We disembarked the horses and, in large part, the baggage train. As a separate section they would proceed overland. Our flotilla now considerably reduced in size, the remainder of us would continue the waterborne transit. Nanking was not much more than the midpoint of our journey.

We left Nanking in mid-November. The winds were favorable. As before, we sailed, or were poled along, at a leisurely pace. With one exception nothing marred the idyllic tranquility of our upstream passage.

*   *   *

The exception was something of a personal nature. It involved a matter to which I'd not given the slightest thought.

Shadowed terrace-tiered hills glided slowly past. A crimson sun hung low above mountain peaks in the west. There was crispness in the evening air. I called out for Wong Sin to bring a padded jacket for me and a woolen cloak for Gentle Breeze to ward off the increasing chill.

Gentle Breeze looked up at me sideways. "Do you want children, my lord?"

The question took me by surprise. What flashed to mind was an indistinct image of a fair-haired lad in England. God's teeth! In a short time young Thomas would turn six. Coming back to Gentle Breeze's question, I answered it noncommittally, "Hmmm . . . Yes—I suppose so. Someday."

"But not now?"

I looked at her sharply. Her eyes were lowered. I could read nothing from her expression. "No. Not now. How can I think of having children when I don't know what the future holds for tomorrow . . . let alone next year?"

Is she trying to tell me that she's pregnant? I wondered uneasily. That wouldn't do. When I discharged this obligation to the khan, I must join a westward caravan in order to make my way back to England. Much as the idea appealed to me, it would be unthinkable to be accompanied by a concubine. It would be difficult enough to part with Gentle Breeze without the added complication of a child.

It was as though, at least in part, she read my thoughts. "I am not pregnant, my lord . . . though the gods alone know why I'm not. Karma, I suppose. I quite forgot to take any precautions. But the red tide came on time two weeks ago and now, since you do *not* want children, your one-eyed monk must not enter to spill his seed in my jade chamber.''

"Huh! What do you mean?"

Gentle Breeze laughed softly. "Do not be alarmed, my lord. The hospitality of the chamber is denied him but temporarily . . . only for a few days. It is during these days when I am wont to quicken. However, as it was when I was afflicted with the moon floodtide, he is not denied his pleasure even though the jade gate is closed to him."

Regardless of my experience with the opposite sex, I thought shamefacedly, in reality I knew very little about their lunar-governed cycles. It was understandable that these should be mysteries. Before Gentle Breeze, my couplings had been sporadic even though plentiful. Now that I was blessed with bed companionship on a regular basis, there was much I was learning.

Once again she divined the thrust of my thoughts. Her eyes twinkling mischievously, Gentle Breeze observed, "If you know naught of this, my lord, it surprises me that you don't already have children. Perhaps, unbeknownst to you, you do."

We arrived at Changsha on the twenty-fifth of December. It was a day of no religious significance to any but me, Marco, and Brother Demetrios. In fact, so occupied was I with the disembarkation of the troops and the off-loading of stores that I quite forgot it was Christmas Day.

Chapter Twenty-One

Disfigurement gave a grotesquely sinister aspect to General Hsü Ch'ien's countenance. A puckered empty socket was where his right eye should have been. A jagged scar ran from his cheekbone to his lower jawline. The wound had angled his thin-lipped mouth upward on the right side, making the moustache bracketing his mouth look slightly askew.

The general sat facing me across a table cluttered with scrolls and maps. My uneasiness was magnified by the fact that his single eye glared at me with every evidence of hostility.

When he spoke, his voice had a grating quality. "You're late," he rasped. "Your cavalry arrived ten days ago."

I could have told him that, due to lack of wind, our passage down the Grand Canal had taken longer than anticipated but the general did not look like the type to welcome excuses. I withheld comment.

Rummaging through the untidy stack of documents on his desk the general extracted a scroll tied with a scarlet ribbon. Without untying it, he slapped it against the palm of his left hand. "This decrees that you be promoted to general of the third rank and assigns you to my staff. It does *not* indicate in what capacity. What military experience—if any—do you bring to this command?"

I bridled. "I'm an English knight trained in warfare, both mounted and on foot, and have acquired reasonable skills with your weapons."

The general regarded me unwaveringly. I found the lengthening silence unnerving. Finally he spoke. "I don't question your bravery. I'm told you're an impressive bowman. I'm told, as well, that you bested a Turkoman in a fight to the death. But skill at arms and willingness to risk your life are not enough. What makes you think that you are qualified to command warriors in battle?"

To that question I had no answer. He didn't seem to expect one. He turned his head slightly and looked down at the scroll he still held. He tapped it meditatively against his palm. With only a slight pause he continued. "But, then, I don't think you were sent here to command troops in battle. What *is* your purpose here?"

That question shook me. What had he been told? "To serve in your command as you see fit," I answered stiffly.

"Yes. Yes, of course. I'll give it thought, *General*. Incidentally, almost without exception, your troops speak well of you, Barbarian. You just may have unsuspected qualities of leadership."

It was a backhanded compliment that did nothing to lift my spirits. "I will turn over command of the *touman* to my tactical commander and await your decision, sir."

The general's eyebrow shot up. "Mangatei? You don't know of his promotion?"

"What promotion?"

The general glanced once again at the tied scroll. "By

this decree the Mongol, like you, is promoted to general of the third rank. In *his* case the assignment is specified. He is to take over command of the cavalry of the Army of the Blue Dragon. I thought you knew of this, but it's not important. What *is* important is the position *you* will fill commensurate with your elevated rank—and lack of experience. I'll send for you a few days hence when I've decided where you can best be employed."

I was allocated a compound in a residential section of the city. It was a property of considerable size encompassed by a high wall. Access from the cobbled street to the main courtyard was through a round-arched "moon gate," but direct access was barred by a marble barrier that had been positioned facing the entranceway a few paces within the courtyard. This partial obstruction was known as a "spirit screen." The superstitious Chinese believe that this barrier confuses, confounds, and turns away evil spirits intent on intruding their unwanted presence.

An imposing structure with a roof of green-glazed tile dominated the courtyard. I was told that this was the Hall of Ancestors but was assured that the ancestor tablets had been removed by the departing former occupants of the compound. I was advised that the property had belonged to the House of Soong—but none could, or would, tell me why or under what circumstances the Soongs had quit the premises.

To the rear of the Hall of Ancestors were dwellings, dormitories, pavilions, and outbuildings such as servant quarters, stables, storage sheds, and cookhouses. Interspersed among this ordered disarray were inner courts and formal gardens. Flagged footpaths and covered walkways provided connecting links. Taken as a whole, the property and its maze of structures betokened that the House of

Soong had been of goodly number and—if not now, at least at one time—of substantial wealth.

As a family seat the sprawling compound lacked the fortress grandeur of Ravenscrest and its drafty keep. Yet, in an odd way—despite the fact that the House of Soong no longer occupied the premises—the compound imparted a sense of enduring stability. I felt like an intruder.

No such feeling restrained Gentle Breeze. She was delighted. She chose as our quarters the dwelling I was told had been the abode of the Soong patriarch. With the assistance of Wong Sin she interviewed prospective candidates and selected the cooks, porters, gardeners, and household staff. I turned over the recruitment of a horsemaster, stablemen, and guards to my newly appointed military aide, Captain Chang.

The compound was a hive of bustling activity. Within a surprisingly short space of time the household was functioning smoothly and harmoniously.

We sat in a comfortable salon. Braziers fended off the chill. Brother Demetrios leaned over and poured himself another cup of wine. He raised it and said cheerily, "Happy New Year, Edmund, my lad."

I grinned. "Happy New Year, little father."

"But," Gentle Breeze protested, "it is yet two moons before we welcome in the Year of the Rat."

"It is the Christian year that draws to a close at midnight," Brother Demetrios explained. "A few minutes from now and it will be the Year of Our Lord 1276."

"Oh. I'm sorry. It *is* confusing . . . Buddhist New Year isn't due until the Month of the Dragon in the coming year."

I smiled at her. "If you find it confusing, little one, how do you think *I* feel? I've been exposed to more religions and beliefs over the past few years than I ever knew existed . . . to say nothing of customs and practices I find strange beyond belief.''

Brother Demetrios laughed. ''About this time last year we came to the Great Wall and you entered Cathay for the first time. What think you a year later?''

''God's bonnet,'' I answered. ''Had you told me then that a year later I'd be a general in the service of a Mongol emperor . . . or have a beautiful woman to attend to every need . . . I would have thought you mad, or roaring drunk. Probably the latter.''

''Drunk or sober, I could have predicted none of what's befallen you,'' the friar said thoughtfully. ''It is of your own making, my lad . . . or perhaps it is God's will.''

''It is my lord's karma,'' Gentle Breeze added soberly.

''Karma, kismet, God's will, or the random spinning of the Greek Fates, it matters naught. What matters is that I'm here, thousands of leagues from my homeland in a land I didn't even know existed, yet enjoying a position of prestige in comfortable surroundings and in good company. What more could a man ask for? I'll drink to that . . . and to we three whom Fate has providentially joined together.''

Brother Demetrios beamed and raised his cup to mine. Gentle Breeze colored in embarrassed pleasure, and did likewise.

Brother Demetrios lowered his cup and wiped his mouth with the back of his hand. ''But what lies ahead?'' he asked seriously. ''You still don't know what post awaits you in the Army of the Blue Dragon . . . or do you?''

''No. Not yet. But I have a meeting with the general tomorrow. I expect I'll know then what post I'll fill.''

''You knew, did you not, that you were to be promoted?'' Brother Demetrios questioned.

''Yes. Kubilai told me . . . but swore me to secrecy.''

"But he said nothing of Mangatei's promotion?"

"No. But, then, why should he? I'm sure that Mangatei knew of his promotion well in advance, but I doubt he knew I was to enjoy a similar honor. I think my promotion came as an unpleasant shock to Mangatei. I know his did to me. I suppose the khan wanted it that way, though I can't think why. There is, however, a distinct difference in that Mangatei was assigned a command. I don't think that General Hsü Ch'ien is at all pleased with that turn of events."

Gentle Breeze extended her cup for a refill. "What makes you think that?" she asked.

"Nothing definite. Just an impression I got when the general discussed Mangatei's appointment."

"Do you think that Mangatei is being groomed to take over command of the Army of the Blue Dragon?" the friar queried.

"It's a possibility that I don't think has escaped General Hsü Ch'ien's attention. He made mention of the fact that Mangatei is related to Kubilai. I got the impression that the kinship is not much to the general's liking."

"What about you?" Gentle Breeze questioned. "Does the general look upon you as a threat?"

I laughed. "I hardly think so . . . but he would like to know why I've been promoted—and why I'm here."

"Why *were* you promoted? Why *are* you here?" Brother Demetrios asked.

"Kubilai doesn't believe the reports he's getting from regional governors and military commanders. Marco and I are supposed to be unbiased outsiders. Marco is to report to the khan on the economic and political climate. I've been commissioned to check on the morale of the troops, the ambitions of the officers, and the disposition and strength of enemy forces. I was promoted to general to give me access to such information."

"In other words," Brother Demetrios observed, "you're a spy."

I grinned. "I suppose it could be put that way . . . but I prefer to think of myself as a neutral observer. And in that capacity, old friend, I need your help."

"How?"

"The disadvantage of my rank is that it separates me from contact with the lowly soldier of the rank and file. I can't frequent the doss houses along the waterfront without inviting unwanted attention—and Gentle Breeze's righteous wrath. No such restrictions hamper your movements. I understand that you're already well known at the Teahouse of Heavenly Happiness. By standing rounds of drink and making the occasional discreet inquiries, you can get a pretty fair reading on the morale of the troops."

Brother Demetrios shot a worried glance at Gentle Breeze and grinned sheepishly. "I suppose I could be of *some* help but I haven't yet mastered the local dialects."

"Persevere," I said dryly. "You will."

Through inquiries from a number of sources I slowly pieced together a reasonably accurate picture of General Hsü Ch'ien. Born in North China, in Kaifeng, Hsü Ch'ien was of mixed bloodline. His father had been half-Chinese and half-Cham. His mother had been half-Chinese and half-Jürched Tartar of the Chin Dynasty. I had not previously heard of Cham nationality. I was advised that the Kingdom of Champa was well south of the Middle Kingdom bordered on the north by Annam and on the southwest by the Kingdom of Kambuja. The Chinese called Champa *Linyi*, which means Savage Forest. It was pictured to me as a tropical land of palm-fringed beaches, dense rain forest, and rugged jungle-mantled mountains. I'd heard the Polos mention Linyi as a source of cinnamon, sandalwood, and ivory, and assumed—mistakenly as I learned later—that Hsü Ch'ien's Chinese grandfather had been a merchant trading in those exotic commodities.

Hsü Ch'ien was forty-five and had been soldiering since he'd joined a Mongol cavalry troop at the age of sixteen. He'd had a distinguished military career. He had lost his eye and received his facial wound in the Mongol campaign in Annam nineteen years earlier. He'd served under renowned Mongol generals such as Uriangkatai and Bayan. Commended for bravery, he'd risen steadily in rank. Under Bayan, at the siege of Lin-an, he'd served as tactical commander as a general of the second rank. Following the capitulation of Lin-an, Hsü Ch'ien had been promoted to general of the first rank and been given command of the Army of the Blue Dragon, a command he now had held for three years with an impressive record of successful campaigns to his credit.

Hsü Ch'ien was a soldier, a redoubtable warrior of unquestioned bravery and a strict disciplinarian. He might not be beloved by his troops but he was a military leader who was highly respected and whose orders were followed without question.

If Kubilai questioned Hsü Ch'ien's loyalty, I could find nothing in the record to support that mistrust.

New Year's Day held two surprises for me. The first of these was that General Hsü Ch'ien placed me in command of the right-wing forces of the army's battle formation. This was a position of trust and responsibility I had not expected. I only hoped that I would prove worthy of the general's confidence.

The second unexpected development arose during that

meeting with the general. He'd been talking in broad terms about our supply of expendable armorer's stores such as pikes, halberds, arrows, and crossbow quarrels. He didn't think that these items had been stockpiled in adequate quantities. He wanted me to look into the matter as it applied to the units now under my command. He then asked me what I thought I might require to supply the war machines I had brought with me.

On our arrival I'd had the mortars, rocket launchers, rockets, and barrels of black powder stored in a dockside shed. I had made no mention of those items to anyone here in Changsha. How had they come to General Hsü Ch'ien's attention?

"No one has been able to tell me exactly how or when they were used in warfare," I replied frankly. "I have tested them and had some soldiers trained in their firing, but they should be tested in battle before we need consider additional supplies. I've enough black powder, iron projectiles, and rockets to conduct such a test."

The general drummed on the tabletop with his blunt fingers. "I was surprised to find that you had located them. I've heard of their use, but have never actually seen such devices. I've been told that bombs, bombards, and rockets making use of black powder were used by the Sung in naval action near Nanking more than a century ago. The devices that hurl iron balls are said to have been developed on instructions from Genghis Khan and were used by him during campaigns in the west. They have not been used here in the Middle Kingdom for well over a century. Where did you come across them?"

"In an armorer's foundry in Cambulac. Mention was made of a long-ago naval action, but nothing was said of their use in land engagements. Why, I wonder, did they fall into disuse?"

"I don't think they were ever used here in land action. After the struggle between the Sung and Chin dynasties, there was a long period of peace. The Southern Sung emperors avoided conflict by paying tribute to the Chin. There were no naval engagements and I imagine the black powder devices simply gathered dust in armories then faded from military memory. Yet they have been put to use in land battle . . . though not in China. My grandfather used them effectively in his conquest of Champa. It was from reading his account of that campaign that I first learned of such formidable machines of warfare. Tell me, Barbarian, how do you visualize their tactical employment?"

"In two ways. In siege tactics the rockets could keep enemy archers from the battlements, and the iron projectiles could breach a city's outer defenses. The second way would be in a confrontation of lines of battle. Instead of having the great drums signal the advance, the simultaneous firing of the mortars and rocket launchers could serve that purpose. Properly aimed, they could make a shambles of the enemy line and sow panic in their ranks."

"Hmmm. Interesting. The latter case is much the way the devices were used by my grandfather. I have, however, reservations. Even with firework displays, black powder has to be handled with extreme caution. If you can satisfy me by a demonstration that the machines pose little or no threat to our ranks I'll authorize you to use them in forthcoming actions." The general's lips twisted in what I took to be a smile, then he added, "Though, as I'm sure you know, their use is strongly opposed by your erstwhile tactical commander, General Mangatei."

Chapter Twenty-Two

My eight thousand troops from the north brought the Army of the Blue Dragon to a strength of slightly more than thirty thousand. That seemed a huge number until I learned that the Sung force opposing us was about four times ours in size.

The Sung warlord had assembled his army at Hengyang, a town six days' march upstream from Changsha. Hsü Ch'ien was in no hurry to march south and do battle. This was not due to trepidation on the part of the general, but to strategic considerations.

The disparity in troop strengths did not trouble General Hsü Ch'ien. Where our Yuan force consisted chiefly of seasoned troops, the Sung army was made up largely of inexperienced peasant conscripts. If the confrontation took place in the field, Hsü Ch'ien was confident of an easy victory. He reasoned that his delaying tactic would force the Sung warlord into taking to the field in preference to choosing a protracted siege.

It was sound reasoning. Having an army the size of the

Sung force encamped on its doorstep would impose an economic burden on Hengyang. This would give rise to friction between the soldiers and the townspeople. The longer the delay, the greater would be the strain. A point should be reached where the Sung commander, unable to count on the support of the townsfolk during a lengthy siege, would choose to rely instead on his superior numbers to guarantee him victory in open combat. With that in mind, Hsü Ch'ien was delaying our march to the south until mid-February.

Why mid-February? To delay much longer was to run the risk of entering the rainy season, which would adversely affect the maneuverability of our cavalry. The general, however, had another reason. Our departure was timed to have us arrive at Hengyang at the start of the week-long lunar New Year festivities. The Sung warlord would be faced with an added incentive to sally forth to do battle. If his troops were allowed to participate in the holiday activities, their fighting efficiency would be reduced substantially.

My demonstration had convinced the general and he'd authorized the use of my mortars and rocket launchers in the forthcoming action. In addition he'd taken time to recount to me how his illustrious forebear, General Hsü Yung, had employed these devices against a Cham army of superior strength. The account wasn't too helpful.

Where I had but two of each at my disposal, Hsü Yung had used four siege mortars and twelve rocket launchers. Moreover, he had fired into an advancing force and had had time to reload his rocket launchers and use them a second time before signaling the advance of his battle formation. Since the simultaneous firing of my black powder devices would be the signal for advance, I had but one opportunity to prove their worth.

About all that Hsü Ch'ien's account did for me was whet my curiosity. How had it happened that a Chinese general had commanded a Khmer army doing battle against a Cham army in distant Linyi? And just what were the "war elephants" that seemed to have played a decisive role in that engagement? I resolved to question Hsü Ch'ien on these subjects if a suitable opportunity presented itself at some future date. For the moment I was content to devise a plan for the effective employment of the limited number of mortars and launchers at my disposal.

A few days prior to our departure I entertained a small number of guests at my residence. Those present were Marco Polo, Brother Demetrios, Gentle Breeze, Captain Chang, and, of course, I as host.

As dinner was being expertly served under the watchful direction of Wong Sin, I glanced at the circle of guests with wry amusement. It would be difficult to conceive of a more disparate gathering. Brother Demetrios, a Nestorian friar of Greco-Uighur origin—who considered himself a Byzantine Greek—was sipping rice liquor. Gentle Breeze, daintily lifting a morsel of food with her chopsticks, was of Syrian-Tartar extraction yet looked more Greek than did Brother Demetrios. Marco, a Venetian Lombard, was as at home with chopsticks as if he'd been born and raised in China. *What about me?* I thought as I reached forward and added several prawns to my bowl of rice. An English knight of Norman-Saxon blood. Of all the group, only Captain Chang was a native Chinese.

The language that flowed back and forth as we ate was chiefly Mandarin Chinese with occasional lapses into Greek and Turkic.

During a lull in the conversation a strange feeling crept over me. What was I doing here in this odd company? What were *any* of us doing here? Only Captain Chang, Wong Sin, and the servants belonged in this country. The rest of us were interlopers. It had been some months since I'd been prey to nostalgic thoughts of home. I was so now. Unbidden, memories flooded in on me.

It was winter now in England. In my mind's eye I saw a pewter sky and snowflakes softly sifting down onto the bare limbs of the oaks, elms, and yew trees of the hushed forest. For a moment I found myself back in the great hall of Ravenscrest surrounded by my kinfolk. English and French echoed in my ears. A roaring fire sent flames leaping upward in the huge fireplace. I saw my chamber as it had been when I'd last seen it. Then, to my shame, I had a fleeting vision of Ethelwyn, softly lit by firelight, standing naked by my couch. With a start of guilt I pushed that vision from me.

At my elbow Gentle Breeze must have sensed my agitation. "What is it, my lord?" she questioned softly in Turkic. "Is something troubling you?"

The spell was broken. "No, little one . . . a sudden chill, nothing more. Don't concern yourself." Then, turning to Marco on my left, I remarked, "So tomorrow we part company. At what hour do you and the good friar leave on your westward journey?"

"Midmorn. I am really looking forward to the adventure. I've been told that the scenery in the Yangtze Gorge is spectacular and that the red-earthed basin of Szechwan is pleasant of climate and incredibly fertile."

"Do you expect to stay long in Szechwan?"

"No. From there we will visit the mountainous former kingdom of Nan Chao, and from thence retrace our steps and return to Cambulac through the western and northwestern provinces. I should imagine that we'll be back in the capital no later than the end of summer. What of you? When do you expect to return to Cambulac?''

''I have no idea. The general doesn't expect the campaign to be of lengthy duration. Following its conclusion we should return here to our administrative base. Is not that so, Captain Chang?''

Chang paused in the act of lifting food to his mouth. ''Yes, sir. The general expects us to be back in Changsha before the first rains fall.''

''And after that?'' Gentle Breeze questioned, a note of anxiety creeping into her voice. ''Do we then return to Cambulac?''

I laughed. ''Never question a soldier about his plans, little one. His plans are made for him from afar. Let us teach the arrogant warlord in Hengyang a well-deserved lesson and *then* see what orders await us.''

From the opposite side of the circular table Brother Demetrios squinted at me owlishly. ''But won't the noble khan want a report of the action from your lips?''

The question annoyed me. The friar was well into his cups but that didn't excuse his indiscretion. I avoided looking at Captain Chang in order not to give weight to the friar's question. ''The khan,'' I said evenly, ''will receive detailed reports of any actions from General Hsü Ch'ien and others of general rank, me included. I doubt that any of us will be called upon to render our reports in person. But if so, I would be most happy to be summoned to Cambulac . . . though I hardly think it likely unless we have to explain away defeat. And *that* is something that none of us anticipates. Don't you agree, Captain Chang?''

''Yes, sir. Most definitely.''

*   *   *

Later that evening, pleasantly relaxed from lovemaking, I lay on my couch with the naked body of Gentle Breeze in my arms. Her breathing was deep and even in sleep. I pushed perspiration-dampened hair back from her brow and gazed fondly down on the curve of her cheek.

I was becoming more deeply attached to my lovely young concubine than I would have thought possible. We were growing closer with each passing day. She seemed to know what I was thinking and she certainly could read my moods. How quickly she'd sensed my momentary detachment at dinner, it was a lucky thing for me that she had not seen inside my head and caught a glimpse of Ethelwyn. Why had that unwanted image flashed into my mind? Perhaps it was because, as Gentle Breeze had suspected, I *was* troubled. It would avail me naught to delude myself. It had nothing to do with England, Ravenscrest, Ethelwyn— or Gentle Breeze.

It was, I supposed musingly, a natural reaction. A week or so hence I would be going into battle—for the first time. The tournaments I'd fought, the skirmish with the Tibetan bandits, and my fight to the death with the Turkoman well might have tested me, but they had *not* prepared me for a full-blown battle. That experience lay yet ahead of me.

"In a sense," I thought glumly, "I'm as ill-prepared as the unblooded peasant conscripts of the Sung army."

Chapter Twenty-Three

We followed the Siang River upstream into steadily rising ground. In the early morning of the sixth day of our march, we wound our way down through foothills onto the valley floor. As we descended, I rode back to the supply train to check my wagon-mounted mortars and rocket launchers. They were awkward items but restraining ropes had been rigged and there seemed to be no problems that couldn't be handled by the soldiers I had detailed to the operation.

As I rode back up the snaking line, I could see the walled town of Hengyang in the distance—and the array of tents and pavilions spread out before it like the extended skirts of a seated woman. There was the army we would fight. They must have had warning of our coming. I wondered why they'd made no attempt to ambush us in the mountain passes. It was what I would have done as a military commander.

The debate going on within me was worrisome. How would I gird myself for the coming fray?

I would have preferred to go into battle in full armor, but the more I thought on it the less the idea appealed to me. If Scimitar were to stumble and I was thrown to the ground, what then? English men-at-arms would come immediately to my assistance in such straits. I could not count on that assistance here. No; appealing as was the idea of the protection afforded by full armor, I'd have to abandon it in favor of mobility. So, I would lead the right wing of our battle formation garbed in my coif and hauberk of chain mail and the circular helm I'd used in my contest with the Turkoman. For ease of identification in the heat of battle I added a yellow plume to the crown of my helmet. That, coupled with my silken tabard with its coat of arms and my emblazoned shield—to say nothing of Scimitar's distinctive size and color and my comparatively towering height—should make me stand out as a rallying point no matter how thick the mêlée. And, in addition to my personal adornments, Chang would ride on my right flank holding aloft my banner of rank.

Which brought me to a choice of weapons. I wouldn't take part in the cavalry charge, which meant that my battle lance would serve no purpose. Mounted bowmen would ride on my right and left flanks. I needn't add to their firepower by encumbering myself with a sheathed bow and quivers of arrows—e'en though I now favored the Mongol bow as a weapon of offense. What I had to bear in mind was that my function as a general was to provide leadership and direction rather than to seek glory in personal combat. The only weapons I'd require were those that would help me to defend myself when the fighting closed around me. What I settled on was my broadsword to direct the fighting—and my battle-ax hung in saddle loops as a backup weapon. I had to keep reminding myself that in the rank I now held, any honor and glory I acquired would be earned for me by the conduct of the troops under my command.

The morrow was the last day of the Year of the Boar. Midnight on the morrow would usher in the Year of the Rat. What more fitting way could there be to round out the year than by a decisive victory for the Army of the Blue Dragon? Now that we'd arrived on the scene, how would the Sung warlord react? Had General Hsü Ch'ien's prognostication been realistic, or based merely on wishful thinking?

It was a moonless night. We sent out patrols to probe the Sung encampment and report back on any enemy activity.

Long before any of the patrols returned we knew what was happening from the profusion of wavering torches and the clamor of activity in the distance. Hsü Ch'ien had guessed correctly. A line of battle was in the process of being formed. The Sung warlord had chosen to face us on the morrow. Short of headlong flight it probably was the only choice open to him. However, since no effort was being made to disguise the activity, he must be in receipt of an accurate estimate of our strength and be supremely confident that his numerical superiority would win the day.

There was no necessity for stealth on our part. We went about positioning our troops in battle formation. But the question was just where were we to form our line? I sent out a patrol to get me as accurate an estimation as darkness would allow of the exact position of the enemy line.

For my mortars and rockets to be effective the distance between the drawn-up lines of battle should not exceed two hundred paces. This interval between opposing formations was considerably less than custom dictated. It had

been one of Mangatei's chief objections. His claim was
that by reducing the distance I was robbing him of room to
maneuver his cavalry before the advancing lines joined in
hand-to-hand combat. His objection was not without
justification. My counter argument had been that any advantage he might lose would be more than compensated
for by the confusion sown in the enemy ranks by my
projectiles.

My confident forecast was purely speculative. As I rode
by torchlight up and down our forming lines to supervise
the positioning of the mortars and launchers, I prayed
inwardly that the morrow's action would vindicate my
judgment.

In the hour of the tiger, as darkness slowly yielded to
the half-light of advancing day, the enemy formation became dimly visible. It was an awesome sight. The line,
though still fluid with frenetic activity, stretched across the
entire width of the valley from the terraced foothills to the
north to those on the south. Commands and responses, and
the thudding of horses' hooves, reached us muted by the
intervening distance, which I now judged to be somewhat
greater than two hundred paces.

I rode to the points where I'd positioned the siege
mortars and rocket launchers, one of each, spaced at wide
intervals, in both the right and left wings of our formation.
I checked to ensure that they were sighted across the center
of the enemy line and adjusted the elevation in the hope
that I was compensationg adequately for the distance.
Then, after cautioning the soldiers not to light their joss
sticks until the cymbals clanged and not to light the fuses
until they saw the commanding general's banner dip, I
rode to report to the general that all was in readiness.

When I reined in at his side, the general turned in his

saddle to bring his good eye to bear on me. As he took in Scimitar's silken trapper and bronze barding, Hsü Ch'ien's eyebrow inched upward. Turning his attention to me, he looked me up and down, his gaze lingering on my mailed coif, boldly embroidered tabard, arms-emblazoned shield, and the plumed helmet tucked beneath my right arm. I took it that never before had he seen a knight and war-horse in such trappings. The left side of his mouth lifted slightly in what I now recognized to be his smile.

"Very colorful, Barbarian. You and your mount present a bold picture . . . and should make excellent targets."

I grinned. He was resplendent in a gold-plated helmet boasting a flowing azure plume. His shoulder and hip armor, and the rectangular plates that faced his blue silk tunic, were also plated with gold. The light-blue cape he wore was trimmed with ermine and embroidered on the back with a fierce-looking cobalt-blue dragon. Officers were *supposed* to attract attention—and the higher the rank, the brighter the plumage. I took his rare smile to indicate approval of my attire.

"The mortars and launchers are trained and ready. They but await, sir, your signal of fire."

"Good. As a precautionary measure I've ordered the great drums to sound on the same signal. Let us hope their thunder is eclipsed by the angry roar of your engines of destruction. Now, Barbarian, I suggest that you take up your position in the wing."

The color of the cloudless sky changed from gray to bronze-green, then to pink tinged with gold. As the rim of the rising sun rose above the low hills to the east, a command was relayed down the wing. On that order wind instruments began to play and the soldiers of our formation broke into song. As far as I could make out, the singing was in the form of triumphant paeans extolling the prowess of Mongol armies in battles long since passed into history.

I'd been told that this chanting was a prelude to battle. How had it evolved? Surely, when the Mongol hordes of times gone by had swooped down upon their unsuspecting prey, they had not advertised their presence in advance by chanting legends of past glories. It was supposed to stir the blood of our soldiers and strike fear in the hearts of our adversaries. Perhaps it did, but to me it seemed a senseless caterwauling. If it served *any* purpose, it was to mask whatever sounds that might have reached us from the ranks of our foe.

Another order came down the line. Now the beating of the drums and clashing of cymbals added to the earsplitting din. But, I had to admit, this was effective. The blood started to pound through my veins in cadence with the thumping of the drumbeats. Tension mounted. The excitement became almost unbearable. It was all I could do to keep my gaze focused on the general's dragon banner.

The banner wavered, then dipped. I heard the great drums begin to rumble; then, seconds later, there was a deafening roar as the mortars belched smoke and flame and thirty-two rockets streaked toward the enemy battle line with a prolonged swoosh.

Although everyone had been warned what to expect, all of us, including me, seemed to be caught unprepared. The human reactions varied from stunned silence to resounding whoops. Horses shied, reared, and whinnied in fright. It took a moment for our force to adjust to the disrupting effect imparted by the explosive reverberations and resume the advance in response to the sonorous thudding of the great war drums. Even before the cloud of smoke from the mortars and rocket firings started to dissipate in the still morning air, our cavalry were sweeping out from the flanks at full gallop.

For a moment or two I was too occupied to give any attention to the damage my projectiles had inflicted on the foe. I steadied Scimitar, and as he pranced forward, I settled my helmet on my shoulders and, with sweeping motions of my sword, I checked the speed of advance of the wing of the formation to conform to that of the center and the left wing. I was conscious of confused sounds drifting toward us, even though partially masked by the booming of our drums, but I was too busy to check out the source. I raised my blade, then brought it sharply down. Bowstrings twanged and arrows arced skyward like a swarm of angry bees. Only then did I direct my gaze toward the enemy lines.

I had been confident that my projectiles would slow the enemy advance by creating confusion in their ranks but I hadn't envisioned anything quite like the havoc they had wreaked when they'd smashed into a yielding wall of human and animal flesh. The center of the Sung battle line was a shambles.

The mortar's iron projectiles had ploughed twin furrows through the enemy formation. While some of the rockets might have exploded early—or not at all—evidently most of them had detonated on target. Soldiers and riderless horses milled about in hopeless disarray. The sounds that I'd heard above the thunder of our drums had been the cries and screams of wounded and dying men and horses. Yet, in all the mangled center, pockets seemed to have escaped untouched. The Sung warlord's banner still waved defiantly. It seemed that, by some miracle, he'd survived the initial onslaught and was rallying the force which now advanced toward us in ragged disorder.

God's teeth, I thought, even as arrows started to shower down upon us, had I had more destructive engines at my disposal we could have chewed their ranks to ribbons and won the day in a matter of minutes. Then the battle closed around me and I had no more time for idle speculation.

My memory of the battle is hopelessly confused. A few images stand out sharply—a flying arm, a severed head, a stumbling steed—yet, for the most part, it's as though I stood apart and watched the rapidly shifting scene through a swirling fog. Still, restricted vision notwithstanding, I was no bystander. From the moment that the battle was joined in hand-to-hand combat I was in the thick of the fray.

I had worried that courage might desert me. I needn't have. There was no time for fear. A madness gripped me. I slashed to right and left until my arm grew leaden and I had to switch sword and shield to opposite hands. I recall switching in this manner not once, but several times.

The pounding hooves pulverized the cracked and rock-hard soil of the stubbled paddy fields. Choking clouds of dust and flying chaff engulfed us. The din of battle was enough to shatter eardrums. To my astonishment I heard my own hoarse voice adding to the shouts and screams. The words that issued from my lips were stranger still: "Death to the infidel! England and St. George!" With that battle cry issuing unbidden from my throat I hacked my way through pikemen, swordsmen, halberd-wielding militiamen, and a hail of crossbow bolts.

While most details are hazy, two things stand out in my memory.

The first of these came early in the conflict. Sweat poured from my brow into my eyes, obscuring my vision which was severely restricted by the visor slit of my helm. This was no tourney with a single adversary charging toward me. The protection afforded by my helmet was

set by the restrictions it imposed. I wrenched the helm
e and flung it carelessly aside. I have not seen it since.
I was learning. The spectacular charge of gallant knights
launch a battle had no place in warfare of this magnitude—
did any of the rules of chivalry apply.

The second incident took place much later when the sun
od high in the heavens. In my vicinity there was a lull
the fighting. I sat wearily in my saddle, grateful for a
ef respite. Scimitar's head was drooping and his chest
aved as he gasped for air. His muzzle and chin were
thed and, below the armor plates that protected his
k, his shoulders were streaked with sweat. His trapper
s ripped and splashed with blood. The noble stallion, I
lized, was near the point of exhaustion. While the
amfron and barding might have saved him from some
rtal thrusts, the bronze was a heavy burden for him to
ar. I inwardly breathed a prayer of thanks that I had not
cumbered myself in like manner.

I was not alone. Where I had led, an escorting body of
ops had followed. What astonished me was that Captain
ang, his horse sweat-lathered but looking fresher than
imitar, was close behind me still with my banner held
ft.

A pikeman stood close to my stirrup. One of his ears
l been sliced from his head. Blood dripped from a
und in his arm. His face was smeared with blood. Yet,
thal, he seemed undaunted. He grinned up at me. A
ackle rose in my throat and I nodded down at him
rovingly.

The battle was not at an end. It simply had ebbed from
momentarily. As I glanced over ground littered with
dies I noted a fierce action taking place not far from us.
the midst of this milling mass there fluttered the dragon
ner of the general.

227

"Chang!" I yelled, pointing toward the mêlée with m
sword. "Over there!" I set spurs to Scimitar.

When we neared the scene of the conflict I realized tha
it would be next to impossible to force through the press c
combatants on horseback. I sheathed my sword, slid to th
ground, and wrested my battle-ax from the saddle loops.
the van of my wedge of troops I carved a path toward th
wavering banner. Out of the corner of my eye I saw
Chang, also afoot, flailing away effectively with a Chines
fighting iron.

On the periphery of my vision I noted a flash of sunligh
as the shearing blade of a halberd swung toward me. Had
been fresher, I might have been able to dodge the thrust.

A strong light seemed to flash somewhere in my head
Then the whirling dust thickened into a curtain of blacknes:

Chapter Twenty-Four

I regained consciousness in my tent. Stripped of all but my underdrawers, I lay on a litter. Kneeling beside me, stirring something in a wooden bowl, was a white-bearded oldster—General Hsü Ch'ien's personal physician.

When I tried to sit up I became acutely aware of some unpleasant realities. One was that my left arm and shoulder were tightly bound. Another was that the modest effort caused a searing pain to knife through my head. With a gasp I sank back onto the litter. Reaching up with my right hand, I determined that my head was swathed in bandages.

The physician turned toward me. "Aha, my young friend, you have decided to rejoin us in this world."

"What happened?" I questioned weakly.

"Nothing that will not yield to ministration. Your ancestors protected you from grievous harm. The linked chain head-covering you wore deflected the blow enough so that it did not split your skull like a ripe melon. You have a broken collarbone. From the bruise I'd say it was fractured by a crossbow quarrel. As for the sword wound in your right thigh, a hand's-breadth to the left and you'd have been deprived of your precious jewels. Now, lie still while I apply this healing concoction."

"What is it?"

"An efficacious salve of my contrivance . . . an equal mixture of moss, mold, and live maggots."

"Maggots!" I protested. "Why not simply sear the wound with a hot iron? I'm sure it would be quicker."

The physician's wispy beard waggled as he nodded amiably. "Quicker, I agree, but the battle is won. You have no need for haste. Where it can be avoided, I don't favor cauterizing a wound. Not only is it painful and disfiguring, but it often leaves the affected limb stiff, if not entirely useless. I leave such methods to less skilled practitioners. You will see. A few days of this treatment and your leg will be as sound as ever it was before this day."

"General Hsü Ch'ien?" I queried.

The oldster chuckled. "Nothing but a trifling cut on the forearm. It seems his ancestors are better versed in matters of protection than are yours. I'm told, though, that your timely intervention when he was set upon saved him from more serious injury."

"Mmmm. We won the day, you say?"

"Indeed. A spectacular victory. The enemy were routed. Even now the Mongol general is hotly pursuing the fleeing stragglers."

The physician must have mixed something in the wine he gave me—some sleeping potion. I slept through until midmorning of the following day. I awoke feeling stiff and sore but my head no longer throbbed.

Ruefully I surveyed my knightly trappings of the day before. My coif was ripped and flaps hung loosely from y torn hauberk. My silken tabard was bloodstained and tattered beyond recognition.

Just because I'd sustained wounds did not mean that I was absolved from duty. My unit commanders were due to report to me concerning casualties and losses of arms and equipment. Following that I would have to report to the general concerning the state of the wing under my command. In addition I was anxious to hear from him what he thought of the performance of my siege mortars and rocket launchers. In that regard, based on what I'd observed of their effect on my enemy phalanx, I had a tactical suggestion to advance. It promised to be a busy day. As it turned out, it was not at all as I expected.

My servant helped me make myself as presentable as possible in a quilted jacket tied loosely over my bandaged arm and shoulder and a cloak draped over my shoulders. I then told him to inform Captain Chang that I was ready to receive the unit commanders. A few moments later Chang put in an appearance. He walked stiffly. His face was pale.

"Chang," I questioned anxiously, "did you suffer wounds? You look terrible."

"A chest wound," he said, then added hastily, "but nothing serious, sir. We were worried about you. You looked half dead when we brought you in from the field."

I grinned wryly. "I have been told that my ancestors were looking out for my interests. I limp a bit, and may look like a turbaned Turkoman, but I'm fit enough. Have the unit commanders report to me without delay."

Chang hesitated. "I've told them to report to you later in the day. If you can ride, General Hsü Ch'ien would like you to join him as soon as possible."

"Ride? I can limp to his command pavilion afoot."

"If you feel up to it, sir, the general wants you to ride

with him to Hengyang. He said to tell you that he will understand if you decline the invitation."

"I can ride," I retorted brusquely. Certainly, I *could* ride, but the physician had told me to avoid any activity that might jar my shoulder. He hadn't prohibited horseback riding specifically but I could think of no activity more bone-jarring. I added tersely, "Tell him that I'll join him in a few minutes. And, Chang—"

"Yes, sir."

"You shouldn't be moving around with a chest injury. Detail someone to take over your duties for a day or two."

The physician must have reported the extent of my injuries. Hsü Ch'ien held his horse to a walk.

He didn't look like a man who had gauged the enemy's probable reactions accurately and, thereby, had achieved a brilliant victory against a superior force. He seemed to be deeply despondent. His face was haggard. He rode in silence, slumped in his saddle.

Considering the scene of carnage all around us, I took the general's reaction to be only natural. We picked our way through a battlefield still strewn with corpses. Details of our soldiers had dug huge pits and were engaged in the grisly task of filling them with the bodies of our fallen. The noontime air was heavy with the sickly sweet smell of death.

The general broke his silence. "They fought well. Our losses were heavier than I anticipated. Much heavier."

"I regret that my projectiles failed to take out the Sung commander. Had he been removed, I'm sure they would have broken sooner."

The general cleared his throat. "Perhaps. Don't mistake me, Barbarian, I was well pleased with the effect produced by your lethal engines of destruction. I've recommended them for future use in my report. As well, I have commended you for bravery.''

I started to stammer out appreciation. The general silenced me with a deprecating gesture. ''Speaking of reports,'' he continued, ''Chang tells me you are expected to report in person to the khan.''

It came as no surprise. I'd suspected that Chang would relay anything heard under my roof directly to the general. I silently cursed Brother Demetrios for having been so loose of tongue. ''If the khan so commands,'' I replied.

''Don't play with words. I didn't need Chang to confirm what I already knew. Like young Polo, you were sent here as the khan's eyes and ears. Do you deny that?''

''No.'' I answered simply, actually relieved that it was out in the open.

''Good. That's why I asked you to ride with me this morning. There is something I want you to see with your own eyes.''

He didn't elaborate. There was no further conversation as we rode slowly westward toward a haze-shrouded foothill that hid the town of Hengyang from view.

The battle had not raged over this part of the valley. Its grim crop of scythed corpses grew ever more sparse. The bodies here were all those of Sung warriors who, I concluded, had been overtaken and felled while fleeing toward the sanctuary of Hengyang.

The path snaked upward, winding its way around fallow terraced fields. Here and there seedbeds of sprouting rice provided splashes of brilliant green but, otherwise, the hillside was dun-colored and drab with no signs of human life. Yesterday's fierce fighting must have caused the peasants to seek shelter in the town. The haze that obscured our view, I now realized, was smoke. Probably, I thought, the peasants had been burning off stubble and had left so hurriedly that they'd neglected to extinguish some of their smoldering handiwork. That assumption, I was soon to learn, was incorrect.

We topped the rise. The general reined to a stop. He said nothing. He pointed downward to the walled town that, though still some distance from us, was now visible. The smoke haze was thicker now and my eyes smarted. It took me a moment to appreciate that, while the stone defenses were intact, the town within the walls had been reduced to smoking rubble.

"God's blood!" I exclaimed. "What happened?"

The general did not respond to my question. "Come," he ordered laconically as he touched spurs to his horse.

As I followed behind him on the descent toward Hengyang, my mind was in turmoil. I could descry but little through the thin curtain of smoke, but I think I knew what awaited me. My thoughts flew back in time to visions of the burned-out villages and bone-heaps we had encountered in the Persian desert.

I'd thought that a few buildings of the town—two pagodas and a flare-roofed temple—hadn't been touched by the conflagration. As we drew closer, however, I could see that I was wrong. The religious edifices, like everything else that remained standing, were smoke-blackened, gutted shells. The fire had been all-consuming.

My vain hope that the mountainous mounds outside the walls consisted of urban refuse was soon dashed. It was as I feared. The larger mounds were corpses piled one atop another. The smaller heaps were severed heads that screamed silently in rictus and stared accusingly at me with sightless eyes. A wave of nausea swept over me. Scimitar whinnied and shied away from this mute testimony to wanton slaughter.

The only sound to assault the midday stillness was the

buzzing of a cloud of flies. The only odor was the stench of death. I reined my stallion to a quivering stop.

Hsü Ch'ien had been watching my face to judge my reaction to the appalling spectacle. He reined in alongside me. "The Mongol answer to resistance," he grated. "A pretty sight, is it not?"

I swallowed the bile that rose in my throat. "Sickening," I replied hoarsely.

"But a good object lesson. A grim reminder to the Sung of what they can anticipate if they continue their senseless resistance to the will of the Great Khan."

I looked at the general sharply. I thought I'd detected irony in his tone. "Did they resist so strongly that this . . . this *atrocity* was warranted?"

"On the contrary. Kubilai's magnanimity to the vanquished is legendary. The townsfolk opened wide the gates to welcome the cavalry—which somewhat simplified the troopers' task. Even so, according to General Mangatei, his troopers labored diligently all afternoon and through the night to achieve their aim. I am assured by that Mongol excrement that not one man, woman, or child escaped the sword . . . or being roasted alive in the torched town. It is, as you say, sickening. It is worse than that; it's madness."

"Then, why didn't you stop the slaughter?" I retorted hotly.

"It was already well in progress before word of what was going on reached me. I ordered an immediate halt, and had Mangatei summoned to my presence. Whereupon he produced a scroll of which I had no prior knowledge. It was a written directive bearing the official chop of Kubilai and further authenticated by the gyrfalcon seal. It authorized Mangatei to use his cavalry *as he saw fit* to make an example of the next sizable town or city to fall to the

Army of the Blue Dragon. I could do nothing, absolutely nothing, to stop the massacre already under way."

"Surely the khan didn't authorize this butchery."

"In effect, he did. Mangatei learned his trade in Persia under Hulagu Khan. He would interpret Kubilai's directive in but one way, the way you see before you. Kubilai knew that."

I was still nonplused. "I cannot understand how orders could be given to your army other than through you as its commanding general."

"Had it come through me, I would have complied with the directive, but not in the way you see here. Kubilai knew that, as well. Though I've served the Mongol cause for thirty years, I do not have the khan's unqualified trust. You see, Barbarian, he mistrusts Tartars. On both my paternal and maternal side my blood is largely Tartar. My grandfather's mother was a Khitan Tartar of the Liao dynasty. My mother was a Jürched Tartar. To make matters worse, my paternal grandmother was a Cham princess. Kubilai has had nothing but hatred for the Cham since their king defied him some years ago. On top of that my Chinese blood is of a noble line. I am descended from the Hsü emperors of the Southern T'ang dynasty. Though I was born in North China, I've strong blood ties here. My great-grandfather, Hsü Ta-kuan, was a mandarin and governor of Changsha prefecture before being sent as an emissary to the Khmer court. My grandfather, Hsü Yung, spent his boyhood in Changsha before accompanying his father to Kambuja. There he saw service with the Khmer king and, eventually, governed Champa as a warlord. My father, Hsü Dhama, came to China from Champa at the age of ten. Before going north to settle in Kaifeng, he lived in Nanking, Lin-an, and Changsha. I have many kinfolk in

South China and enjoy some popularity in this region. Do you begin to perceive why the khan questions my loyalty?"

"Does he see you as a potential turncoat?"

"Until yesterday I would not have said so. Today I see no other explanation." Hsü Ch'ien waved a hand toward the macabre pile of severed heads. "By this act . . . for which I will be blamed . . . I've been stripped of any regional popularity I enjoyed. By overriding my authority, he's stripped me of command into the bargain. No army can exist under divided command." The general's nostrils pinched in an expression of disgust. He wheeled his horse, adding, "You've seen enough. Come, let us be quit of this scene of infamy."

I kept pace with him. "Do you believe this was done simply to discredit you both politically and militarily?"

Hsü Ch'ien snorted. "Not entirely, but it certainly served that purpose."

"What other purpose could it serve?"

"In Cambulac, Kubilai is attended by Mongol hotheads who believe him to be too soft with the Chinese. In part this action, in keeping with Mongol military practice, could be a gesture to placate that warlike faction. Also, it could be personal vengeance. The khan is not a forgiving man and the fact that Sung resistance continues unabated, despite his generosity following the surrender of Lin-an, has both dismayed and angered him. However, regardless of his motives, this punitive act is folly Kubilai will live to regret deeply."

"Why? How so?"

"An army needs food. Rice that was in the Hengyang granaries has been reduced to ashes. When the rains come to soften the earth there will be no one here to do the planting. There is no profit to be had from conquest of a wasteland. Taking a longer view, the impact of this 'example' can only harden, not soften, resistance. Convinced they face slaughter if they surrender, the Sung will fight to the death in every village, town, and city still in their hands. It will be a long and bitter struggle.''

I rode in silence for some minutes. The general had given me much to think about and I thought I could see the reasoning behind his disclosures. He wanted my support in his condemnation of the draconian measures adopted by the khan. Did Hsü Ch'ien want more than that?

"Did you express your sentiments in your report of proceedings?" I asked innocently.

"Of course not," he growled. "I confined the report to bald facts concerning the conduct of the battle itself. Nor did I censure that bloodthirsty pig-turd, Mangatei—at least not directly. I stated that he had conducted follow-up operation as directed. I've sent him to Cambulac to report in person on that phase of the action. For your part in the battle I have recommended that you be promoted to general of the second rank. I advanced no such recommendation with respect to Mangatei.''

It took me a moment to absorb what Hsü Ch'ien had just disclosed. God's teeth, if Kubilai acted on the general's recommendation, my rise in the military hierarchy would be an unprecedented phenomenon. It would, as well, earn me the undying enmity of Mangatei. I put those thoughts from my mind. It was highly unlikely that the khan would act on Hsü Ch'ien's recommendation—which, I appreciated, was intended more as a backhanded slap at Mangatei than as an accolade for me.

"Tell me, as a matter of curiosity," I asked, "what would you have done had the khan's order been directed to you instead of Mangatei?"

The general regarded me thoughtfully, his eyebrows

slightly raised. ''These are my people, Barbarian. Had the khan placed me in that position, I'm all but positive that by today the Army of the Blue Dragon would be in the Sung camp.''

Chapter Twenty-Five

The Army of the Blue Dragon returned to Changsha to await new orders. I was glad of the opportunity this gave me to rest up before embarking on the arduous journey north to Cambulac. It might have been due to the squirming muck the Chinese physician had insisted on applying that the wound on the inside of my thigh appeared to be healing nicely. My broken collarbone, however, still caused me a good deal of discomfort.

Gentle Breeze fussed over me like a mother hen. She questioned me concerning the battle and how I'd come by my wounds. In truth, apart from the glancing blow to my head, I had no recollection of how I'd received the wounds. As for the battle, I recounted the success of the engines of destruction, but gave credit for our victory to the strategy and tactics of General Hsü Ch'ien. But what stood out in my memory was not the battle itself, it was the slaughter of Hengyang's populace by Mangatei's cavalry.

Seemingly indifferent to the grisly fate of the townspeople, Gentle Breeze commented phlegmatically, ''For those in the path of a marauding army, it was to be expected. It was their karma.''

"*Karma!* Had the order gone to Hsü Ch'ien it would have been a different story.''

"Oh. In what way?''

"He'd have spared the city . . . if only to leave people to plant and till the fields. He told me that he'd have defected to the Sung before ordering that the city be razed and all its inhabitants put to the sword.''

Gentle Breeze's eyes grew round. "But that would have been treason!''

"It was a directive subject to different interpretations. How Hsü Ch'ien would have acted on it is open to question. The order went not to him, but to Mangatei. What Hsü Ch'ien told me, little one, must not be repeated. Is that understood?''

"Of course, my lord.''

It was a gradual process, yet I realized that Gentle Breeze was trying to master the technique even before we reached Changsha. Evidently what I'd told her about the esoteric skills I'd attributed to Fatima had made a strong impression. When I commented on her accomplishment, she'd clapped her hands delightedly but didn't enlighten me concerning how she was going about acquiring this skill. It remained a mystery until shortly after my return to Changsha after the Hengyang campaign.

Since my knitting collarbone still troubled me, especially if I was jolted or moved without due caution, Gentle Breeze took the initiative in our lovemaking. I basked shamelessly in this attention. It was during one such coupling that Gentle Breeze held my phallus firmly trapped within her jade chamber and succeeded in bringing it not only to a second erection but, had I not been as drained of

ces as a squeezed orange, she'd have coaxed a third
formance from me. It was exquisite pleasure but, in my
akened condition, one that I had to temper with prudence.
When I restrained her she looked down at me, her eyes
de with anxiety. "Am I not doing it right, my lord?"

Gasping for breath, I managed a grin. "It's not that.
u're fantastic. It's just that you've drained the last drop
ching from my precious jewels. I'm not yet as strong as
ought I was."

"Am I as good as she was?"

I'd thought Ethelwyn unique in her ability. It wasn't so.
ntle Breeze was every bit as competent. I cupped her
rt breasts in my hands and smiled up at her fondly.
es, little one; if anything, you surpass her."

A radiant smile lit her face. "Oh, I'm so glad. I thought
ust be doing the exercises wrong."

"What exercises?"

"Well," she answered matter-of-factly, "when I piss I
ernately hold back then release the flow . . . and I've
cticed religiously with the 'love vase' I bought in
chow."

"The *what*?"

"The 'love vase.' Have you never seen one?"

"Not that I know of."

She giggled. "I'll show you."

Lifting off me, she rose from the bed and went to a
binet. She returned carrying a ceramic vase which she
esented to me with a flourish. I took it from her and
amined it. The bottom portion was squat and widely
red. From that flattened base a neck of uniform thick-
ss extended upward about six or seven inches to termi-
te in a bulbous top.

Handing it back to Gentle Breeze, I grinned. "It looks
mething like a one-eyed monk."

"That's what it's supposed to resemble. It's a porcelai
substitute Chinese women use when their masters are ab
sent for long periods . . . or when they have no man ◆
satisfy their needs. They fill it with warm water and—
She colored as her voice trailed off in embarrassment.

I didn't want to postpone my departure any longer tha
necessary. In addition to making my report to Kubila
there were two other pressing matters to be resolved.

I'd gone south with the *touman* before Roccenti ha
finalized his transactions. My arrangement with Lorenz
had been that he'd leave my share of the profits with th
Polos for safekeeping. The same applied with the sha
that was to have gone to Brother Demetrios. By this tim
the friar and Marco should have returned to Cambulac an
Brother Demetrios would have received his share.

What I intended to do was buy into a westbound carava
but any commitment of that nature was contingent ◆
Kubilai's tacit approval. That meant I had to arrive at
somewhat less nebulous arrangement with the khan co
cerning the duration of my employment. So far nothi
had been mentioned in that regard. In order to mak
definite plans for my homebound journey, I needed
know when Kubilai would no longer have need of m
services.

The overland journey confronting me was in excess
three hundred leagues. If nothing delayed us, we should
able to average seven leagues a day. I was allowing tw
months each way for the trek. Thus it was, accompani
by a troop of cavalry, I set out from Changsha one bluste
morning in mid-March. Summer would be well advanc
before I would see Changsha again. In fact, if my busine
could be concluded satisfactorily with the Polos and
could persuade the khan that he no longer needed m

ervices, I need never see Changsha again. The latter possibility was something I'd not discussed with Gentle Breeze.

I'd no intention of abandoning her, but it was unthinkable that she should accompany me on my return to England. In accepting her as a gift from Kubilai, I'd assumed responsibility for Gentle Breeze's well-being. If things could be concluded to my satisfaction in Cambulac, I'd have her join me there. I would turn over to her a portion of my share of the caravan profits and, if she so wished, take her as far as Turfan to rejoin her family.

Understandably, this would be an important trip. A good deal hinged on its outcome.

As we left Changsha behind us, I glanced back, deep in thought. I noted Captain Chang, riding close on my right flank with my banner snapping in the stiff March wind and, behind him, the cavalry troop. They were smartly turned out. I'm sure that I, resplendent in the trapping of a general of the third rank, cut an impressive figure. But at that moment my thoughts were far from China.

True, I owed much to the fact that I'd found favor in the eyes of the khan. At long last I'd been blooded in battle and brought honor to the de Beauchamps name. I'd gazed on wonders no other Englishman had witnessed and experienced things I'm sure no one would believe. Who, for example, was likely to credit that a young English knight had attained banner rank in a Mongol army? Nonetheless, tempting though it might be to prolong my stay in Cathay, it simply was out of the question. The longer I lingered here the more difficult it would be to retrieve my birthright in England. Ravenscrest, not Changsha or Cambulac, was where I belonged. It was high time I was heading in that direction.

*   *   *

As we neared Cambulac, May came upon us. Fruit trees were in blossom and the fields flanking the Imperial Post Road were burgeoning with greening grain. The air was heady with the scent of spring. Tired though we were, we were in excellent spirits.

I delegated the billeting of the escort to Chang. For myself I sought accommodation in an inn close to the residence of the Polos. I was sure that word of my coming had preceded me and that I'd be summoned by the khan soon after my arrival in the capital, yet I hoped to be able to settle my business with the Polos prior to my audience with Kubilai.

As it turned out, the khan was absent from Cambulac on a hunt and wasn't expected to return for several days. I had ample time to discuss my affairs with the Polos.

"Yes," Niccolò said expansively, "even after we deducted our agreed-upon share, the return was substantial. Of course, it should have been greater."

"Oh? Why is that?" I asked.

"Count Orsini had no background in such matters, which is why we wanted Lorenzo Roccenti to go with the caravan. Unfortunately Lorenzo's experience had been confined to Acre. He was out of his depth when it came to striking a shrewd bargain in trading towns such as Kashgar and Turfan. I'm afraid, in many instances, he was cheated. Then, too, the thieving Nestorian cleric my brother and injudiciously recommended lacks Christian scruples. He overcharged shamelessly in the hiring of pack animals, muleteers, and camel drivers. It is something of a miracle that you turned a profit at all."

"What did Brother Demetrios have to say in his defense? *If* he overcharged, it can be deducted from his share. Was that not done?"

"We haven't seen him since he left with you and Marco.
e friar was to visit Szechwan with Marco, then the two
them were to return here. The khan, however, had a
ange of heart and sent them to Tali. I've no idea when
'll see them back in the capital. As for the share you
:ak of, you must be mistaken. The Nestorian had no
are of the profits. He was a hireling and, in my estimation,
s grossly overpaid for his services."

I stared at Niccolò in consternation. That hadn't been
agreement. We all were to have shared equally—
luding Brother Demetrios. Had Roccenti neglected to
/ise the Polos on that score? If he'd conveniently forgot-
that arrangement, what else had slipped Roccenti's
nd?

"And my share?" I questioned uneasily.

"Reinvested in trade goods for the return journey,"
:colò answered blandly.

"But," I blurted out in dismay, "he was to leave my
are with you for safekeeping."

"That wasn't our understanding. He told us that your
are, which should be substantially increased by then,
uld be kept in trust for you in Acre. We thought you'd
cussed it."

"No," I said weakly, "it was not discussed." My voice
dening, I added, "However, rest assured, I'll demand a
l accounting when I reach Acre."

There was no more to be said. I'd been duped. I vowed
t when I reached Acre, Roccenti would pay, and pay
irly, for his venal treachery.

As I walked slowly back toward the inn, I considered
complications Roccenti's perfidy had engendered. Since
arrival in Cathay I'd given little thought to money. I'd
l no need to. All my expenses had been met from
:side sources. As a result my purse was as empty as

Roccenti's promise to leave my share of the profit with th
Polos. I couldn't do as I'd intended, which was to pu
chase an interest in an outbound caravan. Now the onl
way I could see of leaving would be to hire out m
services to a westbound caravan as an errant soldier
fortune.

Chapter Twenty-Six

The khan returned to the Imperial City in mid-May, the third day of the Month of the Dragon. The following day I was summoned to his presence.

In the palace compound of the Forbidden City I was conducted through a maze of outbuildings and ushered finally into a marble pavilion overlooking an artificial lake. I was left there to cool my heels for the better part of an hour before Kubilai appeared. He was informally attired in an unadorned gown of pale-green silk.

With a peremptory wave of his hand Kubilai cut short my obeisance. He subjected me to critical scrutiny before speaking. "You look much as you did, though I am told you sustained wounds."

"Happily, sire, none of any consequence."

"Your conduct during battle drew high praise from General Hsü Ch'ien, as did your employment of the black powder devices as instruments of war. You are to be commended both for bravery and initiative. Hsü Ch'ien strongly recommends that the engines of war be made standard equipment. General Mangatei, on the other hand, is strongly opposed to the introduction of such devices, which, he claims, reduce the effectiveness of his cavalry. What say you, *Chin man-tze*?''

"In balance, sire, I would say that the advantages outweigh the disadvantages.''

"I'm of two minds. I will authorize their use by the Army of the Blue Dragon for further evaluation before committing myself to wider application. Now, leaving that issue to one side, what thought you of the Sung forces opposing us?''

"Numerically superior, sire, but lacking cohesive leadership and fighting skills within the ranks. The men-at-arms seem to be composed chiefly of peasant conscripts with little or no battle experience. Our victory at Hengyang against vastly superior numbers underscores the Sung weakness when faced with disciplined forces.''

"Will the Sung continue to employ the same tactics, pitting weight of numbers against us? Is there any indication that their numbers are decreasing?''

"Everything I've been able to ascertain indicates that they will continue to outnumber the Yuan forces by a wide margin for some time to come. Their defeat at Hengyang was of such magnitude, however, that I think it will cause them to modify their tactics. I don't believe that they will risk open confrontation. Their more likely tactic will be harassment, then retreat into heavily defended positions. I am afraid, sire, that as the net around the Sung is constricted every defended town and city in the southwestern provinces will have to be subjected to besiegement.''

Kubilai nodded reflectively. "A sound appraisal. Protracted sieges are bound to have an adverse effect on our morale. What thought you of the morale within our ranks?''

"At this moment, sire, I would say it is excellent. There

is nothing like a major victory to boost morale. Of course, there is a certain amount of friction within the ranks, but I imagine that is to be expected.''

"What friction?" Kubilai asked with deceptive mildness.

I knew I'd stepped onto treacherous ground. I chose my next words carefully. "In the main the Chinese foot soldiers have been recruited from the Changsha region. The cavalry, particularly the *touman* most recently attached to the army, is made up largely of troopers from the northern regions. Differences of opinion are only natural.''

"What differences of opinion?"

"The feeling was that the cavalry's tactics in the mopping-up operations following the battle were too harsh.''

Kubilai's facial expression didn't alter, but his eyes glinted like obsidian chips. "Was that feeling shared by you?"

I've no talent for dissembling. I took the bit in my teeth and answered frankly. "In my estimation, sire, the directive should have been relayed through the army's commanding officer. The interpretation put on the order by General Mangatei was too colored by passion. His action was draconian in the extreme. By massacring the townspeople and razing the city, he tarnished your reputation for magnanimity.''

The khan's eyes narrowed to mere slits. He turned abruptly from me to face the window opening onto the still waters of the artificial lake. Behind his back his hands were tightly clenched. For some moments he stood as immobile as though carved from stone. Then, slowly, his intertwined fingers relaxed their clutching grip. His back still toward me, he finally spoke in a hard flat voice.

"I am the Khaghan. No one questions my commands. No man criticizes me, even indirectly—and certainly not openly as you have just done—and lives. You have cause to thank the God you pray to that I have not summoned the guards and had you put to the sword.''

He turned to face me, his hands now tucked from sight in the wide sleeves of his gown. His expression gave no hint of anger. It was difficult to imagine that scant moments earlier I'd been within a hair's breadth of death, yet I knew with chilling certitude that had been the case.

''There are two reasons why I stayed my hand, *Chin man-tze*. The first, and least important, is that you could be echoing sentiments expressed to you by another. The second is that it was I who requested you to be forthright in your observations. In this one instance I choose to overlook your insolence . . . *but it must never occur again.* Is that clearly understood?''

''Yes, sire,'' I replied, keeping my voice steady with an effort.

''I do not give reasons for the commands I give, but I will make an exception for your benefit. It is General Hsü Ch'ien who would have misinterpreted the order. He has too many friends and relatives in the immediate vicinity of Changsha. There is no room in war for sentiment. Mangatei translated my directive into draconian action exactly as I anticipated. You expressed concern about my reputation for magnanimity. In the past I have exercised leniency when it has suited my purpose to do so, but my forbearance has been taken for weakness. It was high time that the Sung were disabused on that score.

''Fear acts as a spur. In the months ahead I must impose heavier taxes on Southwest China than ever were levied by the Sung. Believing now that the alternative to meeting my demands is extermination, the peasants and townspeople will submit to those taxes. Only abject fear could goad them into unwilling compliance. Since I have no wish to nurture the seeds of revolt, that burden of taxes will be eased once the present crisis passes. The peasants then will breathe a heartfelt sigh of relief. You have much to learn about governing in the wake of conquest, *Chin man-tze*.''

I didn't subscribe to his reasoning, yet inclined my head in acknowledgment.

"Now," Kubilai said briskly, "let us turn our attention to other matters. General Hsü Ch'ien recommended that you be promoted to general of the second rank. I approve of the promotion. In addition he requested a transfer of command. Taking everything into consideration, I have granted that request. He has been so advised . . . and informed that you will succeed him in command of the Army of the Blue Dragon.''

If before I had maintained silence due to discretion, now I couldn't have spoken even had I wanted to. I stared at Kubilai in dazed confusion, convinced I'd not heard him aright. If I *had* heard him correctly, surely he must be jesting.

As he watched my face to gauge my reaction, the suspicion of a smile touched Kubilai's lips. "So now," he continued, "let us address ourselves to the employment of your army in the months ahead. The net, as you so aptly put it, must be tightened inexorably. To that end I have placed Marshal Sögatü in overall command of the Yuan forces in Southwest China. That includes your army, the Army of the Jade Panther, the Army of the Golden Boar, and some isolated independent units. He will coordinate all actions mounted against the Sung. His mandate is a simple one . . . *crush the Sung resistance for all time.*''

I was still too stunned to give voice to questions clamoring for answers. I continued to stare dumbly at the khan.

"There will be some changes in the composition of your army," Kubilai continued imperturbably. "General Mangatei will not be returning. He is assuming tactical command of an army being raised at Tali, an expeditionary force scheduled to move westward against the fractious Burmese of Pagan when the rainy season in that region draws to a close. All but six troops of your cavalry will go to that expeditionary force. A new *touman* of cavalry will be raised here as replacements, but you cannot expect its arrival at Changsha before the Month of the Ram. Your army, therefore, must be in all respects ready to move out as ordered by Marshal Sögatü no later than the middle of the Month of the Monkey."

I wasn't dreaming. Kubilai was calmly outlining the employment of an army that was now my responsibility. At least he'd answered one of my many questions. Mangatei would not be on hand to challenge my authority. And, by sending most of the cavalry to Tali, Kubilai was removing the primary source of friction that had existed in the Army of the Blue Dragon since the Hengyang battle.

Finding my voice, I questioned, "If I am to command the army, and General Mangatei has been removed from the scene, that creates a number of vacancies at the unit command level. Am I to fill those vacancies at my discretion?"

Kubilai regarded me intently through slitted lids. "Entirely at your discretion, except that any promotions to banner rank require my prior approval."

"Then I'd like to recommend Toghu for promotion to general of the third rank to replace Mangatei as cavalry commander."

The khan's eyes widened fractionally. "Toghu is a cavalryman who shows promise, yet he strikes me as being overly ambitious. Do you not feel he will, in time, pose you a threat?''

"I fully expect him to be a threat—one day. But until that day comes, sire, he is the ablest cavalryman in the Army of the Blue Dragon.''

Kubilai eyed me quizzically. "The promotion has my approval, but not to become effective until four months hence in the Month of the Cock.''

I had no idea why the khan didn't want Toghu's promotion to become effective until the Month of the Cock, but the fact that Kubilai had acted on my recommendation at all was encouraging. Encouraging! God's blood, what was I thinking of? Nothing was making sense.

Suddenly I realized that Kubilai was speaking to me. I pulled my errant thoughts together and forced myself to listen attentively.

". . . an intensive winter campaign. You will see action aplenty. Beyond that it is an avenue to both fame and wealth.''

"Yes, sire," I answered dutifully. "I appreciate the confidence you have in me.''

"There is one final matter, *Chin man-tze*. A man in your position should have sons to succeed him. I strongly advise you to find yourself a suitable wife, a Chinese girl of good family. She would, of course, have to meet with my approval. Give it serious consideration.''

I returned to the inn as though walking in a trance. It was all happening too fast. I needed time to think.

I had more than enough time to think during the southbound journey. Two things were abundantly clear at the outset. I could forget any plans I'd made to quit the realm attached in one way or another to a westbound caravan.

My resolve to place some sort of time limit on my services had proved equally futile.

Though his reasons escaped me, patently Kubilai had in mind long-range plans involving my continuing service. It wasn't a levy I could avoid by scutage. Indeed, with no fief to provide me with income, I couldn't have exempted myself from military service by the payment of a shield tax even had I been of a mind to do so. Still, e'en though penniless, I should have had no cause for complaint.

My banner rank had been granted solely to facilitate the gathering of information. It had had no real significance in a military sense. Now that I'd been promoted to general of the second rank, all that was changed. Though I still could scarcely give it credence, I now commanded an army that was well-nigh threefold the strength of the English crusading force led to the Outremer by Edward Longshanks. And by Chinese standards the Army of the Blue Dragon was a force of modest size.

In a personal sense I had little to complain about. My every need was taken care of. Did I not have an enchanting bed companion to cater to my sexual wants? My household ran smoothly. I now held meaningful military rank. Even if no lands went with the promotion, had not Kubilai indicated it to be a sinecure that carried with it both fame and fortune?

The rub was that it was Kubilai, not I, who shaped my destiny. He'd gone to some pains to make it clear that he exercised the power of life or death over me. I existed at his whim. As long as he had need of me, my future was secure. What if he felt I was no longer of value?

An analogy sprang to mind. I likened it to a chess game played with living pieces. I could picture Kubilai hunched over the board contemplating his strategy and plotting his next move. Whom was he pitted against? Since the khan was intent on shaping world destiny, Fate seemed an appropriate opponent.

What piece was I on the khan's chessboard? Obviously a knight charging blindly into the fray at the khan's direction. Was I to be sacrificed early in the game, or would I remain until the end game to join in an attack aimed at toppling a king? But what king, and where?

Fanciful? Certainly! I carried it a step farther by putting faces to other pieces on the board.

Roccenti and the Polos I dismissed as mere pawns; Toghu had featured in the opening gambit as a pawn but in no wise could I disregard his continuing presence on the board. The Turkoman I'd fought had been an expendable piece.

Despite his rank Hsü Ch'ien had been nothing more than a pawn. Kubilai must have had him marked for removal long before I'd come upon the scene. That I was the one to replace him was due to a shift in the khan's strategy, a twist of fate that fitted in with the khan's long-range plans for me.

Mangatei was a chesspiece opposing me. Kubilai had exploited the differences between us to promote rivalry and foster enmity. I doubted that I'd seen the last of the Mongol general.

Brother Demetrios was a most unlikely candidate for bishop, yet, as the only cleric in evidence on the board, he'd been mitered by default. I suspected that he, as well, had been but temporarily removed from play.

Gentle Breeze, a Turcople-Tartar concubine of lowly station, probably didn't even qualify as a pawn in Kubilai's estimation, but he'd left no doubt of his intention to introduce a distaff piece into the game. Trying to fathom Kubilai's thoughts was like trying to unravel a tangled skein, but I'd noted that those things to which he attached the most importance he always mentioned last. That I take unto myself a principal wife had not been mere suggestion, it had been an imperial command.

The game had been in progress for a year. Some pieces had been permanently removed from play, others looked to have been only temporarily taken out of the game. Still others, such as Marshal Sögatü and a yet-to-be-determined wife, were about to make their presence felt.

I'm not blessed with prescience. I couldn't discern the khan's game plan. All I knew was that I'd been advanced rapidly up the board and been placed in a vulnerable position.

Everything indicated that I was an important, mayhap crucial, piece in play. Every inducement had been extended to smooth my path and comfort me. I'd been elevated to high rank while yet in my twenty-fourth year and handed a challenging command. Satisfying domestic arrangements had been provided. But the drawback was that my heart was not there, it was in England.

If I accepted Kubilai's dictate, married a Chinese of high station, and sired sons, my chances of seeing England again were virtually nil. The difficulty was, I saw no avenue of escape.

We were being ferried across the Yangtze Kiang at Shasi when the thought occurred to me. There *was* a way of besting Kubilai in this game.

When they'd been forced to turn south in Persia, the Polos had intended to come to Cathay by sea. Had I not been told that Arab seafarers regularly visited ports in Southwest China? If we squeezed the Sung forces in that direction, eventually we'd reach coastal ports frequented by Arab traders.

Surely an opportunity to flee Cathay by sea would present itself if I had specie with which to purchase passage. What I must do now was wrest control of the purse strings from the khan.

Chapter Twenty-Seven

News of my arrival had preceded me. The gates were flung wide. The guards, smartly turned out, stood rigidly at attention with their halberds at the vertical. I clattered through the moongate into the flagged courtyard and rounded the spirit screen to find that Gentle Breeze, Wong Sin, and the entire household staff were assembled before the Hall of the Ancestors to greet me.

Dismounting stiffly, I handed the reins to a stableboy. Gentle Breeze, disregarding decorous custom, ran to me. Heedless of my dust-filmed attire, she flung herself into my arms.

The storm that had been threatening unleashed its fury that night. The wind howled, rain drummed on the roof tiles, lightning slashed the weeping heavens, and thunder crashed and rumbled. Like the drumrolls of combat it provided a strident accompaniment to the "flowery battle" being enacted in my bedchamber.

I must confess that our initial lovemaking fell short of

my anticipation. The fault was mine. I was quickly aroused— and almost as quickly spent. I would have been embarrassed had Gentle Breeze not made light of it.

"We've been too long apart," she said, fondling my flaccid phallus. "Your poor monk is out of practice, my lord. He cannot wait to spill his pent-up *ching*."

She was right. I'd not practiced self-denial during my absence, but very nearly so. I'd availed myself of the services of several "little flowers" in the teahouses of Cambulac, but they'd suffered by comparison. After Gentle Breeze it was like drinking watered wine—it slaked the thirst but failed to stir the blood. On my return journey I'd been preoccupied and had politely rejected the company of young girls available at inns along the way.

I gently caressed Gentle Breeze's breasts, then traced a path downward with my tongue until I reached her pouting portal. Parting the lips, I massaged the pearl within the gate with my tongue and lips until she quivered and moaned in ecstasy and her juices flowed freely. The intimacy we'd enjoyed before my departure returned in full measure. There was little said between us as we ministered to each other's needs far into the storm-torn night.

We awoke to find that the passing storm had swept the sky clean. Morning sunlight slanted into the bedchamber as we made love once again with tender passion.

We breakfasted on the balcony leading off our sleeping quarters. The balcony overlooked a shrub-enclosed garden. The sun smiled down from a cloudless sky. Birds were singing. The air was clean and rain-scrubbed. In the garden pool mauve and white lotus blooms were fully spread to bask in the sun's warming rays. Fat carp swam from beneath the floating lotus pads and lazily rippled the surface of the pond. It was a beautiful morning. I should not have marred it with serious discussion, but I'd much to tell her.

"You've not asked me what happened in the capital," I said mildly.

She favored me with a radiant smile. "I meant to, Emun, but in the joy of your homecoming it fled my mind."

I smiled. *Emun!* She rarely used my Christian name except in our most intimate moments. It would have been unseemly for her to display such familiarity in public. Then, too, she was self-conscious of her inability to pronounce the name correctly.

"Did you know that I'd been promoted to general of the second rank and am to relieve Hsü Ch'ien as commanding general?"

"Yes, we knew that more than two months ago when the khan's messenger arrived to advise General Hsü Ch'ien that he'd been transferred to Korea. You must have passed the messenger somewhere along the way."

I hadn't known that Hsü Ch'ien was going to Korea. That was something of which Kubilai had made no mention. "Were you told that the Army of the Blue Dragon is to join with the armies of the Jade Panther and Golden Boar under the command of Marshal Sögatü?"

"No, I didn't know that."

"Next month a newly raised cavalry *touman* is to join us, and the following month we're to be ready to move south in a final campaign against the Sung." I added glumly, "The khan intends to keep me here. I've had to set aside my plans to return to my homeland."

I could not read the emotions that chased themselves swiftly across her features. "Are you not happy, my lord, that you command an army?"

I smiled wanly. "Of course I'm happy, little one, but

it's a grave responsibility. I don't know why the khan chose thus to honor me . . . and I don't know that I'm qualified for such a challenging assignment."

"You will do well, my lord. The army could not wish for a better commanding general."

My smile became a grin. "I hope they subscribe to that sentiment, little one. They've little choice in the matter."

Gentle Breeze laughed, then questioned, "Is that all that took place in Cambulac?"

"By no means." With some asperity I recounted how I'd been cheated by Roccenti and of the defamatory charges Niccolò Polo had leveled against Brother Demetrios.

"I don't believe it," Gentle Breeze said heatedly. "I just don't believe Brother Demetrios would do that."

"Nor do I. I think it was an excuse to squirm out of paying him his share."

Gentle Breeze's face clouded. She ran her finger along the edge of the marble-topped table reflectively. "There could be more of it than that." Her lip curled in a look of distaste. "The Venetians owe everything to the khan's patronage. They toady to him. If, as you say, the khan wants to keep you here, he could have instructed the Polos to keep your share from you and, since he is your friend, from Brother Demetrios, as well. It well could be that your share *was* left in trust with the Polos."

I was annoyed with myself for not having hit upon that explanation. "It's a possibility," I conceded grudgingly. "It seems he'd go to any lengths to keep me in the realm. He even 'suggested' I take a wife."

"Oh, that you *should* do, Emun."

I don't know what reaction I'd expected, but certainly not such ready acceptance of the khan's proposal. "I'm in no hurry to move in that direction," I said stiffly.

"But it isn't proper for you to have a concubine without

first having a principal wife. It flies in the face of Confucian tradition, particularly for a man of your rank and station.''

''He should have thought of that before he sent you to my tent.'' Then, noting an expression of hurt and anxiety on her face, I added in a softer tone, ''But if you think it to be in my best interest, little one, I'll give it serious thought. His chief concern, however, was not so much the taking of a wife but that she should bear me sons. If sons are considered so essential, why can't you bear them?''

Her voice was tinged with sadness. ''In time, my lord, I hope I will, but I cannot take the place of a lawful wife. Sons of a concubine do not rank with those of a principal wife, or even of a *ying*. It is so ordained by custom. Since I cannot change it, I must perforce accept it.''

''A pox on custom,'' I said irritably, as I rose to my feet. I was sorry now that I'd allowed our discussion to intrude on such a beautiful morning.

General Hsü Ch'ien received me in a gazebo located in the garden of his residence. He was attired informally in a robe of lavender silk over which, despite the heat, he wore a sleeveless vest of black cotton. He motioned me to take a seat opposite him and ordered his servant to bring tea.

''You didn't tell me you'd requested a transfer,'' I observed.

Hsü Ch'ien's twisted lips parted in the widest smile I'd yet seen him display. ''I didn't request a transfer; I requested to be relieved of my command. The khan chose to regard it as a request for transfer of command. In effect I've been banished to the Kingdom of Korea . . . far enough removed from South China that I could not possibly prove a threat to Kubilai Khan. My wives and children aren't taking it at all well, but it really isn't that bad. It could have been much worse.''

"Why Korea? What sort of a command?"

"The khan is raising an army there."

"For what purpose?"

The twisted grin appeared once more. "The khan hasn't taken me into his confidence, but I can guess its purpose. Kubilai covets the wealth of the island kingdom in the Eastern Sea, a realm called Nippon by its inhabitants. Some years ago his demand that Nippon acknowledge Mongol overlordship was rebuffed. Two years ago he sent an army, composed chiefly of Chinese and Koreans, to back up his demands. The Nipponese counterattacked and sent that army scurrying in disarray back to the Korean mainland. Affronts like that Kubilai cannot abide. I've heard he has sent envoys to renew his demands for tribute. If this latest demand is not met, I'm sure he will launch an invasion against the island realm. In that event I'll be part of the invasion."

"When did word of your transfer reach you?"

"The Month of the Snake, about five weeks after your departure. That same directive named you as my successor. I must confess, *that* came as a surprise until I gave it thought. As a 'foreign devil' you'll not be swayed by conflicting interests. You owe allegiance only to the khan and, obviously, you have his confidence. He told you, did he not, that Mangatei will not rejoin the army?"

"Yes, and that most of our cavalry has been sent to join him in Tali. A new *touman* is being raised in North China to replace them."

"I doubt that it will number more than two or three thousand troopers. The Yuan forces are becoming desperately short of manpower."

"If that is so," I asked, "why was the cavalry sent to Tali when it's badly needed here?"

"Ah, another story. Three years ago the khan sent an

envoy to Narathihapate, King of Pagan, demanding tribute. The Burmese monarch rashly had the khan's emissary and his retinue put to death. Since then, emboldened by Kubilai's lack of retaliatory response, the Burmese have been guilty of incursions into Chinese vassal states in the far west. To teach the unruly Burmese a lesson the governor of Tali has been ordered to mount a punitive expedition. Mangatei's cavalry is the seasoned nucleus on which that expeditionary force will be structured.''

"What about replacements for our infantry losses?" I asked.

"No replacements will come from the north. We've been directed to bring the army up to strength by local recruitment. You're going to find that difficult. As you well know, the massacre at Hengyang tarnished our image on the local scene and the continuing struggle has all but denuded the region of able-bodied men.''

I groaned inwardly. Mentally I tallied the army's strength. With the cavalry gone, we were reduced to a force of less than fifteen thousand. When the replacement *touman* arrived, we'd be lucky if we totaled eighteen thousand. By Asian standards that wasn't much of an army.

Hsü Ch'ien poured tea into both our cups. He sat back and sipped the aromatic infusion appreciatively. "You know," he observed musingly, "to be perfectly candid, being relieved of this command doesn't sadden me; yet, in a sense, I envy you. Here, and in the land mass to the southwest, history is in the making. You'll be part of that process while I languish in a backwater.''

It wasn't my intention to be part of the history-making process any longer than absolutely necessary. "I thought," I commented politely, "you said that an invasion of Nippon was imminent."

"A distinct possibility . . . but a footnote to history.

Mongol eyes turn west, not east. To Kubilai the Sung are like a burr under his saddle blanket. No matter how long it takes, he will rid himself of that irritant. In the process he will accomplish something that has eluded Chinese emperors for centuries—the reunification of the Middle Kingdom. Once he's disposed of the irksome Sung, he'll turn his full attention westward.''

''What then?'' I prompted.

He fixed me with his good eye. ''Ah, yes! What then? When Kubilai Khan established the Yuan dynasty, he arrogantly demanded obeisance and tribute from all the neighboring realms to the west, southwest, and the island kingdoms of the Western Sea. Believing China to be racked by civil conflict which fully occupied the khan's attention, most of those kingdoms either ignored his demands or defied him openly. They will live to rue their defiance. That China has been weakened by fully two generations of almost continuous conflict will not deter the khan. Like his grandfather, his uncles, and his father before him, Kubilai is convinced that it is Mongol destiny to rule the world. Conquest, more than the unification of China, is the heady wine that intoxicates the khan. And you, my fine young general, will play a part in Kubilai's grand military adventure. Yes, I envy you.''

It wasn't that I doubted the accuracy of Hsü Ch'ien's predictions. On later reflection what I found jarring was his confident assumption that my destiny was linked inextricably to that of Kubilai Khan.

Chapter Twenty-Eight

I had not expected my elevation to command to be greeted enthusiastically by the officers; yet, surprisingly, it didn't generate the resentment I'd anticipated. To the rank and file it mattered little who commanded. The officers were my chief concern. As I'd indicated to the khan, a good deal of reshuffling was called for and I wanted to effect the changes with as little disruption as possible.

I discussed my selections with Gentle Breeze. I'd learned to value her shrewd insight into human character. There was another reason. Ever since the departure of Brother Demetrios I'd relied on her to provide me with a window through which I could view the Oriental scene.

"Chang was with you in Cambulac," she said. "Why didn't you promote him then?"

"I felt it would be premature until the actual takeover of command. On the trip south I told none of my mounted escort of my promotion, or that I was the new commanding officer-designate."

"Do you intend to retain him as your aide?"

"Yes. I know that he reported my every move to Hsü Ch'ien, but if it hadn't been Chang it would have been someone like him. He's served me well. In battle he never left my side."

"You say you suggested Toghu as commander of the cavalry and that the khan approved his promotion to general of the third rank."

"To become effective in the Month of the Cock. I didn't see at first why Kubilai wanted the delay. I see now that it was in order for Toghu's promotion to coincide with any other banner rank promotions I might recommend."

"Do you trust him?"

"As much as I can any Mongol. In one sense it's awkward. He commanded the troop where I received my training in Mongol weaponry and tactics. At that time he reported regularly to the khan on my progress"—I grinned— "and might still do so, which could explain why he's still here and not in Tali. But none of those things detract from the fact that he's a first rate cavalry officer and the man best qualified to command the cavalry of the Army of the Blue Dragon."

"General Wu?"

"He resents the fact that I was promoted over his head, but he's been passed over so many times he is resigned to it by now. I'm making the old war-horse my second-in-command and recommending him for promotion to general of the second rank. It's higher than he has any right to expect. I don't think he'll give me any trouble."

"Whom have you chosen to command the wings?"

"Liu and Yin Po. I've let it be known that, if they serve me well, they can expect promotion to banner rank, but not until next year."

"You are beginning to think like an Oriental," Gentle

Breeze said approvingly. "You're buying loyalty by dispensing favors . . . or the promise of favors."

I laughed. "In the matter of securing allegiance there's little difference between your world and mine. But, surprisingly, I've encountered very little resentment."

A faint smile touched Gentle Breeze's lips. "The resentment is there, my lord; it's simply hidden from you. It is well known that you owe your command to the khan's favor. No one dares incur your—or his—displeasure. I pray nightly to the Enlightened One that you continue to find favor in the khan's eyes."

The days flew by. The Month of the Horse gave way to the hottest summer month, the Month of the Ram. The cavalry *touman* arrived, and with it the six mortars, four rocket launchers, and an adequate supply of black powder and projectiles that I'd ordered from the foundry in Cambulac. In a month's time we must be ready to break camp and march south to join Marshal Sögatü's combined force. It was a time of hectic activity.

The keystone of General Hsü Ch'ien's policy had been preparedness through training and iron discipline. I have found that soldiers resent and resist change. I did nothing to alter Hsü Ch'ien's policy, adopting it as my stated policy. Mine was the final word, but I delegated much of the authority to my newly appointed unit commanders. I was particularly pleased with the way Toghu stepped in and took immediate charge of the new cavalry *touman*, the majority of whom were Mongols. To my delight the newly arrived *touman* numbered in excess of four thousand officers and men.

I introduced but two changes. Mindful of Mongol inclination toward competitive contests I encouraged such activities between the various units of the army. In truth, such contests were commonplace among English knights where tourneys, jousts between individuals or groups of knights and their retainers, simulated combat conditions in time of war.

My second change was more of form than of substance. Hsü Ch'ien had kept his gnarled finger on the army's pulse through an elaborate network of spies, most of whom had reported directly to the former commanding general. I didn't dismantle this web of informants, but they now reported not to me but to Major Chang.

I found one aspect of my new status amusing. The derisive nickname I'd been given, *Chin man-tze*, had been picked up by Kubilai as a form of address. It had stuck with me. Only the Polos, Brother Demetrios, and Gentle Breeze had continued to address me by my rightful name. It seemed now that the derogatory sobriquet had been dignified through usage. To the Army of the Blue Dragon I was General Chin Man-tze. I'd had it engraved on ivory as my official chop.

The day had been brutally hot and humid, nor had the advent of evening brought much by way of relief. As I strode toward my residence, hot, tired, and sticky with sweat, I had but one thought in mind. I was looking forward to a refreshing bath.

Gentle Breeze wasn't on hand to greet me. I disrobed in my bedchamber and went directly to the bathing room, where I sank gratefully into the jasmine-scented tepid water of the bath.

Absorbed in reviewing the events of the day, I didn't hear Gentle Breeze enter the bathing room. Hearing the rustle as she let her robe fall to her ankles, I glanced up. Smiling fondly down at me as she stepped out from the folds of her robe, she said, "You couldn't wait."

"I'm sorry, little one, I'd but one thing in mind—to sink into this life-giving water with as little delay as possible. Where were you?"

"Attending to your business, my lord," she said primly as she stepped down into the sunken marble bath and settled herself beside me.

"Oh? What business is that?"

"Your pending nuptials."

I'd given little thought to the distasteful prospect of marriage. "Hmmph," I grunted testily. "How does that concern *you*?"

"Custom dictates that a member of your family, generally an uncle or a cousin, arrange the formalities on your behalf as a marriage broker. Since you've no one else to speak for you, I've had to intercede in that capacity."

"Is that considered proper . . . a concubine acting as a marriage broker?"

"It's not considered proper," she said, smiling impishly as she pushed a strand of damp hair back from her forehead, "but do you know anyone in a better position to extol your virtues as a lover and protector?"

"Hell's fire," I rejoined grumpily, "you don't need to be in such a hurry. I had in mind a lengthy betrothal. With campaigns ahead of me I could stretch a betrothal almost to infinity."

"If the khan thought you were playing for time, he'd step in to speed the process. If it looks to him that you're not bowing to his wishes, he's sure to act. Probably he'll suspect me of exerting undue influence on you and—"

"All right," I interjected hastily. Strangely, I hadn't even considered that aspect. I'd thought only of myself. I didn't need her sentence to be completed to picture what could happen if Kubilai suspected her of interfering. "Have you anybody in mind for the dubious honor of marrying a foreign devil?''

"The governor's sixteen-year-old niece, Wang Mei-ling."

"She should win Kubilai's approval," I commented teasingly. "Is she pretty?"

"She's attractive," Gentle Breeze said tartly. "I think I now know how Yang Kuei-fei must have felt."

"Who?"

"Yang Kuei-fei, the 'Precious Consort.' She was a concubine who dominated Hsüan Tsung, an emperor of the T'ang dynasty. Only Yang Kuei-fei, and those women of whom she approved, found their way to the emperor's bedchamber."

"Under my own roof," I said in mock anger. "Is there no peace anywhere for an honest man? Are there none who don't try to manipulate me?"

"Surely, my lord," Gentle Breeze said sweetly, "you aren't accusing me of manipulation. I meant to draw no parallel. Hsüan Tsung was like tallow . . . readily molded. Who could mold you? You are a man of iron."

I glanced ruefully down into the bath water. "Not all of me, I fear."

Gentle Breeze followed the direction of my gaze and smiled. "Even the most stalwart monk needs rest after several nights devoted to hard labor."

"Rest!" I snorted. "He needs more than rest. He needs the ministrations of a physician. His cowl is frayed beyond recognition from the battering he inflicted on your gate."

Gentle Breeze giggled and snuggled up to me. "If he'd enjoyed the ministration of a physician at an early age, he'd have no cowl to fray."

Chapter Twenty-Nine

One vexing question was yet to be answered. How, in Heaven's name, was I to acquire the funds needed to put my plan into effect?

I sat at the table in my command pavilion pondering that question. I was absently affixing my chop to some documents, but my thoughts were elsewhere. They were rudely dragged from a speculative future back to the immediate present by a guard announcing that I had a visitor.

Imagine my surprise when the guard ushered in a somewhat bedraggled, yet beaming, Brother Demetrios. I rose, scattering papers as I did so, then strode around the desk and embraced the friar warmly.

"God's blood, what brings you here? I thought you were with young Marco in Tali. Is Marco with you? Where have you—"

Brother Demetrios held up his hand protestingly. "Stay your questions, Edmund, lad. All in good time. No, Marco isn't with me. He is to accompany the army that will sally forth a few months hence to do battle with the Burmese."

"Why aren't you with him?"

"I can do him little good and, in fact, could do him harm. General Mangatei harbors no affection for me. I cannot act as an interpreter since I neither understand nor speak the tongues of the T'ai of Nan Chao or the Burmese of Pagan and Ava. Then, too, I found Tali not at all to my liking. The mountains are grotesquely twisted humps of limestone. The valleys are veiled with mist and choked with jungle. Savage beasts and snakes abound . . . and the wine is an insult to one's palate."

I couldn't suppress a laugh. "So you reluctantly parted company with Marco, and shook the dust of Tali from your sandals. But I thought Cambulac to be your destination. Why did you return to Changsha?"

"Ah, Edmund. To Mangatei's chagrin—and Marco's delight—news of your good fortune reached us in Tali. I left when you were a part-time spy commanding one wing of a battle formation. I return to find you promoted to general of the second rank and in command of an army. I must say that your rise has been as rapid as one of those rockets of which you are so fond. So I detoured by way of Changsha to offer my congratulations. In a few days I'll continue my journey north to the imperial capital."

I sobered. "Thank you for your good wishes, e'en though they may be premature. If you're journeying to Cambulac to collect the monies due you, I can save you the trip. No funds await you there."

"What?"

"It's a long story. Come, I'll bring you up to date as we walk to my residence."

I recounted all that had taken place since last I'd seen the friar, starting with the battle at Hengyang and its bloody aftermath. Then I told him of my visit to Cambulac and the two jolting surprises I'd received from Niccolò

Polo when he'd disclosed that monies due me had been reinvested by Roccenti, and that no monies were owed to Brother Demetrios.

When Brother Demetrios's anger subsided, I recounted what had transpired at my private audience with Kubilai, and the conclusions I'd reached concerning his disclosures.

Brother Demetrios cocked his head on one side and treated me to an appraising scrutiny. "Why are you so anxious to return to England? Is it just the title that was stolen from you? I'd think that commanding an army in the rank of general would more than compensate for your loss of a title earned solely through birth. What would you have there that you lack here?"

Those were questions I'd asked myself time and again. I gave the friar answers I'd given myself. "I want to return for much the same reason you give for returning to Constantinople—because it's home. A wrong has been done me that must be righted. As the rightful earl I have responsibilities to the people of my barony."

"Kubilai means you to have responsibilities here. Responsibilities that should eclipse any that you have in England."

"God's teeth, why me?"

Brother Demetrios absently scratched the graying fringe of hair above his ear. "It's not just you, Edmund, lad. He's doing the same with young Marco . . . though he's testing Marco in the political rather than the military arena. Were you aware of that?"

"No. But if that's true, why us?"

"I think the answer lies in the labyrinthine corridors of power in the Forbidden City. Kubilai is surrounded by venal courtiers and self-seeking clerics. Corruption is a way of life. He places little trust in those around him and fears that, once he passes from the scene, the avarice of the mandarin class will spell doom for the Yuan dynasty.''

''What has that to do with me and Marco?''

''Everything . . . though I must confess I didn't see it until quite recently. You and Marco arrived in the capital almost simultaneously. You must have seemed to Kubilai like an answer to his prayers. That he looked on you as barbarians was unimportant. What *was* important was that both of you were young, intelligent, had a flair for picking up foreign tongues quickly, and had not as yet been infected by exposure to court intrigue.''

''I still don't follow the thrust of your reasoning.''

''You will. For instance, there was your coat of arms. I was wrong about that. It *was* a test to determine if you placed honor above personal risk. Then, too, it puzzled me that he subjected you to trial by combat.''

''I'm glad it gave you pause for thought,'' I observed acidly. ''It could have been the end of me.''

''Yes, you *could* have been killed. At that time the khan had little invested in you. Nonetheless, he slanted the odds in your favor by giving you the choice of weapons. I think he was curious about your behavior under stress''.

''So you saw in those events some grand design?''

''Not immediately. I knew, of course, that the Mongols are given to placing foreigners in positions of great trust. In theory foreigners are impartial administrators. I didn't see this as applying to you and Marco, due to your comparative youth, until both of you were removed from the corrupting influence of court life on what I took to be a flimsy pretext. You were to provide the khan with information readily available to him from other sources. If you measured up to his expectations, Kubilai would progress to the next step. Marco was ordered to join an expeditionary force as an observer empowered to negotiate trade agreements on behalf of the Middle Kingdom. You've been given command of a Yuan army. You must admit, Edmund, to rise from a trooper under training to a general commanding an army of seasoned troops in just under a year stretches credulity well beyond accepted limits.''

''Why, then, did he threaten my life?''

''Ah, I believe he was acting a part to impress on you your dependency on his continuing patronage.''

Kubilai's words came back to me. He'd said: ''Fear acts as a spur.'' He'd roweled me, and none too gently.

''Do you suggest that this command is but a prelude to a higher station?'' I asked.

Brother Demetrios nodded emphatically. ''I do, though only the khan knows what that might be.''

For a full minute I walked in silence, lost in thought. It was ridiculous, yet, in a crazy way, not without logic. Kubilai was no ordinary man. He was quite capable of such vaulting flights of fancy. What if the friar's hypothesis wasn't as farfetched as it sounded?

At length I broke my silence with a question. ''What if I fail to live up to his expectations? What if he comes to doubt my loyalty?''

Brother Demetrios bestowed on me a searching look. ''I suggest, Edmund, lad, that you not even think along such lines. You'd become a noble experiment that failed . . . in which case I'd not like to stand for a single moment in your shoes.''

Gentle Breeze was delighted to see the friar, as were Wong Sin and the rest of the servants. The presence of the insouciant Nestorian acted like a tonic on the entire household.

When we had dined, Brother Demetrios and I strolled in

the small enclosed garden to walk off the effects of overindulgence in food and wine.

We sat down on a bench at the far end of the garden. My thoughts were, as they'd been earlier in the day, on the sorry state of my personal finances.

A waxing moon rode high in the heavens, its nascent crescent mirrored in the lotus pond. The friar sat with legs extended, feet apart, his cassock drawn above his knees to allow a free play of cooling air. His hands were clasped beneath his ample paunch. He belched contentedly.

I'd been watching fireflies, winking points of light darting through the shadowed shrubbery. The friar's belch broke my train of thought. "Huh?" I queried absently, thinking he'd spoken.

"I said nothing, lad. I've been thinking on what you said earlier. If you're of a mind to return to England against the khan's wishes, it won't be easy. You wouldn't get far along the caravan route without being apprehended and brought back to Cambulac."

"I realize that. I wasn't planning to go that way. My alternative would be to leave by sea, but I don't know how, or from what port."

"The major entrepôt port is Khanfu . . . called Canton by the Chinese. Unfortunately it's in Sung hands."

"It won't be for long," I observed confidently. "Have you any idea how long it would take me to reach the Persian Gulf by sea?"

Brother Demetrios tugged meditatively at his earlobe. "I've not been to Khanfu or, for that matter, have I ever visited the Persian Gulf, but I've heard Arab mariners discuss the voyage. They claim that if seasonal winds they call 'monsoons' are favorable, the voyage from Khanfu to Siraf takes about eight months. They are wont to stop at ports of call on the island of Serendib and at Kulam Mali in India, which extends the time of passage by a week or two.''

"God's teeth! That's about one third of the time we took to get from Aleppo to Cambulac. Why would any man in his right senses opt for the overland route when the sea voyage is so much shorter?''

"I understand the voyage is fraught with peril. Frightful storms batter the vessels, coastal waters are aswarm with pirates, and the oceans abound in man-eating monsters. I've even been told that there exist islands wherein live natives who dine off human flesh. I'd sooner the prolonged company of stubborn mules and foul-tempered camels.''

"I've little enough choice in the matter,'' I said ruefully. "However, we first have to take Canton . . . and I have to accumulate enough funds to pay my passage and get me from this Siraf you mentioned to Acre.''

"You command an army. Acquiring funds should pose no problem.''

"Perhaps it shouldn't, but it does. I was raised in the belief that trade is a demeaning occupation. I fear I'm woefully ignorant in matters pertaining to finance.''

Brother Demetrios looked at me as though I'd taken leave of my senses. "You're expected to exact commissions on all army transactions. How do you think officers acquire property against the day when they'll retire? The perquisite goes with your rank. You're expected to line your purse while on active duty. Didn't Hsü Ch'ien mention this when he turned over the command?''

"No, I suppose he thought I knew how the system functioned. Since the turnover none of my subordinates has seen fit to enlighten me.''

"Mmmm. That makes it difficult. They must assume you already have this knowledge and are delighted that you aren't taking advantage of it. What *you* don't take leaves more for them. No road to riches for you under those circumstances. Have you given thought to how to go about setting the situation to rights?"

I grinned. "Not much, until this moment. Now I have in mind attaching someone to my staff with experience in these matters. Someone I can trust."

Suspicion crept into the friar's tone of voice. "Have you anyone in mind for this position of trust?"

"Yes, I was thinking of asking a Nestorian cleric to join my staff in the dual capacity of spiritual and temporal adviser."

The friar's belly shook as a chuckle surfaced from its depths. "I suppose I could postpone my departure . . . for a suitable fee."

"Let us say a percentage of my percentage. Would an even split suit you?"

"Done!"

I looked at Brother Demetrios appreciatively. For a fleeting moment my imagination, abetted by the moonlight, played a strange trick. The friar's soiled cassock was transformed into a spotless chasuble and a bishop's miter hid his bald pate from view. I smiled inwardly as I visualized the khan's chessboard. A knight-bishop combination can mount a formidable attack. The game might yet develop along lines Kubilai would find surprising.

The friar's question brought me back to earth with a resounding thump. "Have you told Gentle Breeze of your plans?"

"No-o. At this stage it would be premature to do so. I would appreciate it if you'd treat what we've just discussed as confidential."

Chapter Thirty

Why had I not taken Gentle Breeze into my confidence? I fear there is no easy answer to that question, since it touches on ingrained attitudes and prejudices acquired during my formative years.

The trouble was that I'd been reared in accordance with the tenets of my Catholic faith in a strictly monogamous society. The Holy Church allowed little latitude; yet certain transgressions, while not openly sanctioned, were at least tacitly condoned. Many a child was sired on the wrong side of the blanket, and as the bend sinister of bastardy in some family escutcheons attested, paternity had been acknowledged. In sum, however, the dicta of the church were adhered to religiously.

Yet there is more to it. Had I been a commoner, my attitudes might have been somewhat more flexible. Because of my lineage added obligations were superimposed on the prohibitions dictated by the church. As a knight of noble birth I could only consider being united in the bonds of matrimony with a maiden of equally gentle birth.

Accordingly, for one of my station, women fell into but two categories—those of noble birth to whom I might legitimately plight my troth, and wenches of more lowly station.

I didn't delude myself on this score. Verily, I didn't believe for a moment that Ethelwyn of Hebb had come to my father's bed a virgin. But that didn't alter the fact that she was of gentle bloodline. On the other side of the coin was Gentle Breeze. She *had* been virginal when first bestowed on me, yet she was lowborn—and that, too, was an unalterable fact of life. In no wise could she be considered for elevation in higher status.

Polygamy, so much a way of life in Asian realms, confounded me. Yet even here, where the Confucian ethic prevailed, there were clearly defined distinctions. Gentle Breeze could never hope to be a principal, or even a secondary wife for one of my position. She could aspire to no higher status than that of a concubine. In a monogamous society she would have no legal status whatsoever. In England, regardless of the closeness which had developed between us, she could be no other than my paramour.

For Brother Demetrios to have assumed that Gentle Breeze would be included in my plans to return to England astonished me. Yet, mayhap, it shouldn't have come as such a surprise. In all the time I'd known the Nestorian friar, the differences in our respective faiths had never been discussed between us. Perhaps the strictures imposed by the Holy See did not apply to the Nestorian disciplines. But whatever were his reasons, to have included Gentle Breeze in my plans was unthinkable.

Four days hence we would break camp and march south to join Sögatü in his campaign against the Sung. It was September 1276—the eleventh day of the Month of the

Monkey in the Year of the Rat. It was almost a year to the day since the *touman* had broken camp in Shangtu and marched south to join the Army of the Blue Dragon.

That thought was on my mind as I lay abed with Gentle Breeze curled up beside me, her head on my shoulder. I glanced fondly down at the curve of her cheek and the dark tangle of her hair. So much had happened in the year since she'd been at my side. How wondrous a gift was the woman bestowed on me by Kubilai Khan.

She had come to mean much more to me than a sexually satisfying bedmate. She was confidante, helpmeet, and mistress of my household. She gave unstintingly of her strength and warmth. I owed much to this woman who had become such a part of me.

I reached over and gently pushed a lock of her hair from her brow. "Are you asleep, little one?"

"No, Emun," she murmured drowsily.

"Then, listen, carefully. I have something important to tell you."

She stirred and looked up into my face. "What, my lord?"

"In the matter of Mei-ling, move slowly. For what I have in mind, I don't want to be encumbered with a wife."

"Oh, why not? You don't want to arouse the khan's suspicions?"

"No. That we don't want . . . but he won't expect the nuptial rites to take place until our campaign against the Sung is successfully concluded."

"But when will that be?"

"I cannot say. It could well take as long as a year. However, before the campaign is concluded we will have pushed the Sung back to Canton. When we reach that city, I want you to join me there."

"Where is Canton?"

"A seaport some distance south of here. I will send an escort to conduct you thither."

"A seaport, my lord?" she said, her eyes growing wide.

"Yes," I replied gruffly. "When you reach that port, I will start teaching you French and English . . . the tongues spoken in my homeland."